Alumni Hall, Room 34

by Dunn Neugebauer

DUNN NEUGEBAUER

ALUMNI HALL, ROOM 34

The writer acknowledges the use of excerpts from the following movies: Grease, Full Metal Jacket, The Shining, The Poseidon Adventure, Fast Times at Ridgemont High, About Last Night, Fletch and a Few Good Men. Excerpts are noted and given credit when used. Also, Jackson Browne's lyrics are cited from the songs "The Pretender" and "Only Child," both from the "Pretender" album. Finally, the "conversation" wth Andy Van Slyke is purely fictional, and may or may not reflect the feelings and values of Mr. Van Slyke.

ABOUT THE AUTHOR

Dunn Neugebauer has worked at McDonald's in Athens, tended bar in Rome, checked credit in Dunwoody, written for the Neighbor Newspapers in Sandy Springs, coached tennis in Atlanta, fallen through the roof of his high school in Rutledge, kept stats in Buckhead, been rejected by women in Mexico, California and Nevada, worked summer camps in New Hampshire, entered his 150-pound body in muscle man contests in Florida, gotten lost in Canada, London and Edinburgh, ran a half-marathon in Indiana, sung in a choir in Madison, assembled a 2,000 piece jigsaw puzzle in Roswell, and lives with his wife Robin in Atlanta with their collection of books, movies, flowers, dogs and dead roaches.

Acknowledgments/Dedication

To Gary Huff and Brooks Pennington, two people who made a difference. The bad language that pops up from time to time is the author's error, and is not any indication of the lessons they taught.

To Tim Crowley, who I hope is hitting .450 and turning double plays in heaven.

And of course, for Robin, who is always there thank God.

"In the game of life, I'm the player to be named later."
Anonymous

BOOK ONE:

Prologue; A Girl in a Pub; A Phone Call; A Date; Don't Think, Just Live; Depression and a Chat With a Baseball Star

Prologue

First off, let's get all of the crap out of the way, shall we? I mean, before I start this story and you begin to read and you wonder...

It's like this: I'm a college senior now and have been for the last two years. Will probably graduate without honors this May. Something about that real world scares me, though, you know? Like choosing a profession for instance. Or figuring out what to do with the rest of your life. Or finally cleaning up your resume, making your decision, then dealing with the pressures of getting good at it. After all, it's your job.

And as far as writing is concerned, I don't call myself a writer. Never have. Probably never will.

But, for the first part, my English teacher is always busting on us about keeping a journal. For the second - what's going on here is quite simple - I have a lot to say, I must say it, and I'm going to. Period.

Game.

Set.

Match.

It's like that comedian that poured water down his throat, spit it back out, looked at his audience and yelled, "damn it, I'm full."

Well, that's me. I'm full.

And for the more general stuff, for the record, or for that group of people who would say something like, "but what's the setting?" "When?" "What part did you play in all of this?"

Well, I'm saying it doesn't really matter. In fact,

pick a college, any college. Your favorite one even.
Place all your friends out there, books in hand, late
for class, and having a bad hair day to boot. Running
in and out of the library, getting change for the
washer and dryers, looking for a parking spot at the
student center, considering whether to skip baseball
practice or not, wondering why mom hasn't sent the
care package, and pondering just why you never made
the move on this person or that one.

Have you got the picture yet?

No, you haven't. You're still not thinking clearly
enough. Put some more detail in it. Notice what
they're wearing. What's in style these days, anyway?
What music is everyone listening to? What movies are
out? Who is getting it on with who and don't you wish
you were a part of all that gossip? Or are you and you
wish you weren't?

Sorry for rambling, but I'll move on.

Me, I feel there's at least one time in everyone's
life when time just seems to stop and the place or
situation you're in is the only thing that matters.
One pure moment after another, if you will. A world
may still go on, presidents get elected, athletes
still want and get more money, holidays come and go,
and so forth.

That's why I'm seeing what I'm seeing, feeling what
I'm feeling and writing what I'm writing. Especially
since, for me, it is college that does that for me,
though I don't mean just the memory of it all. You
know how people are always saying, "man, those were
the days!"

Truth be told, some of those days were 'the days'
Others sucked.

Just like anything else.

For better or for worse, however, there are things
that always stay with you. I remember sitting there
at freshman orientation on Day 1, hearing some guy
welcome the Class of 1996, and I was thinking, "wow,
will that year ever get here!

Sure enough, damned if you don't run in and out of
one class after the other, a party here, meetings
there, road trips, term papers, sports games, off the

wall outings, food fights, etc., and then … BOOM. All
of a sudden, you're driving back to school for your
last semester.

Or you're studying for a final and it's your last
one.

Or you're sitting in your graduation gown thinking,
"what the hell am I going to do now?"

Or maybe you're wondering whatever happened to the
days when it actually took a year for a year to go by.

Am I making any sense? Probably not, but let's put
it this way. One day, I was standing in the girl's
dorms and there was a big group of my friends there.
Two were studying, one was braiding the other's hair,
one was asleep, using her friend's stomach for a
pillow, others were just taking up good space and my
friend and I were contemplating just how good the
Braves would be this year and who should we put the
move on? Well, for some reason, a thought lodged it's
way up into my head, got past the pizzas and beer and
tests and yelled at me, "It should always be like
this!" I started laughing, right then, right there,
and all my friends just looked over.

"Don't worry, it's just Phil talking to himself
again," they said.

But think about it. Now we're all here, a major
part of each other. Even if a stranger walks into my
room, I hand him a beer, tell him to pull up a couch
and I shoot the breeze with him. In the real world, a
stranger walks in, I call the police and my lawyer.

I'm not saying not to be careful, but don't you
see?

Anyway, after listening to others talking about
"the good old days," I just wanted to try to
experience it now instead of later. I mean, why hear
the song and think, "damn, remember where we were when
he heard that? Remember?"

You may understand and you may not.

You see things the way you see things.

Things happen.

Deal with them how you will.

Regardless, let's move on now, shall we? After
all, I'm full. Remember?

To start things off, I'll begin on a seemingly random day, if there is any such thing, and Fred and I are standing out on a flag football field. Not really sure if that's important or not, but you have to start somewhere.

I can still see him oh so clearly, as he stood across the field, whistle in mouth, penalty flag in hand and …

1: A Girl in a Pub

... he threw it high in the air. It was a fall day
in Georgia; probably fall everywhere else, too, now
that I think about it, and Fred and I were justifying
our existence by earning money on the football field.

We had hurried from class, changed, and jogged
halfway across campus just to get there on time, with
Fred busting his butt while jumping across a rain-
induced creek between the tennis courts and the path
to the fields.

"Damn it!" he yelled. "That's the third time I've
done that this semester!"

It was funny how people kept track of things like
that; where they'd know exactly how mad they were
supposed to be. The first time was probably a mild
irritation, maybe even amusing; the second generally
pissed him off and the third probably put the
thermometer in his head somewhere between bake and
broil.

I didn't want to be around when and if the fourth
time happened.

The day, however, was beautiful; one of those days
a photographer would pull his tripod out of the trunk,
snap a roll or two, then hurry off to the nearest
Jigsaw Puzzle manufacturer and sell them all. This
day would be a potential bestseller, too; would
probably rank somewhere up there with a Vermont
countryside and a winter afternoon in New Hampshire,
if you were into that type of thing.

The leaves had turned, multiplied, peaked and
fallen. They brushed against your clothes as you

walked, left a trail behind you wherever you went,
made a creaking noise when you shuffled across the
campus, reminding you of what season it was as if
you'd forgotten. When driving, you had to turn on the
wipers just to clear yourself a view.

The kind of day that made me wish I was up in the
mountains.

Locked away in a cabin.

Beer in one hand.

Babe in the other.

But for now, flag football at it's non-finest was
going on, and Fred had called me over for our first of
many referee-to-referee conferences. "Phil," he
began, "we have a problem." I glanced over at the
players as if angry, though actually I had about as
much interest in the outcome of this game as all those
Blue-Gray, North-South, East-West 'classics' they
showed on TV when they got tired of reruns.

"The rotund woman over there," he pointed with his
chin, "clearly was pushed in the back by the woman in
green, making this an obvious case of pass
interference. However, the offending party happens to
be a total babe, she's in my Chemistry class, and I've
been trying like hell to get her phone number for the
last two weeks. I hope you understand my dilemma
here?"

It was amazing how much complete and total bullshit
could come out of this man's mouth, and all the while
with a straight face. Never crack a smile. He'd even
won a six-pack of beer off me one night in Atlanta;
bet me he could make a mime crack up and start
laughing. We'll get into that later. Or maybe we
won't.

"That's no problem, Fred, no problem, at all," I
began. "From what I saw, it was obvious that the
rather large woman initiated the contact, making it
offensive pass interference."

He pushed his glasses up on his nose with his
finger, glanced across the field, then back at me;
hyperactive eyes demanding something to focus upon but
rarely satisfied. "I knew you'd see it my way.
Thanks."

"Loss of down?"
"I think so."
"Fifteen yards?"
"Sure, why not?"

I guess most people would feel guilty marking off those yards. Fred, he merely made jokes to the large woman; actually had her laughing by the time he spotted the ball, blew his whistle and re-inserted his penalty flag into his belt.

He glanced up at the Georgia sun, intercepted in spots by robins and blue jays flying across and some occasional leaves that still hadn't settled. I had to laugh, watching him pull out a pen and write something on his hand; a habit he'd passed on to me. After all, notes would come and go, he would say. He really didn't plan on losing his hand.

Knowing him as I did, he was making a notation to make it up to the big woman. She was a victim, but one he'd atone for some way some how, and probably in ways that were a helluva lot more important than flag football. Unfair, you say? Not in the larger scale.

Anyway, we managed to make it through the day without any promises of violence or ill will coming our way. Our only close call was late in the same game, with a mere 2:12 left before calling it a day.

"Fred, we need to confer," I'd thrown my flag and pointed both hands to my chest (the right signal, I think). We locked arms, heads together in our own huddle. "You realize that your babe just ran slap over my friend from my home town. You can see my problem here. I mean, we don't want to discriminate against anyone or anything."

He glanced around, tilted his glasses again. "Phil, you're right," he said. Still serious. Cracking me up. "I believe we have an open and shut case of off-setting penalties. Play goes over, nobody hurt, no yards tacked on or off, to hell with it. We'll just pretend all of that crap never happened. Shall we?"

What a genius.

The game ended at 42-6 if you're keeping score at home; and if so, get a life. With our priorities straight, we first tacked on nine or ten hours on our

time card before sacking up all the equipment. It
wasn't an easy job at this point, collecting flags
from over-enthused athletes who actually wished they'd
had a gridiron career, women who for some reason
didn't think we were being fair and others who just
didn't give a damn where the flags ended up. It took
a while, but … that was our job.

If asked, we would both be quick to tell you the
work helped us pay our way through school - the hours
devoted towards a career in the athletic industry. The
truth? Well, our parents were footing the bill for our
education or lack thereof. As for the officiating? How
else were you supposed to meet women? How much more
visible could you get than wearing a black-and-white
stripe shirt and being armed with a whistle and a
penalty flag?

A waste of time, many would say. Damned good
thinking, we would counter.

Anyway, we were standing outside the equipment
truck - an old van brought back to life by the
intramural director - and it was parked directly
between the two fields. Both fields were surrounded by
rows of faculty houses, with professors able to sit on
their porches and watch all the chaos if they chose,
though they rarely did.

Hearing hundreds of screaming students after hours
in a classroom wasn't usually their choice, thank you
very much.

"You ever feel guilty about putting down extra
hours on our time cards?" It was my conscience again.

"Phil, you must understand something; people will
get paid to keep up with crap like this once we have
real jobs. That is, assuming we ever get out of this
place. For now, our job is to get paid. Period."

Simple enough.

"What's going on tonight?" Me again. Bored and
curious.

"I've got two tests and a paper, all on Friday.
Man, why can't these professors spread all this crap
out a little more. Damn, I don't think I've ever had
just one test per week since I've been here." He
paused, scratched his chin. "And that's a long time."

"Yeah, I know what you mean, I've got some studying to do myself." Eat, study, do a paper and get a good night's sleep for a change." All settled.

He started away and I waited. He got twenty yards or so across the field before I did my best Columbo imitation. "Oh, there is just one other thing," I said. He stopped, faced me, stood there with this totally idiotic look on his face. He had this 'okay, get on with it' expression, but I made him wait. Getting him all worked up ranked somewhere up there with watching late night cable movies and relaxing in hot tubs.

"What?" he finally said.

I continued sorting flags, putting them in burlap sacks, separating red from green from yellow. I glanced around as if that would help jog my brain, reached for my pants pocket, looked at my watch, then cradled my face in my hand. "Damn, would you …"

"Okay, okay, I'm thinking," I answered. I paused a little for effect. "Oh yeah, as I was saying, your babe did mention something about going out to the Pub for a beer. Something about wanting to shoot some pool, play some pinball, hang out for a while. But I'm sorry, it was probably nothing. Sorry I mentioned it."

He looked up, put both hands on his hips, glanced around as if he had a decision to make, then started back towards me. "As I was saying," he began, "I've really been putting too much time into my studies lately. It would do me a world of good to relax, have a beer. I mean, I don't want to get burned out or anything."

I dropped the sacks here, imitated him the best I could by pretending to push glasses I didn't have up to my nose. "You're right. Besides, I can research my paper while I'm out. You know, talk to people, get new ideas for the great American novel I'll never write."

"Exactly, good thinking." He high-fived me for that one, leaving me wondering. About high-fives that is and where and how that got started. Everything seemed to go in cycles, high-fives, low-fives, patting each other on the butt, head-butting, kneeling in end zones, dancing in end zones. It all seemed to spread so quickly.

On the other hand, who the hell cared?

We slung the sacks over our shoulders and started across the field as the Georgia sun began to fade behind the trees. Two carefree seniors we were, deciding once again to blow off studying and hit the town; put off the pursuit of academic excellence for yet another moment. Truth be told, if one were keeping stats between these "moments" and the academic world, it'd be about as close as most Super Bowls, but ...

These decisions one must make, many of them probably innocent. Then again, who knew?

The Pub, to get right to the point, was a hell-hole. The terms 'dive' and 'hole-in-the-wall' could be used if you were in a good mood, but that didn't quite cut it. It was located a mile east of the campus, if you're into directions, though Fred and I had it gauged at a one beer drive, a beer-and-a-half if you were taking your time.

Anyway, the 'decor' consisted of shrubs (weeds) lining a cement block wall, topped off with red paint, probably with its last coat put on somewhere during the Eisenhower administration. The parking lot was dirt and gravel, complete with crater-sized holes in various locations.

One could always tell a rookie by watching him pull in and head to the prime parking spot ... and get stuck in the process. Upon approaching the door, a huge rock sat just to the left, though how and why it got there was a total mystery. We'd often made bets with very large men about whether they could move it or not. We were careful not to tick them off, mind you; something about people that hung out here past their early 20's was scary in itself.

But I always watched, as their eyes bulged out, veins popped, tattoos stretched and grunts started at their mouth and moved deeper within. Friends would gather around and watch, even make bets. Passengers in cars cruising by, if seeing the above, would probably tap the driver on the shoulder and say, "look over there, what's going on?"

"Who knows, probably a fight or something." And they'd drive on.

No one could move it, if that matters or if you care, but I was the type of guy that wondered just who the hell put it there and why. Fred was the type that informed me you could get as many opinions on that as on religion or politics, depending on who you wanted to listen to.

Anyway, upon walking in, a bar looked you right in the eye. Let me rephrase that - you could literally walk in, take two steps and slide a beer mug the length of the bar. We knew this; we'd done it. The glass broke off on the other side. A motorcycle gang member wasn't happy.

Fred approached him to explain himself.

I informed Fred that talk wasn't the rule here.

The man wanted to pound us into submission.

We left and lived.

And I keep getting off the subject.

The inside had picnic tables strewn about, a juke box filled with mostly country music and pool tables and pin ball machines spaced out enough to allow patrons room to pass without ruining your big chance at a free game or plenty of room for the old '8 ball in the corner' trick. You could get around inside easily enough on most nights, with your best chance of trouble being if you interrupted a pool shot during prime time.

Two rooms sat in the corner, bathrooms to use the term loosely, consisting of a trough on the men's side and something I'd never dream of sitting on in the women's. The men's was filled with the usual trivia, though why people stopped to write things on bathroom walls was another one of those questions I had.

The Pub's was no different, however, with this week's graffiti featuring phone numbers, 'x'-rated crap that doesn't belong here and the question of the week, which was "Where's Elvis?"

Several people had answered, of course, with some of the top answers being, "in the brief case in Pulp Fiction", at the mall, or "he's working as a Hoosier under Bobby Knight."

Whatever.

It was a college hangout during the school year,
with locals not always happy about it, but making
amends by getting there early enough for the pool
table, and early enough to fill the juke box with
Waylon and Willie and Hank Williams, Jr. and not all
that rap or pop shit that college kids listened to.
Actually, a journey to the juke box to play such would
draw quick eye contact; not a promise of violence but
a mental click in people's heads; demerits if you
will. Students generally stuck with students, locals
with locals. Sometimes it mixed successfully, others
it didn't.

Regardless, the Pub itself remained uncaring, a
place that wasn't for everyone and would never have
any desire to be. It was more for those who didn't
need or want to put on makeup before going out, for
those who didn't care if they had on blue jeans with
ink stains on their pockets, and for those who just
wanted to get away and not care what people thought,
if only for a few hours.

We took our seats in the back, with Fred taking the
strategic chair (facing the entrance, good view of the
scenery walking in) and I within peripheral vision.
There were a few stragglers around, a greasy looking
couple pretending to be interested in pinball, a
foursome on a pool table and a couple of elderly
gentleman at the bar, perhaps wondering just exactly
when it was that life gave them that swift kick in the
nuts that left them here instead of … anywhere else.

I couldn't look at those two for long – perhaps
something to do with the truth hurting or that line
from the 'Poseidon Adventure', where Gene Hackman
tells Ernest Borgnine that "maybe I'm just like you
and you don't like looking at yourself." I was too
young to even know what that meant when I first saw
it. Now I thought it was a pretty cool line.

Or pretty scary in some cases.

Anyway, let's move on with the story, shall we?

Fred returned with a pitcher and two cups, and
plopped himself down. His attire was 'Pub-Proof',
dirty jeans, faded T-shirt with holes throughout, a

message on the front announcing some 5K road race that
happened in Atlanta years ago, old Reeboks and a hat
with no writing on it. That was the cool thing about
that hat to me.

It said absolutely nothing. Just a plain, blue hat.

"Man, where are all these babes you were talking
about?" He was acting angry as he said this, but we
both knew that when choosing between having a beer or
six and studying …

We sat in silence for a while, two people unwinding
from another non-hectic day in paradise; classes,
lunch, more classes, football, bar, maybe a woman,
maybe not. Such was life. He tried to open with the
"what are you going to do with your life after this
year?" routine, but I gave him that look and he
agreed.

We settled for the Braves, the Falcons, the Hawks,
English Lit, why Dr. Thomas always wore that stupid
looking tie and why in the world didn't Kelly and Gene
just break up. Besides, we all knew how miserable they
both were, didn't we?

"Oh shit, bogeys, two o'clock," Fred announced as
he slammed down his beer. "Don't look, don't look!" he
almost yelled as he saw me swing my neck around
awkwardly, as if connected by some circular hinge.

My turning disappointed my mentor for the time
being, but, if I could play it cool, I wouldn't be …
"wow, must be transfers or freshmen with fake ID's," I
announced, as if I actually knew what I was talking
about.

The first one was tall, brunette, jeans, flannel
shirt, too much make-up and absolutely not in tune
with the proper dress code. The other, I couldn't see
just yet. She was standing behind her, both just to
the right of the elderly losers who were making no
effort to conceal the fact that they were staring. I
guess when you got to that stage in life, you just
didn't bother with petty games anymore.

We wouldn't know. Yet.

"The tall one's at least an '8', probably a '9'."
Me again, getting more knowledgeable with each drop of
alcohol.

Fred slammed his cup down. "Let's clear something up right off the bat," he said and so much for my knowledge. He faced me again, pushing his glasses up with his finger and why didn't he fix that and … "Your old 1-10 scale is totally outdated. Gone."

"Why?" I asked and immediately regretted it.

"Well, I'll tell you," he paused to take a sip (swallow) and pounded the cup back down. "It's a two-letter thing these days, didn't you know?" I didn't answer. "You know, like 'AA', 'BC', 'AD' or whatever." I gave him the common courtesy of looking confused so he continued. "Okay, the first letter is for looks, the second for personality. That way, you get the full meaning right off the bat. I mean, who the hell wants to go out with a '9' if all she does is comb her hair and be seen in the right places?"

"As for now, I'd settle for it," I said.

He cut his eyes over, rather harshly, but I knew he wasn't really mad. "Anyway," he went on, "you have 'A' for babe, "B' for pretty good looking, 'C' for judgment call and I hope she has a good personality and 'D' for better you than me. It's the same with personality; 'A' for great, 'B' is good, 'C' can be moody and aloof and a 'D' is a downright, no other word for it …"

"I think I got it now. But how in the hell can I give them that sorta rating when I ain't even met 'em yet?"

"Not sure, I was just trying to impress you with my new invention." He laughed, drank and pretended not to look over.

Me, I kept straining my neck to get a view.

"They're not going anywhere, they're just buying a beer. Relax." He always had this way of reading my thoughts at times.

"Well Fred, if I was that smooth, I wouldn't be sitting here at the Pub in the middle of the week drinking a beer with a 'CA' no less."

"A 'CA'? You bastard!"

"Just kidding. Actually, I'd sit here and drink anyway. The last thing I need is for some girl.."

"Oh, you've given up already?" Twenty-two and over

the hill? Don't you think there are two nice,
beautiful women out there for us somewhere?" He
stopped drinking when he asked me this. Not sure why.
    "No."
    "Why not?"
    "Maybe because you're ugly as hell and I'm stupid."
    "Wow, nice attitude."
    Regardless, they walked over and took a seat, two
tables over, in front of the pinball couple and beside
one of the many unoccupied pool tables. The make-up
girl just didn't do it for me. She looked too … I
don't know … good, for lack of a better word. The
other one, though, that was the one who poked around
at my insides.
    She wore a baseball hat, no make-up, blue jeans and
a long sleeved T-shirt. Her hair was tied back   shoes
had holes in them and looking at her reminded me of
the saying "dressed for comfort, not to impress."
    Then again, that may not even be a saying. Who
knew?
    "The first one is totally out of the question,"
Fred said to me, referring to the taller one. This was
not good, as it meant he and I had our sights on the
same one. Nothing new.
    "Why, she's a total babe," I countered.
    "Yes, and that's exactly my point," he argued. "Do
you realize that, as we speak, she's standing over
there rehearsing her lines she's going to say to all
the guys that hit on her?"
    "So?"
    "So she's out. Period."
    "Why?"
    "Because I don't want to talk to a tape recorder, I
want to talk to a human being."
    "And you know already that she's not?"
    "Absolutely."
    "Why do you say that?" I'm not sure why I always
stroked his ego by asking these things.
    He lifted his eyes toward mine. He had young eyes
and a young face; could easily pass for a freshman
himself. Even his high-powered, thick, telescopic
glasses did nothing to age him, actually made him look

younger if that made any sense. "Look at her hands,
for instance."
Couldn't say that was my first option, but we'll go
with it.
"What about them? They're pretty."
"No, they're not pretty," he corrected. "They're
lined with rings, jewelry, fingernail polish; all the
wrong things."
"Girls are supposed to decorate themselves up like
that," I argued.
"No, they're not." He slammed his cup down again
for effect; reminded me of a lawyer or a college
professor. "They did all that back in the old days,
before they could vote and work and speak and act and
live. That was then, when they were symbols of beauty
for a man to show off. Those days are gone."
"But women like to do that kind of stuff, some guys
like it, and besides, it's probably a habit," I
countered.
"Yes, but it's a habit that's derived from all the
wrong reasons and I cannot and will not respect that,"
he said.
"You're a sick man," was all I could manage.
We chatted on a little, pretending not to watch the
girls at table four, and our conversation drifted to
the odds of us actually going snow skiing in Colorado.
Out of nowhere, Fred put out his hand and interrupted
me in mid-sentence.
"Phil," Fred began as he gently placed his cup down
and flicked it away as if bored with it. "I've been a
good boy all day, I've minded all my manners, I've
come and gone to class, turned in the appropriate
papers, and I just don't feel like being normal
anymore."
And with that, he burped.
Not just an ordinary burp, mind you, but one where
you'd expect to see his throat lying somewhere on the
table. "My God!" was all I could manage, though I
shouldn't have been that surprised.
"Fred, those girls …"
"What about them? Hell with it, this is the way I
am right now. I'm tired of acting for one day."

I had to look over and catch their reaction; no way I could just sit there. This time I actually swiveled in my chair and looked them head on. They were both laughing. Hard. A lump started up in my throat as I began to speak.

But should I speak? Were they laughing at us or with us? Did they really care? I thought better of it.

Wimp, wuss, chicken, scumbag. My mind barraged me with insults, each as bad or worse than the one before. Why not talk to them? What are they going to do, shoot me?

"I apologize for my friend here, he's had a really rough day," I said as I meekly looked in their direction. *Rough day? A rough day? Is that why you let out a 9.3 burp on an earthquake scale?*

The cute one, not the one Fred had already cast into the pits of hell, but the other one, spoke. "Don't worry, at least he didn't fart."

They laughed.

I breathed a sigh of relief.

But then, the problem wasn't over. There was a silence there, while I stupidly faced them in my chair with my mouth open, a silence that I was supposed to fill with some cute line or something nice or something mean or … That was the point. I didn't know what in the hell to say.

But Fred did, thank God.

"And I would like to apologize for my friend here," he began, actually sounding like a total gentleman. "See, he's really a nice guy, but he's a total closet case when it comes to talking to cute women. Would ya'll like to come over here and join us?" Wow, he was putting on his best southern drawl even. "I promise, we're nice guys," he continued, throwing his hands out in innocence - as if this would convince the two, even after he shattered glass with his paint-peeling belch.

There was a tense second, or maybe two seconds of eerie silence. I could literally see wheels turning in their heads. Turning really quick.

"Sure," Miss Makeup said. My first thought was

that she didn't know what rejection line to pull out
for a guy who burps, shatters light bulbs, keeps a
straight face, then invites them over. Probably has
never happened in her world. Hope not.

I turned back to Fred, swiveled the chair back
around. "My God, you mean that works? You just speak
the truth and they walk over?"

"You should try it sometime," he muttered under his
breath, winking at me as he took another chug of beer.
And as our table for two became a table for four.

Allow me a brief moment here to get through the
preliminaries, starting with the taller one: Shelly
Richardson, math major, 20-years old (I told you there
was a fake ID involved!), transferred from Young
Harris College somewhere way the hell up in the
mountains. Born in the spring sometime (she went out
of her way to point this out, but I wasn't interested
enough to find out why). Drove a BMW, loved her daddy,
fought with her mom, liked to drink and let someone
else drive.

The other one, Leigh, didn't volunteer much about
herself, not even her last name. She just gave a few
courtesy laughs from time to time and kept to herself,
sipping her beer and (*God I wish I was a beer cup*) and
drifting off. Not rude, not trying to impress. Just
glad to be there, thank you very much.

"... and we came straight from the football fields,"
Shelly was saying. That was my cue. And Fred's. And we
jumped all over it.

"Who do ya'll play for? Did you win?" It came from
both of us.

Leigh snapped out of her trance at this point and
my stomach did an extra knot when she did it. I
noticed that Shelly gave way at this point, as if her
wanting to speak required total respect. Then again,
maybe I notice things that just don't exist.

She leaned back in her chair, eyeing the both of us
and answered, "we play for the Jenkins Jockstraps, we
lost 42-0, and the reason we lost by so much is that
we suck."

With that, she killed her beer, slammed it down on

the table and let out a burp of her own. Not as good
as Fred's, mind you, but pretty good no less. Fred,
usually not one to show emotion, started to speak, but
his mouth kind of hung there for a second.

Me, I laughed.

"Who might you guys play for?" Leigh asked.

We looked at each other, as if asking, "do you do
this or me? Okay, go ahead, but don't screw it up this
time. Okay then, you do it."

Fred nominated himself after the silent bickering.

"We play for the Nads, we didn't play today, but we
won 27-6 the other day. Yes, we are a good team, but I
can promise you, Phil and I have absolutely nothing to
do with it."

"And we're also officials," I put in. He glanced
sharply at me for that one, not really thinking our
status as refs would do us any good at this point.
What the hell.

"What positions do you guys play?"

"Fred sits on the bench and I kick the ball off and
go sit beside him," I answered quickly enough. They
both laughed. So far, so good.

There was a moment or two of silence, when Leigh
plopped her cup down and arose. I was already kicking
myself, wondering why I didn't …

"Enough of this small talk," she said as she
gestured towards the bar. "We need more beer."

She returned with two pitchers.

Yes, there was a God.

Fast forward: There were a lot of empty glasses,
cups and pitchers around. Fred and Shelly were
discussing math. I promise, I remember that much.
Leigh and I were having a field day, ripping into
classes, cafeteria food and the new campus radio
station, among other things. Shelly had tried to leave
earlier, after the first two pitchers, but Fred and I
administered the drunk driving test to her. (Are we
cute? If you think so, then you're too drunk to
drive!) She failed. They stayed.

The pivotal moment came. With the fourth pitcher
gone and no money or energy to get up and buy the

fifth, Leigh and I looked over at the math geniuses, who were still discussing why this teacher sucked and why this one was so much better. Didn't you agree?

Leigh just glanced away, looking at her watch, then over at me. She looked kind of bored, to tell you the truth and I was getting tired of small talk. It was time for me to make some sort of a move.

And yes, I was a little drunk (no!). Yes, I really was, though half of my mind was totally conscious, and giving me a hard time at that. *Well … are you going to ask this girl out? Don't you want to see her again? Are you going to wimp out? Again? That'll be the third time!* See, I'm guilty, too. Now I guess I'm supposed to be - mad I think, but who remembered?

As I said earlier, what the hell, give it a shot.

Why am I so nervous?

Aren't I drunk?

"All right, Leigh, damn it," I began as I slammed my cup down on the table. "Let me ask you a question," … *Wow, taking control. Not bad. A little bad on the delivery, but starting every word off with about 16 consonants isn't all that bad.* "There's a party going on this Friday night and …"

"Leigh!" It was Shelly, interrupting. "Oh shit! We've got to get out of here. I'm supposed to meet Sam and Theresa at 7:30. We need to go."

Did that really just happen?

I think so.

But … I was on a roll.

Sort of.

"You guys can't leave, we just decided you were too drunk." Fred.

"Just a second," Leigh waved her hand, looking back at me. "What were you saying?" She stared back over. The problem was, both Fred and Shelly did, too. They all sat there, silent, looking at me. "Well," I began, face getting red and redder, collar hot, neck and throat tightening up. "Never mind. I'll …"

"Speak up you wimp," she said. And with that, she tackled me, right there on that smut-filled, beer-infested, puke-ridden, 30-years-of-dirt-filled floor. I just laid there, totally shocked, mouth open, back

hurting a little despite the beer. Actually, I was
laughing too hard to feel it too much. Leigh had her
butt on my chest, laughing, face turning red.

Fred and Shelly just rolled their eyes, turning
away in that "we don't know them" pose. Leigh started
to get up, then cut her eyes back down. "Call me," she
said, and with that, she got up and grabbed her purse.

"If you people are going to make fools of yourself,
then we're leaving," Leigh said.

"It's been fun, we'll do it again sometime," Shelly
said, grabbing her purse and heading out. The two
walked away and we watched, nothing cool about us.
They were still giggling as they got to the door.

Fred just tipped his hat at the two of them, cool
breeze that he was, pulled me off the floor and poured
me another one. He winked at me from across the table,
knowing what was going through my head. He didn't say
anything. Yet. Though I knew he would eventually.

Oh well, it was a start, if nothing else.

Partial score from Jenkins College: Phil 1, World
0. Details at 11:00.

II: A Phone Call

The next morning in history class, 10:07 and
crawling...

Dr. Higgins was going to town, he always did, going
through American History, top to bottom, start to
finish. No notes required. No chalk. No chalkboard.
Just walked in the room, threw down his notebook and
started firing away.

A man on a mission.

He wasn't one of those "stand behind the podium"
teachers, either, to say the least. He was hyper,
gesturing wildly with his hands, walking up and down
the room, back and forth, grabbing a cigar, never
lighting it, popping it up and down in his hands,
flipping it over, up, putting it back.

The students did one thing and one thing only in
his class - they took notes. Constantly. Never
stopped. It wasn't uncommon to see a student shaking
his or her hand, getting rid of the cramps, flipping
pages, pens running out of ink - an 'oh shit',
expression of panic on their face and 'who had an
extra one?'

All the while, Higgins just rattled away, naming
dates, wars, times, eras, speaking 250 words per
minute with gusts up to 400. Now and again, he'd call
on a student, or mention one by name, just to make
sure they were following.

But most of the time it was all Higgins. Nothing
more. Nothing less.

Fred sat straight to my right, the only class we'd
ever shared. We'd often wanted to take one together,

but now, we both realized, it was a huge mistake. His concentration span was pretty good, though mine was not, and I'd usually interrupt with a note here or there or anything else I could come up with for distraction.

The major difference was, he could stop and pass me a note, all the while listening to Higgins with the other half of his brain, mind cruising at warp speed, concentration split but not overloaded.

It's 10:09 … and I need to be listening. Problem was, I respected history, understood the need to know it, but at the same time, knew it wasn't for me. It was a core class I'd put off, a worry to put off until a date to be named later. Unfortunately, the date was now.

I'd usually make up games to play in my head, you know, listing the counties in Georgia, name the last 10 Super Bowl winners, who won the Best Supporting Role in 1992? What was the count when Cabrera drove in Justice and Bream?

This time, the note passing came from him. No complaints here. Only 10:11 and my mind drifting away.

"She told you to call her? Good for you, stud. What'd you think of Shelly? Write back or I will eliminate you."
                    Fred

It was so funny the way he signed all his notes; as if I wouldn't know where they came from. Anyway, glad to be at least taking notes about something, I blew the cob webs off my pen and responded:

"How can I call her when I don't know her last name? She's funny, hard to read, obnoxious, but cute.. didn't you think? As for Shelly, I've heard she's slept with half of the campus."
"Respond now or have your bed filled with crotch crickets."
                    Phil

Higgins blared on, getting into it now, packing,

walking, gesturing, voice raising and lowering,
raising and lowering. A good teacher, I should try
listening sometimes. Oops, not now. Another note from
Fred.

"Slept with half the campus? What's wrong with the
other half? Where was I?"
                    Fred

I put my hand over my mouth to keep from laughing,
then began to respond. What a nut. Why couldn't …
"PHIL!"
It was Higgins, not Fred. He was - pissed. His
glasses were cocked over his nose, smoke protruding
from his ears, mouth curled in a scowl. He wasn't a
big man, around 5-10 and 160, I'd say, but he did
possess some anger when someone wasn't getting into
his lectures and he could produce fear in a student.
Me, for now.
The whole class looked back at me. My face turned
pink, but got near red. And redder. Collar hot, highs
around 110, throat choking up, red blood cells working
overtime.
"I believe I asked you a question," Higgins said,
flipping his cigar and gazing in, eyes locked on mine;
his and everyone else's in the class.
I looked around helplessly. No holes to drop in.
No bells to save me. Time: 10:14 and creeping …
"You did?"
Laughter, but quickly muffled. He just stared, he
did, the way he always did when he nailed someone. He
wasn't one to let you off easy. If you screwed up on
his time, you paid. The embarrassment technique
worked quite well for him, thank you very much.
My face grew hotter, due to explode in T-minus-10
seconds and counting. Some of the classmates looked
away, glad it wasn't them, shifted nervously,
pretended not to stare anymore.
I just looked up. Wasn't going to speak.
Couldn't. Clueless. *Say something. Anything!*
"We'll forget the question for now, sir, but please
direct your attention to me while in class." Even

after this, he kept staring, as if to say, "I haven't
made my point yet, but …"
Only 10:18. But get me out of here.

"Congratulations, never seen him get quite that
mad." It was Fred, after class, and we were heading
across the quad to the dining hall, him pulling his
back pack over his shoulders, filing his academic
world in the appropriate compartments and carrying it
all with him.
I had mine slung under my arms the old fashioned
way, cradled against the side while I walked, papers
sticking out, books on top of books, notebooks stuck
in there somewhere.
We were cutting through the campus, just past the
signs that warned us not to walk on the grass. A dirt
path gave evidence of how well we listened, and we
passed without thought, two bodies on automatic pilot.
Students were milling around, most heading to or from
lunch, others sitting in the middle of the campus,
books spread out and socializing. It was another one
of those shots photographers would use for the campus
brochure, though they'd probably ask the subjects to
at least look at their books and pretend to be
studying.
I took in the scenery, remembered suddenly that
Fred had spoken. What did he say? Oh yeah - Higgins.
Angry. "Wow." was all I could manage.
"So about this Leigh thing …" He patted me on the
shoulders, letting me know he wasn't going to let it
slide without obtaining information. We hadn't talked
last night; he had gotten interested in a late night
cable movie, one where the opening scene had four
naked people all sitting around a beach, three of them
actually humans. Me? I'd fallen asleep wondering just
where that idea came from and why.
Didn't matter.
I looked ahead, wondering. "I don't know about it.
I was going to ask her out when Shelly interrupted,
then you guys got quiet and I couldn't do it."
"And then she tackled you and knocked you on your
butt," he laughed, picking up speed with the smell of

dining hall food. For some reason, I didn't really
want to talk about this, knowing I was interested, not
knowing how to proceed and knowing he would get after
me until I did something.

"Well, like I said, I don't even know her last
name," I offered.

He threw out his arms, a 'you're hopeless' gesture,
and shook his head. "Don't pull that crap again, damn
it. This ain't gonna be like last year, remember? When
you followed the cheerleader around for a semester and
never even said 'hello'."

"Actually, I did say hello, about 475 times," I
defended myself. "So what am I supposed to do,
anyway?"

"Man, you're useless." He almost stopped; I could
see his wheels turning. Mentally, I prodded him
forward. Ahead. Don't stop. Don't raise your voice, no
calling attention. Food. Two hundred yards ahead. I
promise. He paused, looked up, then kept walking.

There was a God.

"You're going to use the lousy excuse that you
don't even know her last name!? Come on, man, wake up
and live! This is a small school. That kind of
information is so easy to get. Man!" He popped his
forehead with his hands for effect, leaving me tired
of turning red, not wanting lectures, no desire for
further embarrassment.

"Anyway, fear not, I will help you," he said.

I may need that God and soon.

"You'll help me?" I asked, not wanting to hear the
answer.

"Of course, I'm your buddy. I'll take care of you."

I held my breath, wanting to ask but not daring.

"They'll be in the gym this afternoon at 3
o'clock."

"They will?"

"Yes, they will. Didn't you hear Shelly last night
talking about how they work out on Wednesdays and
Fridays?"

No. Didn't register. Wasn't paying attention.

"So what do we do, just walk up and say, 'hi'
remember us?"

"Damn, you're hopeless. Damn it." He sounded like he was really mad here, so I just kept walking and listened.

"Okay, okay …" the professor began, "what is the first thing people have to do when they go in the gym?"

Not a clue. Breathe? Count calories? Change clothes? Walk?

"Come on, Phil, THINK! They have to Sign In! Are you following?"

Not really, but we'll go with it.

"And when they sign in, you'll see her last name. THEN, you open up your Jenkins College Student Directory and you call. See?"

"Sure, nothing to it," I offered, but my 'confidence' didn't fool him.

He stopped me. Put his arms on each of my shoulders. Faced me. Eyes locked in - *damn it, why can't people stop staring at me today?* "Phil, you're going to call her. Do you understand?"

"Okay, all right already, I'll call her tonight for a date this weekend if it makes you feel better."

Didn't fool him.

"Yeah, I'll believe that one."

He didn't let it go, though. Kept at me at lunch, dared me, called me names, threatened my manhood, you name it. Don't know why it was so important to him.

But …

I had a phone call to make.

I had sent Fred away - anywhere away; wasn't about to make a call with him in there. I could just picture him, holding up rating cards, 1-10, critiquing my performance. He had left semi-willingly, off to study, or climb trees, or whatever the hell he did on Wednesday nights.

We had accomplished our mission in the gym earlier; Fred walking up as cool as could be, telling the bored person behind the counter that he needed the last name of the person who was working out because he had a class with her and needed to return some notes.

So smooth.

The person behind the counter couldn't have cared
less - no gym supervision in his future. He just
turned the sheet around as if bored; even held the pen
in place for Fred to use if needed.

It was needed, and Fred whipped out his notebook
and casually jotted the names down. Me, I was wanting
to go in and watch them work out, but for some reason,
he vetoed the idea. "No, you'll use whatever happens
in there as an excuse not to call her."

Whatever.

Our room was basically a box with two beds, two
study desks and room for only one couch unless you
built a loft or did some serious rearranging; neither
of which was on Fred and my agenda for the next few
weeks. The decor of the room blended well, with his
side being a mess and mine no better.

It looked - well … lived in, in my opinion. There
were papers strung out along the floor, empty beer
bottles on the shelf under the mirror, next to the
stereo, and a pile of tapes, CD's and albums, few of
which were in their actual covers, cluttered all
across.

His study cubicle was a little neater, if that
mattered, though books collected over the years fought
for room in limited space. Notebooks, labeled but not
filed, were thrown about, one over the other, and the
wire of his desk lamp sat above it all, a snake in a
den of paper.

My side was a little more creative, if nothing
else, with pictures lined on the back of the shelves
for my viewing pleasure, one of me at the Grand
Canyon, another of Fred and me and a bunch of women
from one of many Panama City Beach, Florida trips and
another of my parents, on a trip in Canada somewhere,
smiling to the camera, assuring us that all was well
and they wished we were here and remember to brush
your teeth and be good and …

And I had my own share of books and papers, but -
I'm totally getting off the subject.

The condition or lack of neatness of our room
wasn't what was important, not on this night. It was

what sat on the night stand between the two beds that
kept bugging me.
  It was the phone.
  Plain white.
  In working order.
  Touch tone, with Pizza Hut, Domino's, Dave and
Johnny and Deah's phone numbers, all on speed dial.
  It had never really haunted me before. Why would
it? We'd played pranks on other students, called beer
buddies, called a radio station trying to be caller
number nine to win the weekend getaway to Callaway
Gardens, played the "sadistic parent" joke on an
unsuspecting innocent faculty member, and even a few
hundred too many 411 calls, if you would.
  But that was all simple stuff.
  Non-threatening.
  Tonight, however, it had a voice. And a damned
loud one. It spoke to me as I threw my books on the
bed, reminded me as I walked to my closet to find some
clean clothes (no luck), and nudged me as I sat in my
chair with my feet propped up. I picked up the latest
"Sports Illustrated", flipped through it, read about
the rumors of the next swimsuit issue slated for next
February, classic quotes from athletes, fans and
coaches, and skimmed a feature on college football and
just who would be number one??
  Didn't care. Couldn't get into it.
  "What in the hell is my problem?" I yelled to
myself, tossing my magazine down in frustration. I
lifted my nasty Nike's off the coffee table ($20 at
the Scavenger Hut and man, what a bargain!) and walked
over to my bed. Propping both elbows on my knees, I
faced the phone.
  There it was, not going anywhere.
  Just sitting there, waiting.
  Laughing.
  Taunting.
  I fumbled through some papers on my bed, tossed
aside my lack of history notes, papers and other
useless crap and I found it - The Jenkins College
Student Directory. Why did I have to find it? That
would give me an excuse, now wouldn't it?

Wimp!

Chicken!

Her last name was Basil. My nerves jumped around a little when I saw Fred taking it off the Sign In sheet at Memorial Gym. It was the fifth name down, right under the reminder for all students, faculty and staff to please sign in when working out. Or so he said.

Basil.

I opened the directory, hoping she'd be listed.

Hoped like hell she wouldn't be.

Opened it up, thumbed through, stared down on the third page … Bailey … Balley … Barton … BASIL, LEIGH.. My stomach double clutched, did one of those drops it does when you shoot down a big hill at the Amusement Park.

Damn it, why did she have to be listed?

Thank God she's listed. Now I can call her.

No way in hell I'm calling her. I'm sober, for God's sakes.

Call her.

She's probably not even home.

You'll know when you call her.

She's probably busy.

Good, call her.

No.

Yes.

No.

Yes.

You call her!

Even I had to laugh at that one, wondering exactly which 'you' was going to make the call.

I stared at the page - 555-2458. The whole nervous system malfunctioned over seven lousy numbers. Seven beautiful numbers. Hadn't been this nervous since having to pinch hit for Calvin in the bottom of the seventh last year with the bases loaded, two outs and us down by three.

The inning ended, us still down by three.

Maybe that's a sign. Maybe.

ENOUGH!

I tossed the book aside and grabbed the phone,

turned it towards me where I could dial. My fingers
stopped above the first '5'. Wasn't there something
else I needed to do tonight? Literature to read?
History to catch up on? Clothes to wash? Walls to
stare at? Cliffs to dive off?

"GOD, you're pissing me off," I yelled again, being
oh so thankful that Fred wasn't around to see this.
He'd have a field day jumping on me, would never, ever
let me forget it.

I could actually hear his voice, fighting in there
with mine. "She's just a woman, for Christ sakes! Man,
I'd hate to see you in a serious pressure situation.
Wow …"

I put the phone down. I picked the phone back up.
Why did I have to be a guy? Wouldn't it be easier to
be a girl? *Right … And go through periods, have
babies, get cramps a few times a month and stare at a
phone that never rang because some micro-brained wimp
was too much of a chickenshit to pick up a phone and
dial. Ouch.*

The truth really sucked sometimes.

I rubbed my hand together, as if this would help.
Breathed deeply. Slowly. Laughing at myself and
hurting all at the same time.

My right hand took action. Five … five … five.
Pause for effect … two … four … five. I stopped.

No way.

I ain't calling that damned number.

Not now.

This was getting tough. I needed a break, yeah,
that's what I needed. Walked back to the other end,
picked up the magazine, threw it back down.

Came back over. Sat by the phone. Got myself
pumped. *Get it over with. You can do it. You can do
it. You can do it.*

I did it.

All seven numbers this time, no pause in the
middle, no pause in the end. My heart, like the world,
stopped after dialing that sacred '8' at the end. I
waited for what seemed like hours (half a second for
the connection to get through). Pause. Click at the

other end. Busy.

"Yes, there is a God!" I screamed, slamming the phone down. Jumped up and pumped my fists into the air. Breathed out a huge sigh of relief. Walked back across the room, propped my feet up.

Wait a minute. What the hell are you so happy about? Do it, damn it, do it again.

Are you serious?

Hell yes I'm serious, get your butt back up, pick up the phone and call her. Now!!

This was getting tough. Wouldn't a Miller Lite be good right now? Or did it have to be a Miller Lite? Where was Fred? Couldn't he come in and suggest we go somewhere? A movie? Skating? Talking? Drinking? Swimming in funk creek? Anything? Anywhere?

No, you ain't getting out of this one. You will talk to her. Tonight! I surely hoped no one was walking outside my window, staring at a supposedly sane 22-year-old who talked to telephones and threw fits for no particular reason. I laughed again, though it didn't release me from the fact that I, and no one else, was pissing me off.

Don't think. Just do it. Use the force. Be the ball.

I did it again. Quickly, before I came up with some other excuse. It rang. *Oh shit. Maybe nobody's home. Maybe they're all outside studying. Or they're in the shower. Right! Two hundred women are all showering at the same time and absolutely not one of them can come to the phone. Sure, happens all the time.*

Second ring ... *Good stuff* ... *I can go ahead and hang up. After all, I've given it one helluva college try.* "Yeah Fred, I called, she wasn't there. Too bad, too, I was really looking forward to asking her ..."

"Hello?" came a voice. My throat responded - by doing nothing. My mouth opened, tongue laying down and ready. Consonants, vowels perched at the tip, waiting to form words and communicate.

Nothing.

"HELLO!" Louder this time, generally angry, getting hotter. Speak now or I hang up.

"Uh, yes, this is ... I mean, is Leigh Basil there?"
I managed.
"This is Leigh Basil," she answered, questioning
and curious.
Holy shit. No time to regroup. Can't hang up
while they're going to get her. No time to think. Full
speed ahead. Damn the torpedoes.
"Hi Leigh," I managed. *Brilliant comment.*
Wonderfully creative. Grace under pressure. A non-
artist in action. How'd I ever think of that one?
Bonehead!
"Who is this?"
I can do it. Simple question. Go ahead. Try. "This
is Phil, you know, from the Pub yesterday." Silence.
No help. "Remember?"
"HI, PHIL, how are you?" she sounded happy to hear
from me. Thank God, I just lost eight pounds.. *Wimp!*
"I didn't mean to bother you ... I ..."
"It's okay, I was heading out the door to study,
but ..."
"I'll let you go, I mean, I can call some other
time."
"No, go ahead, I've got some time."
Good try, gutless.
More silence.
I hate myself.
The system kicked into overload. Had to get to the
point and get there fast. Still nervous, not sure
why. The thought of a root canal or a filling without
the novacaine sounded better at this point.
"Phil?"
"Sorry, I'm still here. I had a question for you ..."
Beautiful! To the point. Get on with it.
"What's that?"
"I won't keep you long, I was just wondering ..."
Even my radio turned itself off at this point, the
campus stopped, students quit what they were doing,
the anchors on TV quit reading their scripts and stuck
their faces in, Chevy Chase paused from his monologue,
Jay Leno silenced his audience, begged for quiet, even
my older brothers appeared out of nowhere, faces in
the window, smirks on their faces, laughing at little

brother and laying odds on the outcome.

More silence, though listening to her breathe was kind of kinky.

Get on with it!

"Listen, I understand if you think I'm crazy, Leigh, but … we're having a party Friday night and I don't have a date and I figure you do or you probably have about 362 boyfriends but … even if you did, going out with me would probably make you appreciate them a whole lot more. Anyway.." Her laughter interrupted. It made me feel good to make people laugh – even if I didn't do it on purpose. I wanted to just pause and hear the laughter. Couldn't. No time. When you're on a roll, you haul ass.

"Sorry to ramble, but, would you like to go with me to a party Friday night?"

My stomach dropped.

Not gradually, but straight down.

The earth shook. Slowly at first, a short rattle if you will, then pried itself loose and turned over. Roller-coaster style. Me, I held on to the bed post. Not sure if that would help.

And why the hell was I so nervous about someone I hardly knew?

Another pause. Another eternity. Finally, the voice.

"I don't know."

She didn't *&%#$@ know! All this and she didn't #$*& know? Wars were fought over answers like that. Innocent people killed, property destroyed, children starved. I started laughing at this point, not sure why, but I believe it reminded me of when my mother told my oldest brother to eat all his food because of all those starving people overseas that didn't have any. He just looked at her and answered, "Name one."

Mistake.

Dad didn't laugh nearly as hard as I did.

Mom kind of chuckled, then held back.

Older brother laughed his ass off.

Got kicked under the table.

Why am I thinking about this?

"What are you laughing at?" It was her, bringing me

back.
    "I'm sorry, I …"
    "Phil?"
    "What?"
    "I was just giving you a hard time. I'd love to go
with you Friday night."
    "You would?" *Oops, wrong move, bad statement, lack
of confidence.*
    "Of course I would, what time are you picking me
up?"
    No idea, hadn't thought that far ahead.
    "Eight o'clock?"
    "That will be fine."
    "Okay, see you Friday night, Leigh."
    "Goodbye."
    "Bye."
    Click.
    Click.
    That wasn't so hard now was it?
    I exhaled 37 more pounds out of my body, pumped my
fist into the air, and went into the hall, searching
for Fred.
    Where was a good roommate when you needed one?
    I needed a beer. Now.

III. A Date

"So you have a date?" It was Fred and it was 3 a.m. and it was probably the last year of our lives where it being 3 a.m. didn't matter at all.

I rolled over onto an elbow, accidentally bumping into one of last week's shirts I'd forgotten to clear away in the 'get ready for bed' process. I pushed it onto the floor. It plopped down among plenty of company, with our first semester cleaning session already put off until some time next month.

"What's wrong with me having a date?" I tried to sound hurt here, wondering why that was so odd.

"I don't know, I just thought a 'date' was a rare fruit not found in Georgia, that's all." He laughed at his own joke, then continued. "You're taking her to a beer party? One of ours?"

He asked this in a penetrating tone, as if disappointed. I rolled back over, cupped my hands on my pillow and propped my head on the both of them.

"You're suggesting I take her out, like to eat, to a movie or something like that?"

Silence from his end … *and answer me, damn it*!

Fred rolled over, propped himself on his elbow and faced me; two guys about to solve all the world's problems except for tennis elbow and the common cold.

"No, and I'll tell you why." *Somehow, I knew he would*. "Let's look at it this way," he began, shuffling some covers around, probably needing diagrams or something to get his point across. "I think you're showing coconut-sized balls in taking her to this beer party." I laughed at this, wondering why.

"Let's say you take her out to some nice place; you know, Cracker Barrel, Calvin's, one of those joints," he continued. "She's thinking two things right off the bat; either, a) this guy really likes me, or b) he's just trying to get me in the rack." Another pause. "Either way, this is no good."

I laughed again, following his logic.

"So is there a point here?" I asked.

"Hey!" he sounded genuinely offended. "You just be thankful I'm your roommate and can take care of you like this."

"Sorry."

"No problem, let me continue."

By all means.

"Anyway, you're just taking her to a beer party, nothing more, nothing less. It shows character."

"Taking her to a beer party shows character? I'd have thought it was the other way around."

"So would everybody else, and you and all of them would be wrong."

I wasn't going to ask.

"Anyway, now she has a totally different scenario playing out in her head," he continued. "She knows one of two things: First, this guy just goes about his business come hell or high water and couldn't care less whether I go with him or not. Girls like that kind of stuff. It shows initiative, direction." I had to laugh again. Something about a beer party and direction. "Or, the second scenario is - and this is where you need to fall in - is that here is a guy who is who he is and to hell with it. Not out to impress anyone, just knows who he is and what he's about. Just going to a beer party on a Friday night. Plain and simple. Nothing fancy. Take it or leave it, you're there either way. Deal with it. That's you."

I could feel his eyes looking over. Me, I'd never given that much advanced thought to this, to tell you the truth, only a little guilty about taking her to a beer party. Then again, I'd never had to process drinking a water tower full of beer, trying to ask a girl out and screwing it up the first time, then having her burp into my ear and tackling me onto the

floor and then …
  "Are you with me over there?"
  "Oh sure, I just hadn't given it that much thought,
that's all."
  "Yes, Phil, you have. And I'm just putting your
mind at ease."
  Why don't I learn? Lying to friends doesn't work.
  We both lay there for a while. I considered asking
him whether I should shave or go with the Don Johnson
look, but I thought better of it. When he spoke like
that, it took me a while to digest these things, not
always necessarily from what he said, but more from
where he got it all from. Who knew?
  Trying to figure out how people's minds work was
pretty fun. With his, I never knew.
  Anyway, I tried all the advanced techniques to
induce self-hypnosis, sleep, or anything that would
silence my mind. Millions of sheep leaped over a
fence. Reminded me of milking cows back home with Don
Stanford, how hard he'd laugh at me and my overalls.
Or were they his? And how funny his hair looked at
4:30 in the morning and what kind of hell was it that
made somebody get up every single day at 4:30 in the
morning to milk cows when there were perfectly good
things to dream about? And thick, feathery beds to
sleep in?
  Moved on to Technique #2.
  Visualized every number of the 24-second clock,
backwards and forwards. Wrong again. Reminded me of
the region finals. I'd dribbled too much with my head
down as usual, cutters open for days underneath,
Cookie swinging around a screen on the weak side
screaming for the ball, Marv breaking away from his
man in good position. Never saw them. Something about
dribbling, calling a play and thinking at the same
time. Couldn't do it.
  Shot clock went off.
  Turnover.
  We lose.
  Cheerleader didn't want to sit with me on the bus
on the way home.
  Sat with Cookie and Marv. They were polite, but …

I'm trying to get to sleep here and why am I thinking
about that?

The 24-second thing never worked anyway. Reminded
me of the '24-hour rule' in college, pertaining to
when someone leaves beer in your refrigerator. Next
day, it was yours, unless they called and reminded
you.

Made me laugh. On our hall, it was the 24-second
rule, just like the shot clock. If it's not claimed in
24 seconds, the horn goes off. A turnover. Other
team's ball. Or beer.

Technique #3.

Stared at objects on the wall until dizzy. No, the
Braves team picture didn't do it. Too many days and
nights with the radio, huddled underneath the covers,
listening to Skip Caray. Remembering the intensity
when the game was close, the humor when we were 30
games out in August and the lack of humor when the
folks told me to turn that damned radio off. Lived and
died with those guys, totally lived and died. Them and
the Boston Red Sox, of course. And man, if those two
ever hooked up in the Series? Then what? Who would I
cheer for? Who would you rather have in the outfield,
Hank Aaron or Carl Yastrzemski? Who would you rather
meet in person, Greg Maddux or Mo Vaughan?

And how about that homer Justice hit in the top of
the ninth in Cincinnati back in October of '91? The
bar went nuts; the band thought we were cheering for
them. They ran back onstage and did an encore we never
asked for. We tuned them out while the Braves retired
the side in the ninth and kept pace with the Dodgers.
Never mind.

Dead file … Move on to other objects.

How about the poster of the rock group The Clash?
Didn't work. Took a girl to a Clash concert in Atlanta
last November - the 18th if you're into dates and how
about that for memory, Professor Higgins? We got
along so good. She was so beautiful. So alive. We had
so much fun. Loved spending time with her. Never
argued. Never fought.

She dumped me one day, out of the blue, no reason
given.

Bitch.
Didn't need her anyway.
Technique #4. Or is it #5?
Time for a different approach, like naming all
teachers grades 1-12. Terrible idea. Got through
grammar and middle school okay, but bogged down
totally in high school. Too much went on. Women or
lack of, sports, pep rallies, study halls, meetings,
drinking beer after school in broken down pickup
trucks, slipping in past the parents, drunk, tired and
stupid. Too many memories. And I'm supposed to be
sleeping.
But I'm not tired.
Friday is only two days away.
Excuse me, one day away. It's after midnight. It's
Thursday now.
And if I went to sleep right now … and I'm not even
tired, I'd get only four hours of sleep. And I'm not
even close.
I've turned a perfectly comfort zone filled
situation into one of - nervousness?
I eventually slept, tired of calling myself names.

"You're going to wear that?" It was Fred, hunched
in the corner of our room, perched between the
Domino's pizza boxes, the Lite beer cans, Chemistry
papers and a lot of books; none of which could catch
our required attention.
He was sitting on his bed, browsing through the
latest issue of Playboy for the tenth-through-fiftieth
time, (of course he only got it for the articles!) and
he was giving me the once-over. He was in boxer
shorts, dirty socks, a T-shirt and his hat, and he
paused from his 'articles' long enough to stand and
critique.
We were ending our 'study hall' session - me
listening to R.E.M. on the head phones and he stirring
up his hormones. Nothing was accomplished as usual,
but at least we tried.
Sort of.
I looked down to do a quick inventory, remembering
all of mom's finest tips. Shoes are on and tied. Good.

Socks, do they match? Never could figure why that one
mattered, I'd have on long pants anyway. But they did,
so I guess that was good as well. Jeans fastened and
zipped. Unfortunately, yes they were. Shirt on
straight, got it. No visible zits or substances
hanging out of ears, mouth or nose. Did I shave? No,
but you can't do everything.
     "What's the problem?" I looked down at my shoes
and looked myself over as best I could.
     Fred grabbed his magazine and sat back down. "You
look awful," he said, shaking his head and returning
to his scenery. He started to get up again, then
thought better of it.
     "I looked awful when I met her, so what?"
     He scratched his chin, considering. "You know, you
have a point, but wouldn't you want to get rid of that
shirt?" I started to remind him of the above "late
night conversation" but didn't have the time. After
all, he would answer.
     I picked up my coke that was sitting on the
dresser, probably bought sometime during the calendar
week; took a chug and defended myself. "We're not
going to a funeral or a wedding, we're going to a
party. A beer party."
     He picked his magazine back up and returned to the
horizontal position. "You're probably right." He
looked back at the January babe, then cut his eyes
back at me. "But ace the shirt, anyway. Put one on
that has a collar. Grab that new one your mother sent
up." Pause. "Oh, and don't forget to take the
cardboard and the pins out of it."
     He laughed at this. I'd made the cardboard mistake
before on an earlier date and man, I just couldn't
figure out how she knew it was a new shirt. Really
felt like a fool when I told her she must have ESP,
while she just reached across and yanked.
     We don't have to get into that, do we?
     I obeyed as ordered, though I didn't worry much
about the pins. I was a little nervous at the time and
besides, pins had a way of reminding you if you forgot
one. She was the type of girl who would probably laugh
at something like that, anyway. She was …

"You like this girl, don't you?" Fred looked at me
with a straight face, inquiring eyes.

Me, I gave him my own idiotic stare, all the while
thinking - damn, don't you just hate those penetrating
questions? He should be a lawyer or a …

"Don't you?" And what an ignorant question.

"What difference does it make whether I like her or
not?" He dropped his magazine again, took off his
glasses for effect, and spread his arms out wide.
"You're the one going out with her." He stopped,
dropping his head as if figuring out how to proceed.
He was coming with something serious. I could feel it.

"Don't worry about what Richard and Mike and all
those guys say."

Oh no, the old peer pressure routine.

"What do …"

"I mean, be yourself, Man, why would you take their
advice? Richard has no girlfriend, the jury's still
out on whether Mike's walks upright or not, Jimmy's
talks like a goat in heat and who can figure if Bob's
is even female or not?"

"Doesn't matter these days."

He tossed his magazine at me. *Wow, don't mess up
that magazine!* He made a dress code change or two,
gave me advice I didn't really hear, then flipped his
hand up as if dismissing me.

"Get out of here. Have fun. Go away."

So I did, though my body wasn't used to leaving my
dorm with those new clothes on. The shirt was nice,
had a blue horse on it, the pants were new but faded
blue jeans and the jacket - well … I wasn't really
sure where the jacket came from. It was suede or
leather or was there a difference and it hugged my
chest just a little too tightly on this not so cold
Friday night.

I walked out the back way to the car, not wanting
to risk walking past the guys, who were already
brewing down at the other end. Didn't want to hear
their words of lack of encouragement at this point. I
sneaked out on the tennis court side, ducked as I
crossed their window, then sprinted up the hill to the

parking lot.

Unlocking my car, I quickly removed all evidence of my slob-ridden habits. Throwing open the trunk, I poured my front and back seats inside. Hardee's, McDonald's, Miller, Miller Lite, Arby's, papers, books, what was that? Who knew? Pens, pencils, notebooks, tennis balls, a picture of an ex-girlfriend. Hold on … might want to get rid of that one.

Anyway, Leigh lived in the upper quad for those of you familiar with the Jenkins College campus, and if you weren't, so what? The bottom line was, it was about a mile drive, the cruise taking me past the Chemistry Building, Green Hall, Trustees, the Emerson Center, Cook Building, Hermann Hall and hell no, I didn't know what went on in all those buildings.

After the campus part, there was about a half-mile patch of open fields with fences, hay, tall, sweet smelling Georgia grass, deer sometimes darting in and out of the woods in the back, and then, the castles of the upper quad.

It fit that she lived in a castle, it really did, though that did nothing to stop the butterflies from screaming at me as I approached the dorm. *My God,* I thought as I combed the left-over candy bar crumbs from who knows when underneath my seat, closed the door and headed up the path, *I'm off to pick up the princess.*

Walk slowly, damn it, not so fast, you don't want to appear too eager, said the voice as I walked between the shrubs and up the stairs. Were these voices going to follow me all night? Did I have to listen to lines from the "Universal Handbook of College Studs" from start to finish? Probably not, it would switch over once she was with me, over to the one from 'The Dating Game'. *Well, everything started out fine, I was minding my manners, all ready with my clean shirt on, but then …*

To hell with all that, couldn't I just be myself?

No way, that would never do. Would it?

I concentrated on the cement steps to calm my turmoil; made myself walk slowly to the top. It was a

big, wooden door that was kept locked on the weekends.
Actually, pausing and looking around me at the castle-
structured buildings, the surrounding shrubs and the
magnificence of it all, it wouldn't have surprised me
if there had been a moat surrounding the doors.

But no, it was seven steps and up and then the big,
brown barrier at the top. I paused before climbing, at
least being relieved that it wasn't like high school -
where you had to go in and shoot the shit with the
parents. My ex's father would always make it a point
to be cleaning his gun when I walked in; polishing,
cleaning, waxing, and how clean did it have to be? And
he'd look me square in the eye, hell yes he would, as
he'd put it down on the couch, walk over and extend
his hand. And holy shit, that man could grip a hand!
My little ink-pen-holding, money-grabbing-from-parents
hand couldn't do a thing under there - except scream,
wilt and threaten to break under the pressure. And his
eyes, those military eyes that would lock into mine
and wouldn't consider letting loose. My civilian eyes
not daring to look away, but not daring to stare back,
either. All the while, he'd go through his speech and
I'd try not to shake and I'd try not to laugh. I could
never help but to think of Louis Gossett, Jr. in "An
Officer and a Gentleman," when he got in Richard
Gere's face. "You'd better stop eye-balling me, boy!"

I'd hold it back while he rattled off the
questions. "Where are you two going? When are you
coming back? What time is the movie? Do you have
reservations for dinner? What time are you bringing my
daughter back? Do you have gas?"

I shrugged this off, being almost relieved when I
caught her tangled up with another guy, arms and legs
piled, stretched and bent so many different ways, I
should've thrown a penalty flag right there, went in
to untangle, find out who's was who's and how many
people were under there and THANK GOD I didn't have to
stare at her father's shotgun anymore and have him
break my hand and …

I actually found out later he liked me. Thought I
was respectful, proper, possessing all the social
graces and amenities, if you will.

Enough already. Let's continue. Shall we?

My nerves reached the top of the stairs before I did, but once my body made it, I paused again, then knocked. *Let's get this little show on the road, shall we?*
SHUTUP!
"Who is it?" Oh no, it sounded like her. No time for mental preparation whatsoever.
"It's Phil. I'm here to pick up Leigh."
"Who?"
"Leigh, is that you?" My stomach did a quick drop, you know the feeling, like the one on the first or second downhill of the Scream Machine AFTER you've eaten the cotton candy and the nasty hot dog and have had two hours of standing in line inside those terminals with all those sweaty, smelly, greasy, nasty people and your stomach just … doesn't quite know what to do.
I waited for the doors to open; stood there, tucked in my shirt again, flicked my hair back with my hands … and waited.
"Would you like for me to come out?" I could hear her laughing at me from within and once again, I knew not what to say or do. Oh well, they say there's a time in every person's life when you're made a fool of by the opposite sex. Maybe I'll get mine out of the way right here, right now and …
In an instant, the door opened and out it came. Water that is, emptying from a big, silver bucket, held by the North American Queen herself. It hit me right across the chest. - Oh *no, new shirt* - melted the jacket against my chest and dribbled down to my jeans.
You know, I had expected a lot on this date, even had plans for idle conversation if it came to that. But what do you say about a woman that throws a bucket of water on you, point blank, when you don't even have her in the car yet?
She stood there, mouth open and poised, a face that simply couldn't wait to start laughing. She herself, was already soaked to the gills, her blond hair matted

up around her eyes and mouth, her jeans and T-shirt drenched from head to toe.

She looked … great.

Not knowing what to do and feeling I was being severely tested, I just started laughing.

"Leigh," I began, shaking water from my hands, "these are not my …"

"Those are not your clothes? Why not? Who dresses you anyway?" She asked, her mouth still hanging there, ready to absorb whatever was thrown her way. "Come on in. You're wet, you have a date with me in five minutes and you're simply not ready."

With that she stepped aside, gestured towards more stairs and winding at that, and she took me into her quarters. Oh shit, it was my English teacher's voice, competing for time in my head. Why couldn't I ever hear her in class?

"What did the room look like? Details. Please!"

Okay, okay, it was big, huge even, four walls, one floor, one ceiling, two beds, two closets, two desks, shitload of posters on the walls, do-dads or knick-knacks or what-me-nots or whatever the hell you call those things lined up on a bookshelf in a corner with books that probably hadn't been touched. Dust on the radiator in the corner, gobs of it even, spiders playing kick the can in the web in another corner next to a sweater that was hanging from a hook that came from a ceiling. THE ceiling, I mean.

"What kind of posters? You're so general."

No, damn it, I'm so wet, but since you ask, there's The Beach Boys, the cast from "Friends", David Letterman and where did that poster come from?, and "Olympics, Atlanta, 1996."

There, you happy?

"The room was a mess, you say?"

Not a chance. It was heaven. Pure, unadulterated (is that a word?) heaven. Dear Mom, The world is good. Don't need money, don't need clothes (well, maybe a dryer), don't need medicine, don't need anything. I told you I did the right thing by coming here. Man, you never seem to listen to me.

"Sit down," Leigh awakened me from wherever I'd gone. "On the bed."

I just stood there, looking around helplessly, not wanting to be rude, but …

"But I'm wet."

"Do I look like I care? Sit down or I'll throw you down." And with that, she did. She hurled her body into the air, crashing sideways into my chest and pinning me right across the bed. Jumping to her feet, she placed both her knees on my shoulders, nailing me to my spot.

"Were you about to argue with me?" she asked. And she laughed again. I was getting close to conversational, but not yet. I wasn't really sure.

She jumped off me suddenly, and started across to her closet. "Seriously," she began, "I've got a shirt you can borrow, your jeans are okay, and man, where did you get that ugly jacket?"

I laughed, she glanced over semi-harshly, wondering where the humor was and I answered, "It's Fred's, he was..." I wasn't going to say it.

"What was he doing? Dressing you? You look fine. Just throw me the shirt and I'll wash it for you."

It was a full moon, that much I won't forget. And her giggling and laughing. And burping after her first beer. And kicking me in the butt with her foot while walking. And constantly switching the station on my radio.

We had circled the campus a couple of times; she didn't want to get there just yet. Me, I didn't care if we made it at all, but that's beside the point. We reversed direction back towards my dorms, circled the tennis courts, old gym, funk creek and the academic buildings and had started back up to her place.

"Those cows look like they're playing a game of football, don't they?" was one of her first comments as we started back across the fields. She looked at me after saying this, her mouth taking on that 'O' shape as if waiting for reinforcement. Truth be known, I couldn't really say I'd noticed a whole helluva lot about the cows, one way or the other. But, since she mentioned it, it did look pretty much like a football game. Or not.

"Sorry," she apologized, "I just seem to notice these things." It was a small, simple statement, one that slowed down my innards somewhat. The voice took advantage of the silence, letting his presence be known. Again. *Don't you think maybe she's a little nervous, too? Can't you just be yourself and have a good time? Will you relax?*

I managed not to wreck with these comforting thoughts and we pulled into the party at around 10:45. Most of the fashionably-late people had already arrived, so we were really pushing it a bit.

I parked along the street and walked up, beer in one hand, babe at my side, and man, wasn't life just great? Dave and Johnny lived here, for the record. They were baseball teammates, lived on our hall for three years and decided they were sick of all the petty rules (were politely asked to move off by the dean of students, never to return, but we'll forget that for now.) and had moved out.

It was a two story, run-down house they'd planned on fixing up once they moved in. With a semester and six beer parties already under it's belt, it appeared the house would have to wait a while. For now, we were glad; with no need for guilt after spilling a beer. Or generally trashing the place.

Kevin Smith, or "Stretch" if you knew him well enough, was the first sight as we walked up the driveway towards the house. He was leaning against an old Chevy, probably between puking bouts, and he made an attempt to stand up straighter as we approached.

"Phil? And is that … Leigh?"

Bastard. Why was he so shocked that I was with such a cute girl?

"Have you already thrown up or were you just about to?" It WAS Leigh, coming across with the point blank, penetrating question. Kevin lifted his head upright at this, as if answering a correcting parent.

"NO, no, I was just … you know … getting some fresh air."

"How's the party?" I asked, trying to save him from

embarrassment.
"Be careful of the punch, it's rough." And with
that, he turned a corner and - well, never mind.
We could take a hint.
We walked inside, our eyes adjusting to the
piercing cigarette smoke and the smell of liquor,
mixed with beer, mixed with … not sure what the last
smell was. People were sitting around on the floor, on
couches, standing in groups, listening to music,
smoking, drinking; a bunch of people happy to be out
of the school environment for a couple of days. It
always amazed me what people would do once they knew
they didn't have to work or be at school the next day.
Fun to watch in one sense, made me wonder how well
they enjoyed their lives in another.
Each room was more of the same, with people filling
the chairs, lingering in doorways, grabbing beers from
the refrigerator or walking back out to their cars.
Leigh and I walked through, me wanting to impress
her with all the people I knew and how glad they'd be
to see me. To tell you the truth, I didn't recognize
some of those people and this was supposed to be our
party. A combination third floor/baseball team thing.
Didn't matter.
We stood off in the corner in the kitchen for a
while, neither of us seeming to be into it. My friends
were scattered about and she knew a few people, but
all of them were about six shades drunker than we were
and neither of us felt like catching up. Or maybe we
didn't want to be around other people.
We watched it from the corner, like bad kids in
kindergarten that got sent to the Chair. I made it a
point not to look at my watch after a while, though
reminding myself of it made me only look at it more.
11:15 - and slowly creeping - Is she having fun? Do
I suggest? No … we've only been here for a beer and a
half. It's way to early to suggest …
"Let's go get a 12-pack of beer and get out of
here," Leigh said this as if on cue. This time, it was
my mouth that curled up in confusion and my silence
almost screwed it up. I was almost thinking that I
didn't even need alcohol on a night like this.. But -

what the hell. since she suggested it.

"Never mind," she continued, "we can stay."

"No, no, I've been ready, that's a great idea," I answered.

We headed out, my lungs glad to be free of cigarette smoke and whatever else. Actually, aside from the smell of Stretch's earlier deposit, it was a great night to be outside anyway. The moon was full, winds calm; one of those nights the weathermen would raise hell about. He would point his or her pencil right in your face and insist that this night was so similar to an early summer's night and ...

Whatever.

We got back into the car, me fastening my seat belt out of habit, she hers just to be polite, and that was when it first hit me.

This was it.

There was no turning back.

There was nobody to blame.

There were no excuses.

This was THE MOMENT OF TRUTH.

We were in a car, just the two of us, heading out ... where? Just out.

Just me.

And just her.

And oh shit.

And it was time enough for me to start thinking something stupid and laughing aloud. And fearing she would ask me what I was laughing about and I wouldn't be able to explain it to her.

And that's exactly what happened. I couldn't tell her what it was, but I'll tell you. It was that damned movie, "Fast Times at Ridgemont High" when Damone was teaching Mark Ratner how to hit on women.

"When it comes time to making out, always put on side two of Led Zeppelin Four. It works like a charm," he'd told his friend.

"You mean you're going to just crack up laughing and not even tell me what you're laughing at?" It was Leigh, with a trace of anger in her voice. She actually looked hurt as she said this. And boy did she look cute when she looked hurt. Her tiny little mouth

seemed to drop a bit, her eyes focused more on me
instead of all over the place and these small wrinkles
creased the corners of her cheeks. I wanted to pull
those cheeks and - never mind.

"I'm sorry, sometimes I just think funny things."
And then I laughed again, because that was a line from
another movie, though at the time, I couldn't recall
what it was.

She turned away and, as if to change the subject,
began to rummage through my car. She kept turning
between the back and the front seat, a hyperactive
mind demanding to be stimulated. I just looked over
and watched, sensing the wheels spinning in her head
and …

Then she found it. Or she found something, anyway.

"Oh my God!" she exclaimed, clutching two tapes in
her hands as she pulled them up between the two seats.

"What?"

She looked over at me with curiosity, eyes now
sparkling. "You've got a John Denver tape and a Bee
Gees tape. Right here. In the same car! This is a
first."

Actually, I loved both John Denver and the Bee
Gees, but damned if I was ever going to tell anybody.
"I'm sorry, they're actually …"

"Don't give me that shit," she jumped in. "They're
yours. I know they are." She stared back at them as
she said this, "An Evening With John Denver," and
"Spirits Having Flown" staring right back at her.

What could I say?

A closet John Denver/Bee Gees fan. Busted. Guilty.
Of enjoying hearing JD sing while in the mountains, or
listening to the Bee Gees when I was sick of rap. *Rap,
no, don't tell her.* Sorry, I have a conversation to
join.

"Well."

"Well, what? You let your friends dress you and you
hide your music. Why do you do these things? Just put
on your clothes, play your music, be yourself, and if
other people don't like it, they can go screw
themselves."

Oh my God, I was in love.

I started to comment, but the voice shut me up. And then she spoke, thank God, so I wouldn't ruin the moment.

"Actually, I kind of like John Denver myself, though I think the Bee Gees sing like they just go kicked right square in the balls."

No comments from the wordless wonder. Just my mouth hanging open, with drool approaching fast if I didn't close it soon. Miraculously, a thought crept inside, one that I could actually share with my listening audience.

"I'm a little curious about that."

She turned in my direction, ears eager to hear and react. "About what?"

"About the Bee Gees and John Denver. How in the world can they have sold millions of albums and yet, nobody ever admits that they like them?"

Not a bad comment under pressure. My inner self patted myself on the shoulder. Good diversion, self-defense with humor, dodging one bullet, preparing for the next.

"Oh, everybody likes them," she said without a pause. "It's just that everybody hides all the tapes under their car seats. I mean, if you turn your stereo down when you're at a red light, you can hear all of that stuff you can handle. As long as the person in the other car is alone, that is. Otherwise, it's pretty much Pearl Jam, Counting Crows, the Beatles, the Stones or some of that disco shit that people never got out of their system."

"You like disco?"

"Only when I'm drunk and feel like dancing."

Okay, enough of the small talk. And there was plenty of that. We covered astronauts, what our mothers made us eat for breakfast before school, Miss Hinkley's music class, Bill McClendon's clothes he never washed, music, sex, drugs, rock and roll.

The digital clock had made it's pivot as the car sat parked across from the lake, hidden from security behind a clump of trees. We'd bought the 12-pack and she'd instructed me to head back to the campus. This was scary, she was reading my mind.

I'd driven up past her dorm, away from everything, down a narrow road where thick trees surrounded both sides, with fences flanking the road with shrubs in front that were well manicured by the maintenance people. Another brochure piece, if you will. "See, we even keep the back of the campus clean!"

Cross country runners trained here, students drove these parts to cure claustrophobia, beer drinkers came back when tired of sitting in their rooms and couples made their way to these parts only to get run off by security at one point or another.

It was quiet.

The Jenkins College weekend was going on outside the gates at the time.

But who cared? We parked, drank and talked. Constantly. Never paused. Higgins would've been proud. No notes needed, thank you very much, just two college students hashing it out, shooting the shit, throwing words around like they'd never stop, our own little gusts, though not as high pitched and with a lot less care.

I looked at my digital clock that sometimes worked. 4:00 a.m.

4:00 a.m.? What the hell happened to 1, 2, and 3? I heard my mother's voice, asking me what we did until 4:00 in the morning. I always shrugged my shoulders and had the exact same answer.

"I don't know."

She'd always shake her head, but it was always the truth. I didn't. You tell me. What did you do? What exactly did you talk about for five hours? You mean, you sat around and talked for … how many hours?

Really?

About what?

Mother's voice settled down, as did my own. The CD player was changing tracks, with the Counting Crows getting ready to change over to R.E.M. Or was it Dave Matthews? I should know this by now.

Anyway.

At approximately 4:14 a.m., eastern Jenkins College Time, Saturday, October whatever the hell date it was

now, we stopped talking. Her head was perched on my
shoulder (and gee, her hair smelled terrific! And damn
it, I started laughing again.)

She cut her eyes up at me, but this time didn't
ask. Her eyes locked into mine and clamped down. Blue,
round, curious, intense, funny little eyes all rolled
into one face; an expression for every situation. My
natural reaction was to try to say something funny,
but …

Would you hurry up and kiss her you stupid,
ignorant, incompetent, miserable, wimp, scum, gutless,
big mouthed, chicken shit?

I'm no genius, but I figured the voice was really
starting to get a little angry. And make me angry in
the process.

Anyway, the world just stopped. Nothing moved.
Anywhere. Even the crickets stopped chirping, the
frogs stopped bumping their butts, the clouds stopped
drifting, even the moon peered in.

Her face got closer to mine.

I looked her square in the eye.

Her eyes never blinked.

Nor did mine.

If you don't kiss her soon, you're probably going
to shit in your pants!

Oh no, please don't laugh.

I closed my eyes, moved my face forward, and at the
last second, she turned her head and I ended up
kissing her somewhere between the cheek and her left
ear. God, how loud I could hear the laughter, coming
from my friend's mouths, if they ever heard about this
one. I'll never tell.

"I was just kidding," she said.

Then she giggled.

And then we did it right.

For the record, I entered my dorm room at around
5:45 a.m. Feet never touched the ground once as I
parked the car, complete with extra bird shit on the
hood, and cruised towards Alumni Hall, Room 34. Made
it a point to walk slowly, I did. Something about the
beauty of not hearing a bell or having to rush to

class. Or tracking down a teacher, missing him or her
in their office by ten minutes; told to make yet
another appointment. Or beating people to the chow
line. Or …

This slow thing could be a good habit, I thought,
though I knew it wouldn't happen for a while. Life, or
college life even, wasn't designed that way. Time was
only equated in money, self worth was only in how much
you'd accomplished in other's eyes.

Walks, relaxation and peace of mind so underrated,
so buried, so forgotten, so cast aside for technology,
committees and "progress reports."

Not for me and not for now. I cut across the
campus, slowly, appreciating its silence, walking past
the signs that told me not to walk on the grass
(sorry, again!), past the academic buildings, across
the road, across funk creek and the tennis courts and
into the dorms. It was a tad colder now, getting
toward jacket weather, but I knew I'd have to
appreciate this night even more since the jackets
would turn heavier in short time.

Fred was standing in the hall as I turned the
corner. Why was he there? This late? Who knew?

He glanced at his watch, then up at me. "Man, you
must've gotten your brains …"

"Fred, no, it was nothing like that," I answered.

"Right, I wish I could stay out all night doing
'nothing like that'. Man!" He thought for a second,
tilted his eyes to mine as if sensing something.

"Never mind," he continued, "I'll just leave you
with your moment."

"Don't," I said as we walked into the room and
plopped ourselves in neutral corners.

"Why? What the hell do you want to talk to me for?"
His eyes stung me as he said this, as if I'd lost
points in the friendship.

"Because."

"Good comeback, dumb shit."

"I mean …"

"Relax, you can tell me all about it if you want.
Or you can't. Whatever." He took off his shoes after
this, tossed them in the correct place (wherever they

landed) and lay back. A thought seemed to strike him,
his head jerked a bit and then his whole body froze.

"On second thought, you can get drunk with me. You
don't want to go to sleep now. If you did, then the
night would be over."

Perfect statement.

" … always glad to see things work out for
somebody; you haven't had many of these nights in a
while."

No shit.

"Are you okay?" His eyes were on me again,
evaluating. I could feel them without looking as I
took off my own shoes, threw them towards his, opened
a beer, tossed the crap off my bed and leaned back.

"Yes," I managed.

"Damn, you've got a way with words tonight. You
should really think about becoming a public speaker."

Another pause. "Do you remember back when you were
a little kid and … "I tried to ask, this time with my
eyes traveling across the room.

"I still am. So are you," he broke in.

Another perfect statement.

"Relax, you're thinking too much." Fred again.

"Tonight was really …"

"Great, so leave it like that."

"But what if …"

"Such is life."

The night ended that way, with Fred sucking down
both a beer and a Mountain Dew, and me falling asleep
fully dressed on an unmade bed. I was kind of mad at
the time, I mean, I wanted to talk, but Fred taught me
something without saying it, as he so often did.

Sometimes it's not always smart to play things out
in your head. They happen. Some things good. Some
things bad. Sometimes you don't want to be anywhere
else other than where you are, other times, your
parachute don't open and you bust 152 percent of your
ass.

So be it.

She might have seven boyfriends back home.

Or wanted by the police for raping a golden
retriever.

Or she could leave school tomorrow.

Whatever.

All I could do for now was keep cruising, full steam ahead.

IV: Don't Think, Just Live

Monday: Fred's alarm clock went off, as most days
it did, waking myself, third floor, and probably most
of the western civilization in the process. Everyone
but Fred, that is.

"Jesus Priest! How many families do you wake up
with that thing?" I yelped as I tossed the covers off
onto the floor and bounded out of bed. I looked over
at the still sleeping Fred as I realized I had never
gotten under the covers. He wasn't close to answering
me or anyone else. His coiled hair and his mouth
seemed stuck to his sheets; those non-macho sheets
that featured bikinis with blue parrots on them. And
man, who designed those and how?

Never mind for now, the clock blared on, waiting
for a human touch. Realizing he wasn't going to supply
it, I tiptoed across the room to shut it off.

"What in the hell am I tiptoeing for?" I laughed to
myself as I started back to my corner. If that siren
didn't wake him, my little sized nine feet damned sure
never would.

It was extremely early, about 7:30 a.m. or so, and
it was much too early for me to consider getting out
of bed. Class wasn't until 9, so the Standard
Operating Procedure was to sleep until 8:50, brush the
teeth, put on the hat and knock over about five people
trying to get to class on time.

Today, however, was different. Sure, there were
English papers to write for Dr. Taylor, philosophy
pages to read for Hammond, Higgins to listen to and
make another effort to keep up with, but, all that

could wait for now.

I wasn't eager to get into all that, not mentally
anyway. I searched the closets for something to wear,
quietly though I knew not why, and eventually chose my
"Disco Sux" T-shirt I'd won the week before at
Bogart's for having the most hairless chest in the
place. My jeans were already on, never quite got out
of them last night and - though I needed a shower, I
didn't really want to yet. After all, instead of the
normal smell of Red, White and Blue Light Beer or
perhaps a tequila shot that never quite found it's way
into my mouth, I could still smell the scent of
Leigh's perfume, left over from our evening together
consisting of a campus movie and dinner. What kind was
it? Who cared?

I laughed to myself as I thought this, recalling
the old joke we used to pull on women in bars. We'd
con some unsuspecting and innocent female into asking
a guy what he had on, then have him tell her it was a
hard-on, but he didn't know she could smell it.

My "Party Till You Puke" hat again saved me from
having to comb my hair and after brushing my teeth
(even squeezing it from the bottom just for you, Fred
baby), I was ready to roll.

"Where are you going?" Speak of the devil.

He'd rolled over on his side, adjusting his eyes to
the light and was looking at me with a combination of
'I'm confused/why are you up?/what time is it?' look
on his face.

"What?"

"What are you doing up so early?" he asked as he
threw all but a third of the bikinis and parrots out
of the way, exposing his boxers and mattress marks
throughout.

"What am I doing up? Your time bomb over there went
off, waking up the dead and the living."

"My alarm went off?" He looked towards it as he
asked me that, a temporary look of panic on his face,
as if the Panasonic Boomer would actually answer.

"Yeah, it was on the news," I answered, shaking my
head and clearing away my own mattress marks.

"You're going to breakfast."

I just looked at him.

"Phil, you haven't gone to breakfast since Ronald Reagan was president."

"That guy was president?" I joked as I headed towards the door. "I'll see you, I'm going to eat and then head over to class."

I didn't really expect to get away with that one. You don't just fool the people who know you, even if you say something perfectly logical.

"Wow, you must be in love." Damn, don't you hate it when they use that word?

"Just kidding babe, enjoy yourself, I'm happy for you." He plopped back on the bed, the morning cobwebs not close to being gone. He smiled as he said it, I think, though his teeth were still pasted to his mouth somewhat. Still, the shape of his hair drew more than smile as I waved once more.

"Hey Phil, you might want to take your books along."

Eleven o'clock. That's what mattered on this day. Not the breakfast (not sure what it was anyway), not the English class (how can so many women get engaged in one class), not calculus (but I promise I can now draw the infinity sign without turning the paper sideways and drawing an '8'!) and not history (I think Higgins is mad at one of the Generals of the Civil War, but I'm not sure which one).

I got through them all, promising myself that I really would start studying and keeping up, though not now. Perhaps this weekend or even tonight.

Right, have another beer.

Anyway, at precisely the stroke of eleven, I stood on the stairs of Green Hall, overlooking the quad, the Cook Building, and Trustees. Usually, Leigh would walk out of Cook, books in tow, heading back to her dorms. The path she would take would split all of the above buildings, but went closely by Cook. The only negative that could happen, besides her telling me to go screw myself, was if she drove. The parking lot, unfortunately, was in the back.

Different path.

Out of my view.

Jesus wept.

I was pretending to listen to Bill McCloud as my eyes focused on the campus. Students, everywhere. Some taking a cigarette break, others mingling in the quad, several throwing a Frisbee, some rather talented, others bad but wishing they weren't. Others moving along with a purpose, classes, appointments to keep, a life to lead. Some biking to class, others deciding not to go no matter what means of transportation. It was neat to watch it all drift from chaos to conformity with a glance at a watch, or a sound of a bell. Not as quickly as high school, not as structured, but the same result.

McCloud was rambling on about last week's quiz and how it dealt mostly with the notes and he had studied the book and did I get Number 12 right? Number 12? Did I look like the kind of guy who would know or actually give a shit about a question a week later? Sure, the law of averages said I missed it, but, I'd long ago learned about the perils of discussing a quiz afterwards. It's over and dealt with, for better or for worse.

Apparently Bill didn't share my philosophy; he was talking up a blue storm with his arms waving and the whole nine yards. "I was hoping I could exempt this final, but if he puts some heavy weight on these pop tests, I could be… "

Over there, coming down the steps. We have spotted our mark.

Wow, the voice was actually a police officer today, coming at me like that guy on Dragnet.

She looked tired, thank you very much, and she still was beautiful. Blue jeans, white sleeveless shirt, a hat with purple whales on it (and what is it with all these animals today?), tennis shoes, no makeup, perfection in motion.

I left Bill with his quizzes, papers and finals, probably even walked off in mid-sentence, but so what? Hang in there, Bill, and don't forget what Jackson Browne tried to tell you on the "Pretender" album. "Among the thoughts that crowd your mind, there won't be many that ever really matter."

Leigh was moving at a rather rapid pace, heading my
way, books in hand, calculator on top (still didn't
trust those things.) and I knew I had to head out just
about … now.

"Hi" I said as she was at ten yards and closing.
*Hi? You stay out with her until the roosters start to
scream and all you can come up with is "hi"? Zero for
creativity and I expect more from you in the future!*

She smiled, her widening mouth making her tired
eyes look almost refreshing, though that may not make
a damned bit of sense, and she angled over towards me,
never breaking stride.

"Where's your headphones?" she asked me and who
knew where that came from or where it was going.

"Headphones?"

"Sure, you know, where you can listen to …" she
stopped, dropped her Chemistry book, cupped her hands
over her mouth and yelled, "WHERE YOU CAN LISTEN TO
YOUR FAVORITE SINGERS..JOHN DENVER AND THE BEE GEES.
THAT'S RIGHT FOLKS, JOHN DENVER, BARRY GIBB AND … what
are those other two geeks names?" she asked me, her
mouth closed trying to suppress her laugh.

I just stood there and turned red. Right there in
the middle of the academic quad complete with
buildings, students coming and going both on foot and
on bicycle, some milling around, all within ear shot.

Most looked over or maybe it was my imagination,
but truth be known, yelling and screaming on a college
campus day wasn't all that unordinary. Probably
happened all the time and all over the place.

Didn't help my face, turning orange and moving over
to red. And quickly.

I picked her books up for her, what a gentleman!,
and I continued walking, trying to shake the color off
my face as I went.

"Phil?" Oh no, what now, I promise I don't have any
Barry Manilow or …

"What?" Actually I was scared to ask that, but it
seemed the thing to say at the time.

"Where are you going?" Simple question.

"Uh, well, I was …" Nothing.

"Were you waiting for me, Phil Baby?" she laughed
again, bringing her left foot around behind her and
kicking me in the butt. Her eyes glanced off of mine,
gauging my reaction.

The face went deeper, the color of my T-shirt.

"I'm just kidding. Sorry, I do these things
sometimes."

"Okay, okay, damn it, I was waiting for you. I just
wanted to walk with you and talk to you for a second."
Painless enough, might get away with it.

"So what would you have done if I'd have walked
into road over there and gotten run over by that
truck?" she laughed again while gesturing at a campus
school bus. Fred used to drive that bus, but that
really doesn't matter at this point.

I just shook my head and kept walking, eyeing the
ground with false intensity, trying to give a damn
about the pine straws, fallen leaves, wadded up pieces
of paper, footprints.

"Phil?"

"What?" Almost angry.

"I'm hungry."

"Me, too."

"WELL, WHAT IN THE HELL ARE WE WALKING THIS WAY
FOR? THE CAFETERIA IS THAT WAY!!" She was amusing
herself so much she dropped her books again, though I
think I was immune at this point. She kicked me again
in the butt as we changed direction, though I wasn't
really sure how to proceed. I was remembering that
line again, about being made the proverbial fool in a
relationship. Did I enjoy this?

Pretty much.

My mouth opened, but not a syllable, consonant, or
vowel made itself known to the world.

"Would you like to go eat?" she asked, her mouth
curling in that 'O' again, waiting for my response.

"Yes."

"Boy, you've got a way with words. You know, you
really ought to consider a career as a writer or
public speaker." Let's see, I'd heard that somewhere
before, rather recently at that. "But that's okay, I'm
not going to bother you anymore. I'll just walk with

you to the cafeteria. Before I leave, however, I just
want you to know that I eagerly await your next
syllable."

Five steps, ten, fifteen. Increasing pressure with
each placement of foot to the turf. For some reason, I
heard that voice on "Full Metal Jacket", the one where
the drill sergeant went ballistic on the guy he called
Private Pyle.

"You've got to be shitting me, Private Pyle! You
mean to tell me you can't …"

"Leigh?"

She patted me on the shoulder after this one,
pumped her fist into the air the way Jimmy Connors'
used to after hitting a winner. "I knew you could do
it. I had faith in you the whole time. I swear!"

More laughter.

More silence.

More pressure. I'd never noticed my shoes in such
detail before. So faded, torn, hole-ridden, and
perfectly comfortable.

"Would you like to study with me tonight in my
room?" *Pretty bold question if you ask me, especially
throwing in the 'my room' part.*

Silence.

Nothing.

Did she hear?

"You study?" Her voice finally came, knifing the
air.

"No, but …"

"I would be happy to," she interrupted. "It will be
a pleasure. In fact, whatever will I wear?" She
flipped her hand up to her forehead, eyes bulging,
like the woman in the commercial who had just washed
her hair and couldn't do a thing with it.

"Is nine o'clock good?" I asked, trying to pinpoint
the time where I could plan for my nervousness. And
clean the room. Wow, there was a job.

"Nine is fine, just promise not to play any of your
music or anything."

She laughed.

I shook my head.

We walked.

I almost didn't want to eat with her now, in fear
of screwing something up.

For the record, she did come to my room that night,
thank God, and I thought I'd done a semi-excellent job
of getting the room ready. Fred had even pitched in,
for a while, though once he started looking at his
watch, I told him to take off.
He did.
And what a great roommate.
Anyway, the beds were made (and God, I couldn't
remember the last time I got to actually turn the
covers back before getting in) papers and books
stacked, shelves dusted, floor void of any pizza
boxes, beer cartons, toilet paper and other academic
and non-academic accumulations.
Would she be impressed?
She knocked on the door, right at nine, fashionably
on time. Me, I'd paced a while (hours) and Fred had
long since gone away to do some studying or frog
gigging or whatever Fred would do when sent away.   He
acted angry about the inconvenience. He wasn't, though
he did admit to jealousy due to his lack of success in
the love life department. "I'm holding my own, you
might say," he said, and it took me a while to get the
joke. He loaded up some books and headed off.
I answered the nine o'clock knock and there she
stood. She was wearing shorts … *Surgeon General's
Warning: Do not attempt to walk upright until at least
20 minutes after viewing. Do not ponder while driving
or operating dangerous machinery.*
God I was a sick man.
Let's finish the description, shall we? They were
dolphin shorts, yes, more animals, with a T-shirt and
a necklace around it. No hat, hair sitting on
shoulders, little to no makeup. This was her, deal
with it.
"Where is it?" was the first thing she said. I'd
moved aside, admitting her to my abode. Her eyes were
darting everywhere, gears in brain on overdrive,
wheels spinning out of control, in need of answers. I
had learned at this point not to answer when her mind

took off like that, just sit back and watch and see where it takes her. Or us.

Her eyes, suddenly thin and piercing, dashed across the room, up and down, top and bottom, over and back. I remained in my seat at the couch, strategically sitting where there was room for another.

"I found it." Her face lit up as she walked to the closet and threw open the door.

Out it came.

Everything.

Boxes.

Papers.

Letters.

Albums.

Even my old cassette tapes (not the groups mentioned earlier, though the old "Grease" soundtrack was clearly visible.)

And above, below and in the middle of it all was laundry, more laundry, and even still, more laundry.

"I knew it," she laughed as she plopped herself down right in the middle of it. (And so much for my strategic seating arrangements) "There was no way you had a neat room. Couldn't happen. I've seen your car. And why did you clean up for me?" Her eyes nailed mine dead center, target sought and found, demanding an answer, and a serious one this time.

She brushed me off with her hands. "Never mind, I don't want to hear you stutter right now, you amaze me."

So there I sat, on the couch, pretending to give a damn about Maslow's pyramid of needs (and my God man, how many classes would I have to study those needs?,) and I watched Leigh play in my stuff out of the corner of my eye. She didn't ramble or pry, mind you, never held a letter up to the light, never touched anything she felt I might consider private. She just probed. Looked around. A rabbit sorting through food. Curiously, non-curious and I know that makes no sense.

She reminded me of a girl in a sand box, just playing, as if figuring out every detail of my life by all of the crap I'd amassed. How else would you do it? Her mind was being fulfilled and she had this pleased, "wow, I'm having fun" look about her.

I quit pretending to study and just watched.

The "Grease" tape didn't get a response, though she did hold it up, turn and face me with a smile. The expression said it all, so I just threw up my hands and starting rolling my pelvis around like John Travolta did. You know the part where he sings about "we made out, under the dock?"

She seemed to love the picture of my mom and dad, the one of them up in New Hampshire or somewhere. "They still together?"

"Yes."

Earlier in my life, this made me normal. Now, I think it made me weird.

My dirty underwear didn't get much of a comment, though the rabbit's foot made her eyes crease at the corners, and she merely tossed it to the side.

"Laundry day isn't until next week," I said with a smile, holding my hands out at my side.

"Don't worry, you can use dirty underwear and socks for weapons. Put them together and kill an intruder," she never looked up as she said this, leaving me wondering if she was ripping into my non-cleanliness or just saying something funny.

"See, no Barry Manilow albums," I offered as she seemed to get to a stopping point.

"Why not? Is he too macho for you?" Her comebacks were way too fast.

"No, actually, a friend of mine got killed in an accident one afternoon and later that night, all I heard on the radio was that damned song, "Can't Smile Without You." I paused, remembering.

She looked up at me, quit playing in her sand box, if only for a moment. "Wow, that was a serious answer."

"Sorry, it won't happen again."

"No, I love to hear that kind of stuff about people. It interests me."

My brain unfortunately turned back on at this point, wondering briefly if I in general interested her, but the voice of my high school tennis coach paid me a casual visit. "Patience, Phil, patience. Don't

force the action. Wait until you have the opening."
    It seemed that I should have mentioned in my non-
illustrious two-year tennis career that I never seemed
to find an opening, nor did I really know what one
looked like. Maybe that's not important for now.
    Eventually, her mind grew weary of my play things
and she, too, popped open her Physics book and began
to study. I tried to tackle American History - had
that solid 71 average in there and was sitting pretty
in my mind - while she and her 3.4 had no worries at
all.
    Well, I wasn't concerned, but …
    Can I take this time to tell you that studying next
to a total babe is really not a good idea? Do you
really think I learned a whole helluva lot about the
Industrial Revolution or any war during this time?
    "You're not studying." It was her and maybe what
gave it away was my book being upside down, or closed,
or maybe my eyes were closed. Something.
    "Sorry."
    "It's okay." And with that, she put down her book,
grabbed my face … *and oh shit, I forgot to shave*!, and
I started laughing, so she didn't kiss me. "Sorry," I
said.
    She ignored my weirdness and kissed me.
    No problem.
    We'll worry about that grade point average later.

    We moved on, to that perfect feeling; you know, the
kind that comes around about once every twelve years
or so. The kind where you start looking over your
shoulder and behind your back, you watch your feet
wondering when the door's going to open. The ground
looks smooth, but there's got to be a mine out there
somewhere. Or maybe it's a formula and it's all
planned. And God is sitting up there saying, "Well,
old Phil is way above the normal happy line now, but
make a graph of that one, angels, we'll have to bring
him down soon."
    Or perhaps I'm totally out of line and who am I to
be telling you what God is saying? Perhaps he has more
important things to think about than Phil and his late

nights and his "Grease" soundtracks and …
Anyway, the beauty was, I no longer had to play stupid games with Leigh anymore; you know, like standing in front of Green Hall and pretending to listen to Bill McCloud. Oh, he did great on that quiz by the way. Unbelievable. Got Number 12 right, hell yes he did. He told me.
Do you know how hard it is to act like you give a shit?
Sorry, I'm getting off the subject again. But way to go, Bill. Seriously. Hope you exempt the hell out of that final and each one thereafter.

I would wait for her in front of Green, actually, and we'd eat together in the dining hall. She would call and I would call. And more naturally this time, I might add. No more arguments from the brain, name-calling, jumping up and down and cussing at a phone; none of that. Just pick it up, dial, talk, hang up.
Isn't that easy?
Even better, I didn't have to clean my car, my room or hide any of my albums. (Okay, I lied. I hid at least a third of them, but who's counting?)
For a while, we were that stereotype couple that just made you sick. You know the ones I'm talking about. The ones that are always touching each other. Even if you were doing something like playing tennis, when each of you were supposed to be across the net. Laughing. Always happy. Always doing perfectly stupid stuff and getting away with it. Staying out late, wondering when we'd catch up on sleep, putting it off.
I know that one catches up with you somewhere.
But as I told Fred one night in a "Late Night Conversation" that I forgot to write about: "Fred, I haven't slept in two weeks. Then again, I haven't wanted to."
I think he liked that. He didn't say anything, he just gave me that nod, that "rock on" look. Another Jimmy Connors passing shot down the line.
We did some of the stupidest things, by the way. We drove to Atlanta in the middle of the night to watch "Rocky Horror Picture Show" on a whim. We wrestled

outside of Trustees. (See above Surgeon General's
Warning) We played racquetball and I'll be honest with
you and tell you she was probably the worst I've ever
seen. Couldn't figure out an angle for shit. She
teased my hair, and gee, it didn't smell terrific. We
sat in the attic of the chapel under the bell after
midnight and looked out over the campus. She even ran
out onto the flag football field one day and tackled
me as I was approaching the ball to execute the
opening kickoff.

Did my friends have a field day with me for that
one?

Yes, yes, and yes. Will never hear the end of it.
Never.
Ever.

And besides, my one moment of glory. "All we put
you in for is to kick the damn ball and you even screw
that up." Fred said that, couldn't keep a straight
face when he said it.

Regardless, we moved ourselves away from the
mainstream and never once missed it.

Do you expect me to tell you all the places where
we did it? Well, have another beer. The truth was, we
didn't. She was a virgin. Me, I was not, but I managed
to control myself most of the time. Now Fred, he had a
little trouble with that one. Every time he'd see
something blue, he would point it out to me and make
comparisons to that and the color of a portion of my
anatomy. "They have to be at least that blue, I'm
amazed you're still walking. We should do a feature on
you for the "Campus Carrier."

But on the same subject, the only time we got
really hot and heavy a damned security guard came up
and banged on my window and told us to move along. I
understood that rules were rules, but I got the
feeling the little weasel had stood there a while and
watched while we rolled around. Started to ask him if
I needed to get my butt up a little higher or follow
through a little more, but I refrained. Maybe next
time.

As for the roommate thing, the "ratio" that Leigh
spoke of one night was definitely in effect -- the

closer you got to a person of the opposite sex, the
less you got along with your roommate. This wasn't so
true with Fred and I; we'd been through a lot worse.
Leigh's was a different story, though, as she was a
freshman who'd gotten attached and counted on Leigh
for a link into the Jenkins College world.

Oh well.

Fast Forward …

It was late afternoon on a Tuesday when I picked up
the phone to call her. Fred was studying for a
Genetics test, whatever that was, and he was curled
over his desk lamp, peering at a space he'd cleaned
for his books and notes. He never really complained
about me making noise, unless of course I farted, so
making a call was nothing.

She answered on the second ring, and, like usual,
was still talking to her roommate even after picking
up.

"Don't worry about it, it's just a philosophy quiz!
Hello?"

"It's me." I leaned back, ready to talk, pillows
propped up and shoes off.

"No shit."

"Fred tells me that college is the best years of
your life. Is that true?" I kicked the pizza box off
my bed, clearing space.

"Of course it is."

"You mean, it gets worse."

"What's wrong with college days? What do you want
to do? Work?" Her questions had that piercing tone,
one that drove into my brain even through the phone.

"No, but …"

"Are you not happy, Phil? Do I not make your day?
Are you …"

"No, no, I mean, yes, yes … never mind, you know
what I'm saying." A little pause here, and I sensed
her silence as another test. One of those "I'm eagerly
awaiting your next syllable" type things.

"Let's go to Waffle House and play spades." *Good
subject change on my part. An '8' for creativity, '7'
for coolness under pressure.*

"To heck with Waffle House, let's go get hammered!"

Wow, an even better answer on her part and why can't I think of stuff like that?

Clone this woman.

"I'll pick you up in five minutes."

"Four or I'm kicking your butt."

So much for the pillow prop, the kicking off the shoes and an afternoon of studying. I had to stop and wonder just how much trouble I'd be in at test time, but, when you're on a roll, you don't call time out.

I wonder if my parents would understand that.

"Where are you going?" It was Fred and he knew, he just wanted to let me know that he knew that I knew that I had to weigh things here. Keep a balance, if you will.

"Fred, can I be honest?"

He rolled his eyes at me, started to make a smart crack; decided against it. "I'm sorry about all this, I want us to do stuff, but …"

"But what?" Sometimes he enjoys giving me a hard time.

"Well, you remember when you were going out with Debbie and …"

"Debbie! Don't ever mention Debbie," he practically yelled. In fact, I could detect traces of smoke oozing from both ears; he'd even stuck his hand in one of them, as if reading my thoughts or holding it back or whatever.

"I thought you guys had made up and were friends?" I asked.

"If Ted Bundy were alive, I'd give him her name," he responded. Laughter on my part, but holy shit, I hope he don't ever get mad at me.

"Okay, I screwed that one up. But, we'll hang out. I mean, I think you're a great person even though your socks smell like total dogshit and your alarm clock could probably wake up Buddha himself and …"

His look silenced me. Not an angry look, just one of those, "what the hell are you babbling about" kind of things. I started laughing here, because it reminded me of that scene in the movie "Fletch," where the people in the airplane hangar started talking about the guy "that just had that look," which was

just before the part about "everything's ball bearings
these days," and I lost it.
   He shook his head, not even bothering to ask. He
pretended for a second not to be happy, but I could
always tell when he was winging it. Besides, the smoke
from his ears was gone, his finger was removed and his
glasses were on, ready to study; easily done without
me pacing the floor, picking up phones, rattling
papers and all the millions of other things roommates
can do to crawl from first to last nerve in 2.5
seconds.
   He glanced over at me, but didn't pierce his mouth
together that way … you know that way.
   He tipped his hat and I was gone, though at the
time, I knew not where.

   She was standing outside her dorm holding a
football when I drove up. What in the world she was
doing with that, I couldn't begin to tell you. But
there she was, wearing pink slippers, blue jeans, a T-
shirt that read "Drunken State" and a red hat.
   She looked up as she saw me approaching and yelled
her roommate's name. They lived all the way up on
third floor, and I couldn't imagine the roommate
actually hearing, but once again, I was wrong.
   "It really is a lovely evening to be out carrying a
football. Seriously," I said as I approached. She cut
her eyes at me after that one, then trotted over,
tucked the ball into my arms and tackled me, right
there in the parking lot.
   On the cement.
   In the cold.
   For no particular reason, whatsoever.
   She helped me up, then hollered back to her
roommate, who was poised at the window, head resting
on her hands, viewing the scene with no telling what
kinds of thoughts running through her head.
   Probably something like "Dear Mom, why did you send
me here? People are soooooooo weird."
   I got up, dusted myself off, and composed myself.
"I'll wait while you run the ball up." Her eyes
flickered as I threw my arms out. "Or we can bring it

with us. I mean, you never know when a good football
could come in handy."

She almost hit me with it on that one, but instead,
walked across the parking lot and loosened her arm.
Glancing over at me, angrily, she answered, "run it
up, hell, watch this you chauvinist."

And with that she gave it one of the best punt,
pass and kick efforts I've seen in a while. The form
was a little rough, but my God man, was it ever
accurate. I almost closed my eyes and ears here, not
wanting to hear the shattering of glass, the screaming
of coeds, the conversation with the dean when he asked
you just what the hell you were doing with a football
for Christ sakes?

No glass, no shatter, no dean.

And what a pass!

Hit her roommate right square in the hands. One of
those passes where you'd feel guilty about dropping
it.

She didn't.

She caught it, waved goodbye and closed the window.

Perhaps I should take back every bad thought I've
had about that roommate.

That was pretty awesome.

One of those moments that was really cool, but when
you try to tell people about it, they just look at
you, waiting for the rest of the story that doesn't
exist.

We walked to the parking lot in silence, me with my
hands near my sides to catch her foot if she gave me a
boot, her a little angry that I was reading her mind.

"Oh no," I said as we approached the dirt-filled
wonder, "somebody stole my Porsche and put a Sunbird
here. Hate when that happens."

She didn't even smile, just looked at me with
that," my God you're weird" look, though at this point
in the relationship, I knew. She didn't have to say
it.

"I'm driving your car," she said, and with some
intensity I might add.

"You're what?" I stood, keys in hand, at driver's
side, totally prepared to do the honors.

Her mouth curled up again, she looked at me rather curiously, wheels grinding, full steam ahead. "Do you get angry when other people drive your car, Phil?"

"No, I've just never sat in the passenger side of my own car, that's all."

"Always a first time," she said, snatching the keys out of my hand, unlocking the door, closing it almost in my face and looking up at me. She rolled down the window. "Besides, I'm tired of shoveling all the crap out of the seat and throwing it into the back. You do it this time!"

So I did. And it took two loads, both hands per load. History notes, and boy those were accurate, English packet with a bunch of stories by a bunch of people that I was supposed to read, sports schedules, McDonald's and Hardee's and Arby's all represented. Ticket stub to a game I went to sometime in the 80's. An unstudied English book. A picture of one of my brothers and where the hell did that come from? And last, but not least, a handout of some story about a grandmother and her thimble.

I organized my thoughts, while tossing back my disorganization. Maybe it'll be next semester when I ... oops, there's only one more left. Maybe I'll hit my peak in time for finals and ride the momentum into spring semester. Heck, while I'm at it, I'll clean my room, wash my car and ...

"I'm starting to realize something here," Leigh said, breaking through my thoughts of ambition. She turned the key, forgetting it was a five speed and sending us both lurching forwards and backwards in prime, whiplash fashion.

"Yes, you're realizing that this is not an automatic."

Bad move, not funny in her eyes. The lady driver stereotype went out in the 80's, now everyone shared a piece of the action and drove like bats out of hell.

She got it right the second time and started us rolling past the fields where the football playing cows were ... *in the back by the trees, probably huddling, or maybe half time, or maybe the quarterback was just pissed off because nobody was blocking.*

Sorry. We headed towards the back of the campus; that place where I attempted to kiss her the first time and planted one right on her jaw, getting a good taste of a combination sweat/make-up and lots of embarrassment.

Oh, those memories.

"I'm not going to talk," was her next comment and speaking of, where in the hell did that come from? I knew my mind was thinking of cows calling plays in a huddle in a cornfield somewhere in the sticks, but I got that from her. I promise.

"You're what?"

"I always talk and you always respond," she said. Made perfect sense to me. The nuts and bolts of conversation even. "I mean, you're pretty good, but do you realize you never say or offer anything? You know, I bet you didn't even score on that assertiveness test you had to take in high school, did you?" She looked at me, eyes slanting, darting, wondering.

"Never had the nerve to take it," I countered.

"See! You always do THAT," she pointed with her finger, as if that would show me exactly what 'THAT' was..

"Do what?"

"That's just it, you know WHAT, you just won't and don't say. You say all these funny lines and they're cute and all and I'm not saying you should stop, but the bottom line is, you avoid things."

Pause for a second Surgeon General's Warning: *Be wary of people with goals of studying philosophy, psychology, or any similar topic. Tend to ask questions at the strangest times, trying to make sense of total randomness, even questioning the beauty of randomness in itself. An occasional relationship with these people could be helpful. Too much of it, however, could lead to one shooting his or herself, talking to trees or urinating in strange places.*

Sorry, back to reality. And quickly. I think she's angry.

"What do I avoid?" I managed. Mistake. Giving away control of conversation totally and completely. Why not pull down your pants, roll over and wait for daddy to whip out the belt?

"Like … hell I don't know," and boy did she look cute when she said that. She, like Fred, always knew. That's why I never had to. You just surround yourself with brains and you … Never mind.

She made a circular motion with her shoulders to bring me into the conversation, shrugged them completely, leaving the steering wheel totally unattended. She caught it with her knees.

I was getting worried.

"I don't have anything to say." Someone hit me harder. Please.

"Wrong! Guess again. Tell another lie. Pull another leg." A bang on the steering wheel here for effect, but at least she was holding it. I didn't want to break up the cows and their game, wanted to see how the second half came out. "I see you talking to your friends. They're all gathering around you listening to you while you're moving your hands all around and talking up a fucking blue storm." *Wow, the "f" word. Effective when not overused. Never use in church, however, and make sure …*

"They obviously know you have something to say." She looked over with finality. The moment of truth once again. There was no denying it, no Fred to hide behind, no coach to take me out, no dugout to sit under.

I had to speak.

Oh no.

Jesus wept again, and much louder this time.

"Do you want me to tell you about the old man from Nantucket?"

Ding. Thanks for playing. Total stupidity. Probably the least funny thing I've ever said, attached with the worst timing, the "Gong Show" people would have stood up and knocked that damned bell in half, pushing each other out of the way in the process, beating it without mercy and into submission and the host would have to call for a commercial and try to restore order.

Her eyes supported my thoughts, she probably wishing she had a club or two right now.

She spoke. "Seriously, what are you thinking? And I mean right now." Another bang on the steering wheel. Harder.

"You really want to know?" Am I shy, tense or just totally and completely ignorant? Is there help in the future?

"Did I stutter? Are these questions complicated? Open up that brain. Spit it out. Talk to me you ASSHOLE!!"

Sorry, but I have to quit thinking and talk for a while. As Columbo would say, "bear with me."

So what the hell. I folded my arms and began.

"Actually, I was thinking of a World Series from a few years back, I don't know, '85 or '86 or who knows? Anyway, the Mets came back and beat Boston, good series if you were a Mets fan. Boston had the thing won in six games, but with two out and nobody on, the Mets rallied. You may remember it, the famous grounder that went through Bill Buckner's legs. He was the first baseman and it just made me think of how unfair everything is. I mean, shit, Bill Buckner was a damned good first baseman. He was solid! But afterwards, he even got death threats over one ground ball, one damned ground ball! How can people be so cruel? How can people put things so out of perspective? One play, one little thing totally takes over your life, overshadows all that's done, for better or for worse. Besides, I wanted Boston to win so bad. I mean, they never do. And if there's a God, then some day, some where, the Red Sox will play the Cubs in the World Series. That's right, the Red Sox and the Cubs and do you know what else? The score will be tied in Game 7 after nine innings, just like the '91 Series with the Braves and Twins, but this time, both teams will shake hands and just walk off the field. Hell yeah, two champs, Red Sox and Cubs. But besides all that, I remember the picture they put in Sports Illustrated, of the before and after of the Red Sox fans in a bar, one where they were about to celebrate and tear down Quincy's Market, the Boston Garden and everything else in happiness, the other in total dejection, shock, defeat. It was so sad. Such a quick change of

emotions. Broke their hearts, the Boston people's
hearts and mine, too. And let's not forget my dad's.
He's from up that way, New Hampshire somewhere,
Bedford or Manchester or hell I don't know. My mother
had to nurse us back to health. Took her three days. I
loved Bill Buckner. I loved the Red Sox, almost as
much as I do the Braves. And we always seemed to lose
in the end. ALWAYS! Besides that, I had a bet with
Kenny Watkins. He didn't really give a crap about
either team, but he loved to get me all worked up
about it. I had to bring him a Snack Pack Pudding, do
you remember those things? Whatever, I had to supply
him with those things for a week. One week. I mean,
how do you tell your mother that she needs to run to
the store and buy a shitload of Banana Puddings? How
do you explain these things at the ripe age of …
eleven? Twelve? Man, don't you remember how tough it
was being a kid? Or how tough it was in high school?
It wasn't like the movie "Grease", where you'd walk
into school the first day, meet a girl as pretty as
Olivia Newton John and then dance on top of cars the
whole time. Hell no, it was tough. I mean, if you got
rejected by a woman, the whole school knew. If you
missed a layup and blew the game for your team, the
actual game depression was only the beginning. You
don't just get on a jet and fly to another city and
hole up and regroup. No way! You get up the next day,
walk into school and face the same damn people. The
same ones! The teacher calls role at 8:30 a.m. and
you'd better say 'here' or you get one of those marks
by your name and she confers with mom and dad and … It
goes on. Every day. You live with it, for Christ sakes
and even worse, you have to live with yourself. And
your parents. And those people. And there is NO PLACE
TO HIDE! Nowhere. I mean, heck, look at it now, if you
don't like your college, you can leave. Hate your job?
Big deal, go someplace else. Or maybe you can find a
spot in the library, grow zits, glasses and extra
brains and study for four years. You can even be weird
and people will call you colorful. Hell I don't know.
Whatever. It's freedom. It's choice. Back in those
days, not a chance. Your butt was stuck. Right there.

Like clockwork. Same path to school, same seat in the
same row, same chalkboard, even the same damned apple
sitting on the same damned desk. And man, you
should've seen what happened to Billy Baxter, for
example. Great guy, good athlete, decent looking. Too
bad, doesn't matter, he was scared of needles. Took
him to get a physical. The dude went running out of
the office, screaming, yelling, raising total and
complete hell. Poor guy. Hell, he was a great guy, but
so what? Don't you see? Don't you? I mean, they spend
all those years trying to teach us fair from unfair,
right from wrong, and then we get older and see that …
or maybe we wonder if it ever comes into play. Ever.
There has to be a God. There has to be something after
all this. How could there not be?"
     I stopped here. I had to. I was out of breath.
Besides, I think my teeth and tongue were about to
fall out, my throat was starting to rebel, the inner
voice was asking me where the hell all that came from
and finally, I think that whatever point there was for
me to make, I'd probably made it. I think.
     She just sat there - and can I tell you how wide
her eyes were open? Remember those posters of Charles
Manson? Him and those scary eyes. Nope, he was a total
and complete wimp compared to these eyes. They were
stretched way out, to the corners, to her ears. In
fact, if she had worn glasses, she could've seen right
over them, the lenses wouldn't have come close to
blocking her view. She'd have thought they were for
her nose.
     Her hands were now stuck to that steering wheel.
Totally stuck, in the ten and two position. I mean, I
wasn't sure where the road was going, but I had no
doubt, we were going straight. Please tell me the
construction people planned for this when they built
this place? Two hundred or so years ago?
     There was silence, but this time, I didn't care.
I'd done all I was capable of doing, was actually
getting a little winded and dizzy if you want to know
the truth. For a while, I thought she wasn't going to
say a word.
     Tells you how much I know about the opposite sex.

"How do I begin?" She gestured with her hand, but quickly regained the death grip on the steering wheel, her world altered only for a moment. "You're talking with me and you're thinking of Bill Bucknell or Buckner or whatever his name is... Baseball, for God's sakes. And no, I didn't eat those pudding things because I packed my own lunch."

I was getting depressed here. She was going to take 159% of my heart and soul I'd just cast into her lap and was going to use it all against me. Wrong again.

"Why don't you do that more often?" She still looked weary, as if we'd just had the most advanced session of collision sex known to mankind. Late night cable couldn't touch it. No words written could …

"You want me to spill that kind of crap? Often? On purpose? And expect someone to listen?"

Silence. Okay, I get the point. This is one of those sessions, one of those 'work through your anger' things.

She just looked over again.

And said nothing.

"Don't tell me I have to start talking again. I think I'm spent. Man, I feel like I just had sex with a tribe of moose. I …"

"Listen," she interrupted and yes, this confused me somewhat. "You need to live a little, take some chances, speak your mind, open your heart. Why must you always feel your way through things? Why do you edit yourself?"

Quick thoughts raced to the top of the brain, all wanting to be first. Let's see now, feeling your way along … Well, it helped to keep you alive for starters, watching others screw up and learning would be another good one. And live a little? Wow. Had I not leaped some sixty some odd feet off a ledge in Blue Hole, Alabama, wherever the hell that was, to what I knew was instant death? Put that on your resume. I had never had my male organ jammed so far up inside me in my life, had to scare it out just where I could take leak. Had a craving desire to put on makeup and curl my hair for a while, I did. I promise. Take some chances? You try stealing second base in the Little

League All Star game with Donny Curtis on the mound.
Man, that dude could hum the ball the allotted 60 feet
in a second or less, leaving most runners, the few
that were, caught in a run-down. A run-down for Christ
sakes! Do you know how embarrassing it is to get
caught in a run-down when you're trying to steal?
Couldn't believe the coach gave me the 'steal' sign.
Cussed his name and I wasn't even old enough to,
cussed his belt that he rubbed, twice with his left
hand, the first being the key, the second being the
sign. My one good, clean hit, in front of parents,
brothers, God and everyone and I couldn't even enjoy
it by getting to run the bases. Hell no, I had to
steal. Even my own parents folded up the chairs on
that one. "Got to go, got to take care of that leaky
faucet," they would say. All the while, my little
once-white, now red ass darting back and forth, back
and forth, trapped in a run-down, sixty feet and
closing, caught between first and second, large
enemies with gloves looming closer, ball whizzing past
my head, faster, closer, quicker, second base so far
away. An eternity. A thud on the back and wow, that
bastard didn't have to tag me that hard and then
having to get up and trot back to the dugout, flick
the dust off my back, just flick it, mind you, if you
rub it you were considered a … Never mind. Anyway, you
trot, damn it. Get your head up! If you don't, then
the coach can drop the esteem lower, sit you down with
his face in front of yours, giving you full view of
his molars, tongue and all dental work done in the
last 12 years.

This living thing is not easy. May I interject and
give huge, total and complete respect for any man or
woman who lives to be old and can smile about it. May
tears roll out of my eyes in respect, and any failure
to refer to them as "ma'am" or "sir" should be
punishable by whippings, no Banana Puddings and five
years in run-downs. Five years! And give them a day to
draw a crowd to watch. And laugh. And what the hell,
why not sound Fred's alarm clock to get the show
rolling why don't we? Let it be a lesson to all young,
all brats of the world. May non-respectful children be

taught so quickly, may court cases never intervene on
teachers and let them discipline with free will. Let
parents understand if junior had to have the shit
knocked out of him a time or two.

I'm sorry. I rambled. There's a conversation going
on here. Let me return.

"Are you hearing me over there? Are you still
alive? Have you gotten your quota out for the day?"

A 'hell yes' response came to mind, but we'll
suppress that for now. She was getting angry again,
now, and my training had always taught me that anger
was brought on by doing something wrong. What …

"Now you're pissing me off." With that, she punched
the seat and the steering wheel (my poor car!), she
blew out a breath that probably released at least
eight pounds of weight and focused again on the road.

More silence. Live a little, huh? Open your heart.
Take some chances. Don't just keep it in play, babe,
go for broke.

Boy, my tennis coach was going to be pissed.

"Okay, you win," I said, throwing my hands up into
the air. "I think you make me happy. I think I want to
take you out to the lake and let you take full and
complete advantage of me while I'm still vulnerable. I
think the high school junior-senior was an overrated
crock of shit, almost, but not quite as bad as the
Super Bowl. I think you're beautiful, even more so
because you don't try to be. I think that if Bruce
makes as many errors as he did last year we're going
to suck again and I think we should go to the lake,
right here, right now, because I don't want to talk
about myself anymore." I threw up my hands, flicked
them at her. No more, no mas, game, set, match, or
strike three if you will.

She just smiled, she did, and I promise you the
sight of those pearly whites cut the knife in my air
like a chain saw to a twig. Her whole face got into
the act, the mouth going all the way up towards her
eyes, the eyes flying at half mast, almost closed,
almost the way you'd look if you were stoned (not that
I'd know, I'd read about it!!), her forehead kind of
creased a little and she flipped her hair back.

It would've been the perfect moment, you know, except I screwed it up again. It was when she flipped her hair back.

Remember the movie, "About Last Night," where Demi Moore and that other girl make fun of their friend in the bar for the "giggle with the hair" flip and Demi Moore gives her a 'nine' rating and they both clap?

I started laughing and she asked me why.

How do you explain these things? Being weird is a silent, yet unappreciated pleasure.

Anyway, we went to the lake.

She took full advantage of me.

Almost.

A security guard ran us off.

Leigh shot him a bird.

I shot him a moon.

Good night.

V: Depression and a Chat with a Baseball Star

I remember it now so clearly, these small things
that happened; things that should've warned me. It was
a week before homecoming, not that homecoming was that
big a deal on our campus, and three weeks before
finals.

To give you a time frame, it was a week and a half
after above `Phil speaking mind and Leigh shooting
security a moon' incident. I'd sat through my three
morning classes and man, let's not discuss my grades
right now, okay? I felt sort of low.

I guess it's the equivalent of the sugar high on
the way down; the same in relationships. Everything
goes perfect for a while and you're just … way the
hell up there. Then you peak out, you start expecting
things, you take things for granted and …

Me, I always blame myself. Maybe I wasn't supposed
to talk about Bill Buckner that day, maybe I was
supposed to tell her what she wanted to hear. Maybe.

I don't know. At least, for better or for worse, I
didn't edit myself.

Well, I met her in the dining hall that day,
Wednesday if that makes a damn, and we sat at our
usual table in the back. The Jenkins cafeteria was
divided clique-wise from back to front, with the nerds
and geeks up front, the jocks in the center and the
back divided up among people refusing to be cliquish,
the ones who didn't belong to one or the ones who just
didn't care.

She plopped her books on the table, muttered a
`hello' and went off to get her tray. No life in that

'hello', none at all. This concerned me, my innards immediately told me something was wrong.

No, I was just paranoid.

No again, I'd made a lot of decisions in the past ignoring my instincts and gut feelings. They were always wrong.

Let me repeat that.

I'd made a lot of decisions in the past ignoring my instincts and gut feelings. They were always wrong.

Whew. I feel better.

Anyway, we ate that day and, for the first time in the month or so we'd been dating or whatever you called it, there was this uncomfortable silence. Dead air had never been a problem with us two; in fact, others never wanted to join us at our table. They would throw their hands up in despair, unable to understand our laughter, unable to be on the same plane, for better or for worse.

"Something wrong?" I finally asked.

She looked up from her food as if interrupted. "Oh. No, not at all," she answered. She laughed as she said it. Totally forced. Not her at all.

My innards did some shifting inside, alarms sounding, screaming for reinforcements. Code Red, This is Not a Test.

I backed off, didn't pry, walked her to class, didn't ask. Maybe I should've asked. *Shouldn't you be assertive and ask her what the problem is? No, leave her alone and let her work it out. Do you …*

I don't know.

The mind can be a totally dangerous thing.

Anyway, she called that night, "interrupted" my studying. Fred and I were again in neutral corners, him kicking in hard down the stretch, me just glad to be there.

"Hi,!" I yelled with enthusiasm, the way I'd done so many times before into the phone.

"Hey, Phil, what's up?" Not good. She usually yells something, rips into me.

Something.

Anything.

We made small talk, we hung up, I tried to get some

sleep. None of the above sleeping measures helped,
and I hadn't read about any new ones.
    Just laid there.
    And on the next day …
    It started normally enough, Fred got up and went to
Calculus, I thought about going to English, but
decided to take a mental health day instead, and our
radio informed us that life indeed was in full swing
outside the campus.
    The Atlanta Hawks were in season and had an
excellent shot at making the playoffs. What team
didn't in the NBA? Atlanta was still basking in the
Braves World Series title, Michael J. Fox was
commenting on his role in "Back to the Future," and I
can still remember my dad's reaction when that one
came out. "Excuse me, but just how in the hell can you
go back to the future?" Regardless, all of this had
nothing whatsoever to do with college life as we knew
it.
    We had food to eat, sports to play, women on all
corners of the campus and hopefully, just hopefully, a
few more decent days before fall collapsed and gave in
to winter.
    In short, hearing that there even was an outside
world was more an inconvenience than anything.
    And then the phone rang.
    It's rather strange, now that I think about it, how
the ringing immediately gave me a bad feeling in the
pit of my stomach. It rang and I knew. I was a mother
hearing bad news about her child.
    Besides, my phone wasn't supposed to ring at 9:15
in the morning.
    Mom and dad knew I was alive, drunk and stupid.
    Fred didn't give a shit if I went to class or not.
    Anyone on the hall would just come by, not call.
    It was a noise that just wasn't supposed to be.
    But it was; so I answered it.
    I reached across the end table and questioned,
"Hello?"
    "You need to meet me by the lake at 8:00 tonight."
It was her.
    "Hot damn, I can't wait," I yelled as I threw the

covers off of me and onto the floor.
No laughter.
Nothing.
What did she say about speaking up or …
"I'm serious, I need to talk to you." No hint of a
smile on that face, no trace of humor, life, vigor,
pep, or whatever all those crossword puzzle words
were. I think "elan" and "verve" were a couple of
them, but why in the hell was I thinking about
crossword puzzles?
"Are you there?" It was an order, not a question.
"Yes, I'm here. Sorry. I'll see you there."

Can I tell you it was a long day? Eight o'clock
just never seemed to get there. Didn't see her at
11:00, while standing on the steps of Green, didn't
even pretend to listen to post-class conversation
about finals, almost walked straight into a cyclist
heading off to class, barely made it to my classes,
didn't listen, what a shock, didn't see her at lunch.
Didn't see her.
Anywhere.
Felt so empty.
So alone.
So shitty.
For the record, (and why am I always keeping them
anyway?) she had on blue jeans, a T-shirt that
announced a Florida half-marathon and her hair was
tied back in a bow. She had on tennis shoes, no makeup
or jewelry or anything unnecessary.
I had a flashback of the Surgeon General's Warning,
but it negated itself, dropped back down, a panel
inside telling me this wasn't the time or the place
and to put a lid on it.
"Come sit by me." She patted her hand to her right,
taking a seat on the bench, overlooking the lake. It
was beautiful out, though I wonder why I noticed in
any detail. Ducks were everywhere, a blue sky, trees
opening up, fighting off winter for at least another
day. Birds squawking, marking their territory, blue
jays raising total and complete hell, a cardinal here,
a woodpecker there and where are all these birds

coming from?

I was in need of a quick underwear change.

Something was wrong.

My nerves got to the seat about three steps before I did. My sweaty palms wiped off the pine straw and I sat.

Nice seat, too.

Leigh's head was down, lifeless; she let out a deep breath, another pound-releaser, and she glanced over at me.

Silence.

She spoke.

"You don't want to hear this and I'm sorry." Her voice broke. She wiped a tear away. She was right. Didn't want to hear this at all. I was frozen. Solid. Holding my breath. In another run-down. Sixty feet and closing.

"Perhaps you remember my roommate speaking of Dennis?"

Perhaps not, but I hate the sonofabitch already.

"Well, he's back. Damn it, he's coming back." More tears. I guess a real man would grab her here and console. I was still stuck, locked and loaded. Mouth open, heading nowhere and fast.

"He's … I'm sorry, let me start from the beginning." *Start ANYWHERE else, I don't like where this is going.*

"He's my boyfriend from home. He left school early this semester. Something about being mad at me for flirting with other guys. Something about us growing apart."

And he's back? Don't even ask that. Man, I can ask some idiotic questions in the clutch. My friends would've literally slapped me for that one.

"He's coming back and he wants me back and he wants to talk and he's registered for school again and they let him back in even though he was failing everything in sight when he took off."

She paused.

And I wish she hadn't, because my nerves were getting a little angry. Kind of like when the bases are loaded, two outs in the bottom of the ninth, the

score's tied, here's the pitch … and the damned batter
keeps fouling the pitch off.

Enough already.

Let's win it or lose it.

This is killing me.

And so she did; dropping down the proverbial
hammer.

Hurt like a bastard. Like getting your foot stepped
on when it's five degrees outside, getting thumped in
the head by your granddad, getting your teeth drilled
for the first time.

I'm rambling. Besides, the above examples aren't
even close. Not even …

"These last couple of months have been absolutely..
perfect," she continued. *So why screw it up? Quiet!*
"We have so much fun together, you're such a neat guy,
you're …" *A nice guy who's finishing last!* She threw
back her hair as if telling herself to get through it.
"we can't be together right now. Not now." She reached
over and patted my knee, tears rolling down her face.
I'd never seen anything close to this type of emotion
from her - it was always rock-n-roll, laugh and sing,
dance and drink, dare and get to me.

She continued. "I think you're great. You make me
happy. All the things we did - the lake, the parties,
the studying, the racquetball." she stopped and swept
her arm across her body, as if that would explain it
all and save her from it.

So that's it.

It's … over?

"What did you tell him when he said he was coming
back?" I asked. For the record, I had to have at least
opened my mouth. I did, and felt not one bit better
because of it.

"I told him I was seeing someone. I told him I was
happy. But, I don't know, he's a stubborn guy and he
really loves me. And he's coming back and this is a
small school and …" *holy shit, she's dumping me.* "We
just can't be together right now and I'm sooooo
sorry." A pause. Tears. "But…" *No 'buts' please, these
damned things are killing me..* "I have to worry about
his feelings right now. I don't want to hurt him and I

want to see if I can figure out what's going on. I
don't know what to say. I just … We have to be apart."
    Another pause. Another pat on the leg. "I'm so
sorry," she said again. Briefly, she lowered her
forehead and put it on my shoulder, then quickly
removed it, perhaps already getting used to pulling
away.
    "God, I hope things work out all right somehow,
Phil…" *they were, damn it* - "and I hope we can get
along and be friends. I want you always to be close to
me." She paused here as I waited for the 'but'.
    Perhaps greater men could speak at this point, talk
her out of it. Tell her I'm her man. Tell her Dennis
was a penishead. Tell her … Maybe… Never mind. Perhaps
I don't have the slightest idea what to tell her and I
should leave it at that.
    I said nothing. Nothing. Nothing. But I did reach
over and hold her. And neither of us wanted to let go.
I'll take my small victories, damn it. And speaking
of, her pretty little fingers were digging into my
back at a fierce rate, so fierce in fact, that when I
go to take my shower later, people are going to think
that … QUIET!!!
    Never mind. I guess I'd like to say that we stayed
there forever.
    Seriously. Like - the snow came and went and there
we were, it rained a few times, major windstorms,
Super Bowls and World Series' came and went, hockey
strikes, political nominations, debates, Nike
commercials, all that stuff just kept on going and
going and going and that damned battery commercial
didn't have a thing on us.. We … we … well, we just
stood there by the lake. Summer, fall, winter and
spring and we're still out there, her and I, though my
knees and feet are tired and my back's a little sore
and my shirt is wet from where she's cried all over it
and her T-shirt is a little moist and …
    Eventually, her grip loosened somewhat.. and that
SUCKED.. and she drew herself away and looked me over.
Me? I looked back, yes I did. "I don't know if I'll be
that carefree little girl anymore." Her head dropped
here. I just stood there with my mouth open. "I have

to go now. Please understand and I hope we can still be friends."

FRIENDS!!

She walked away. I know this because I watched. Every step. All the way to when her pretty hand reached into her left pocket, pulled out her keys (large key ring, Mickey Mouse on it), inserted them, opened the door, stepped inside and I watched still more while she and her tears drove away.

Me, I just sat there. And how long I sat, I don't really know or give a shit. In fact, I don't want to talk about it. Can't believe I'm sitting here writing about it.

She was gone.

Outta here.

Later days.

How do you even describe this in writing terms?

Screw the writing terms, it felt like shit. It sucked. The pits.

I remember looking out over the lake and watching the mallards wash themselves. I remember hearing the blue jays and black birds cackling and maybe they were playing some football. NOOO. I remember seeing the trees rock a little with the November winds, dancing over the lake, protecting it for now.

And I remember just last week when Leigh and I were here.

I got to go.

So I did, or I tried, anyway. I sat in the car for a while, must've been a pretty good while. The Cars Greatest Hits played through a couple of times (four or five) and that's a pretty long CD. Birds chirped themselves hoarse. It seemed to get colder. Frogs bumped around, hollered, croaked, or did whatever the hell it was they did on November nights in Georgia.

And you know the funny thing (hell no, and why do I think everything is so damned funny?) is, for some reason, I found myself thinking about that time in 1992, you know, when the Braves beat the Pirates in Game 7 of the National League Championship, when Francisco Cabrera hit a 2-run, 2-out single that scored Justice and Bream and put the Braves into the

World Series.

Well, Andy van Slyke, the center fielder for Pittsburgh, just sat in center field in shock. Sat on his glove, chewed on a blade of grass and just sat there. I remember it because the Braves announcers commented on it and morning show disc jockeys had a field day with it. "Could somebody come get van Slyke out of center field? We've got a game to play tonight." And the Braves players, fans and the city celebrated so much that we forgot to win the World Series, but that's not the point for now.

The point is, I felt for Andy van Slyke at that time, though I had to laugh at myself again for thinking of it now. *My God, you just got dumped and you're thinking about Andy van Slyke for God's sakes.*

But I was, and I felt his and a lot of people in Pittsburgh's pain even though this didn't have shit to do with baseball … and … the thought just wouldn't go away.

It really wouldn't.

So I quit fighting it.

And I walked out there, I did, right out to center field, right back on that October night in 1992, with Atlanta people going ballistic and the city coming apart and if Larry Munson would've announced it the way he did Georgia football games, he would've been screaming, "Oh my God, the girders are bending, now we are gonna have to renovate this place. MAN, is there gonna be some property destroyed tonight!"

But Skip Caray was the announcer and he, too, did a damned good job, thank you very much, but why do I keep getting off the subject? I don't know.. why not? Do I have anywhere to go? "Little busy tonight are you Lloyd?" Jack Nicholson. The Shining, I think, but can I get back to the point?

The point is, I walked out to center field at Atlanta Fulton County Stadium and I plopped my goofy ass right down beside Mr. van Slyke, hell yes I did. Made my entry about ten feet behind second base, docksiders knifing through the immaculate grass, smelling the popcorn, feeling the intensity and the celebration, the depression and the pain, and all the emotion that flew that night in the Georgia air.

Felt the pain of the Bill Buckner's, the celebrations of the Kirk Gibson's, the excitement in the crowd, the agony. The emotion. The beauty. And the shit.

And I was there.

I walked straight, no hesitation, straight to the man in center field. He glanced over, almost as if expecting me. *Like, sure, it happens everyday, Mr. van Slyke. You just sit out in center field long enough, weird people will just walk right up, have a seat and talk to you.*

Well … I did. And I plucked a blade of grass of my own as I sat myself right down.

Even though I'm a HUGE Braves fans. In fact, they almost had to put me in a mental home during the 1991 World Series when we were … QUIET!!

Sorry, but I'm doing the best I can.

Well, Mr. van Slyke glanced over at me, he did, then back at home plate. Atlanta people were jumping on top of people, screaming, yelling and generally throwing shit. Pure and simple bedlam.

Everywhere.

Fans weren't even thinking about leaving.

He reached over and picked up another blade of grass. And another. Threw them both back down. Glanced back at home plate. Up at the sky. Over at me.

"Sucks, doesn't it?" He said. *Wow, he spoke to me. Wait'll my friends hear this one! Yeah, me and old Andy had a talk, just him and I …*

"Er.. Yes sir, it definitely sucks."

He eyed me with some intensity. Threw down the grass and continued. "You don't have to call me 'sir'. We're in this together, you know." Even the voice got prepared to shut up at this point. *That's right, just listen to the man and shut the hell up!!*

I suppressed it all and spoke myself. "I feel a little guilty, you know," I began, "you see … I'm …"

"I know, you're a big Braves fan. I understand. Nothing wrong with having a little passion and cheering for your team. Nothing wrong with that at

all." Another grass blade got picked and plucked,
another got tossed back down. Nice grass, though.

"Son, you have a decision to make here." He kept
looking away as he spoke, his voice soft, calm,
effective, no need for heavy volume in spite of the
chaos that was going on around us.

"You can get to a point where you can drive
yourself crazy if you don't be careful. Me, I could
sit here all night and figure what would've happened
if Belinda had thrown this pitch or that pitch. What
if Drabek had stayed in the game? Pitched a helluva
game, you know." He looked over at me for
reinforcement. I gave it to him. I was glad to see
Leyland pull the dude in the bottom half.

"And what would've happened if the home plate
umpire hadn't gotten sick in the early innings and
didn't have to leave the game? What if he had still
been back there calling the balls and strikes? Some of
those balls to Berryhill looked pretty good, you
know." He had a point. Fact. Even our sports editor,
Furman Bisher said it and Furman Bisher was the shit.

He continued.

"You can't go there, son, you can't." He looked up
again, convincing himself and me. Plucked another
blade of grass, spit, rubbed his pants, folded his
arms again around his legs, cradling them. Another
glance in the stands where nobody had gone home. Noise
level still high. Tears. Laughter. Joy.

"You get to the point where you start questioning
things, and people, and life. And you start wondering
if there's any point; and whether or not you can trust
anything, sometimes including yourself. You do have
these thoughts, Phil, or you wouldn't be sitting here
right now talking to me." *Holy shit! He just called me
Phil! Then again, what else would he call me? That's
my …*

"I'm going to tell you something, right here, right
now, and you're going to listen. It's not that you
can't believe in people, places and things, it's just
that sometimes you get caught up in using the wrong
people, places and things for gauges. Do you
understand? Do you? You can't give up on yourself,

life and so forth and make that mistake. Can't quit
trying and become cynical. Do you know what the
definition of 'cynical' is, Phil? Do you? Well I'll
tell you. A cynical person is nothing more than a
person who refuses to keep growing; a person who
expects the world to come to them. Frankly, I don't
know if I read that or just made it up, but who cares?
It's a fact. And don't go there. And I'm not going to
sit here and tell you it's going to be easy. It's not.
If it was, me and six million other jerkoffs would
play in World Series games every year and it would
have no meaning."

Another pause. He slapped at the field at this
point. Me, I reached inside my wide open mouth with
hopes of pulling out any flying insects or whatever
else was getting trapped in there. I was hanging on
every word, I swear I was, though I couldn't silence
my inner spirit that kept yelling, *"can you believe
this? This is Andy van Slyke you're talking to."*

He brought me out of it when he continued. I faced
him, as if telling my innards that it was he I needed
to listen to, not me. "You have to be able to dig down
inside … in here." He tapped his gut, twice for
effect. "There's a place in here nobody can touch.
Nobody. A place nobody can get to, nobody can destroy.
It's sacred. The trick is, you have to KNOW that that
part of you is sacred and take care of it. Don't let
these people change your values and warp your mind and
spirit. And they're out there, damn it, they're
everywhere." He opened his hands out for more effect.
Worked for me.

"I'm not saying don't be nice to them. Do. Please.
Remember the advice your mother gave you when you were
a kid. Be nice. Smile. Speak to them at parties. Help
them up when they fall. Loan them a handkerchief if
they need one. Help fix their flat if it's flat, drink
beer with them in a hot tub, teach them how to play a
sport if you want to." Pause. "But don't ever let them
into your soul, Phil, don't ever let them into your
soul."

He reached under his butt, grabbed his glove and
plopped it onto his lap. I was still sitting there

with my mouth open, wondering if words would ever come
again. Didn't matter.

"You are hearing me, Phil, you'd better be, because
this is important. Me? I'm going to get up off this
field, wipe the grass off my butt, change, shower and
fly back to Pittsburgh. I'm not going to watch one
second of the World Series, mind you, not one second.
Can't do it. It'll hurt. But one day at a time, it's
going to get a little better, each day easier than the
one before." Pause. He wipes his nose here, empties
all grass from mouth, regroups.

"I suggest you do the same." He stood, cradled his
glove against his chest with his left arm while fixing
his pants with his right. "It still sucks though,
doesn't it?"

"Yes sir, it really does," I answered. Sorry I
spoke, but I had to get my two cents worth in.

He got up, he did, and me the spectator just
watched. He took one more glance at home plate, one
more look into the stands and another up at the sky
just for the hell of it. He took a step or two away,
stopped, then turned back to me.

"You hang in there, man. There's good out there,
you just have to be strong enough to find it."

And with that, he tossed me his glove. *Holy shit,
he just tossed me his glove*! And I felt like that kid
in that Mean Joe Greene commercial years ago, a Coke
commercial, I think, but who knew? I caught the glove,
held on to it, stared at it, felt it.

I couldn't get up. Wasn't ready to. I watched as
Andy van Slyke walked off the field, headed out of
Atlanta Fulton County Stadium. He looked into the
stands almost peacefully, walked with a purpose and I
watched until he strode by first base, past the foul
line, and headed into the dugout.

Me, I started laughing, could picture my own self
in the next day's newspaper, sitting in center field,
on top of a glove, clad in jeans, docksiders, T-shirt,
no belt, no hat, with a caption under the photo
saying, "Who the hell is this guy?" Laughed a little
harder. Couldn't help it. How could I not?

I cradled my arms against my own knees. Looked up

into the Georgia sky. Felt the emotion, the tension,
the good and the bad, dreams born and bred and teased
and dead. I felt it all.

I gave it a long look. Touched the glove. Chewed
some grass. Closed my eyes … and …

… stared at my clock radio and it was 5:00 in the
morning. And there was no baseball field here, no
glove in my hand, no smell of the grass, no noise of
the fans. I wondered how long I'd sat there talking to
empty space. And where'd everybody go? And was I
talking to myself? Did people walk by and go, "check
that dude out in the car. Never know about people
these days."

It didn't matter. It was worth it. The lake was
still out there, my car still the same. The moon was
still up, ground still down, sky still up. I felt my
head, body parts to make sure of what I don't know. To
make sure I was back, I guess. Shook my head, stared
into the mirror to make sure I was all there.

I was.

It sucked.

I was so weak, so confused.

Not sure about anything.

Not strong at all.

Didn't trust a thing or a soul.

Felt I had no one to talk to.

I laughed again. Not a 'ha-ha laugh', but one of
those 'how do I get into these things' kind.

I would have to fight to get through this.

Wondered if I could do it.

Wondered how things can happen so fast.. So high,
then so low.

In fact, I had no idea what the hell just happened,
but I knew I had no desire to see any human being in
any form, shape or fashion at this time. I laughed to
myself, imagining a conversation with Fred.

"Where you been? It's late."

"Oh, sorry about that, I've been sitting out at
center field, shooting the shit with Andy. Sorry, I
should've taken you with me. Seriously, you'd have
enjoyed it. Never know where and who you can get good

advice from. Who knew? Just walk out to center field
and there he was.. just waiting."
    I eventually did what I had to do. Cranked the car.
No, not ready. Turned it back off. Wasn't ready for
human intervention. I laughed again, recalling the
shocked look on Leigh's face the other day when I
broke out with my baseball story. Couldn't imagine the
look on mine.
    Well, eventually I did have to crank the car, drive
it back, park it in the upper quad, walk across the
tennis courts, jump funk creek, walked into the double
doors, unlock the door to Alumni Hall, Room 34 and
regroup.
    I would see her tomorrow and probably start
throwing shit.
    Or I would meet Dennis and go ballistic.
    Or maybe I'd be strong, conquer, learn, make it in
this world just to piss her off.

    Fred was asleep. Didn't roll over or budge when I
came in. He and his parrots and blue bikinis were in
dream land; he looked oh so peaceful. The room was
still oh so messy.
    Sat at the foot of my bed for a while.
    Tried to prepare for sleep.
    Tough times were ahead.
    But who the hell said they were supposed to be
easy.
    Would I ever laugh again?
    No, not for a while.
    Yeah, yeah I would.
    Some silent voice, deep inside, knew that I would.
Can barely hear him, but he's in there.
    Cheering for me.
    Keeping me strong.
    Hard as it may be.
    I'll be back, damn it, though I hope my journalism
teacher doesn't get mad at me for missing a few
assignments.
    Good night.
    I'm trying, damn it, I'm trying.

BOOK TWO:

A Letter From Fred; A Late Night on a Baseball Field

"People always say they'll only live once; but when you get right down to it, they don't really know what they're saying."

A drunk in a bar

Dear Phil:
   We interrupt this program. This is only a test. If
it were an actual emergency, you would be instructed
to... Never mind, you know the ropes.
   I'm sorry about doing this, but I had to. I had to.
I mean, what could I do? I was just sitting in the
room one night, just farting around, bored, nothing
but naked vampires groping at each other on late night
cable, no drinking buddies around, no desire to study.
   You, you were off trying to straighten things out
with you know who.
   The point is, I found your journal. Read the whole
damned thing. Every word.
   Now, before you blow a gasket and have this
irresistible urge to pound me into submission, bear
with me, if only for a moment. Besides, I will give
you the opportunity to strike me at least twice in the
head if you so desire.
   Why twice?
   Well, I figure the first time would be one of those
'don't hit him hard, he's my buddy' type thing. The
second one, you'd probably get past that and really
club me one. (Please don't hit me on the left side,
however; Dr. Denton just put one of his infamous
fillings in there. The man is too stingy with his
novacaine, but never mind that for now).
   Let's get back to this journal and please, don't
get me wrong. I enjoyed it. I really did. There's some
landmark shit in there. Seriously. I mean, it's not
every day you cruise back through time, sit around and
shoot the shit with Andy van Slyke. Wow. Rock on! Good
for you. And while I'm at it, what kind of glove does

he have? Always wondered what those famous bastards
played with.

Do you think they just walk in a Champion Sporting
Goods or something and pick one off the shelf? Are
they special made? Do you care?

And while I'm on the subject, don't feel bad.
That's my luck, too. To be sitting around one night
having a perfectly good dream, ready to be off in
paradise, tied to the bed post by six or twelve babes,
only to end up sitting on a baseball field with some
guy!

Hate when that happens.

Never mind, I'm getting the feeling you don't care.

In fact, you don't. Not about that or anything
else. And I'm sorry that I'm writing this, invading
your privacy and getting onto your ass all at the same
time. But … you need it. If your head was any further
up your butt you could roll when you walked.

I knew you were in trouble in Higgins' history
class yesterday morning. Big trouble. We were all
taking notes, writing away, except you. You were
staring out the window, notebook closed, pencil not in
hand, brain as far away as those dates Higgins kept
rattling on about.

The note I sent you, that's what made me worry. Did
you even read it? Did you? It was an effort to cheer
you up, one that should've at least drawn a laugh, a
smile or a response.

I realize I'm not a poet or anything, but "Hickory
dickory, dock, your woman's running off with a cock,"
is at least something to acknowledge.

Making up rhymes doesn't come easily for me.
Actually, it does and why am I lying to you?
Regardless, Shakespeare's job is still safe.

And don't think I'm laughing at you, either. I'm
not. I've never said I didn't believe in ghosts, ESP,
spirits and stuff like that, and who's to say that you
and ole Andy didn't solve most of the world's
problems.

But, I never said I did, either. I mean, I know I
didn't exactly sit around the dorm and shoot the shit

with my great grandfather or anything, so I'll just
try to be open minded. If you show me van Slyke's
glove, now, that would be a completely different game!
Actually, I'd probably have to dash off to the john
and change my underwear. Wouldn't you?

But in moving forward, I was sitting there reading
this thing, I got to around page 30 or so, and I
started thinking. Sure, I'm sure she's a pretty neat
girl and all, but what about everything else that's
going on in the world? What about his buddy Fred? What
about the baseball team? What about anything else in
the world besides that girl that talks so loud that
half the time you wrote about her, you had to use
capital leaders, for Christ sakes!

An off the wall point to be made here: Actually, it
never has bothered me that she's so loud. It's just
standard operating procedure to rip the shit out of
anyone who's broken your buddy's heart. A courtesy
thing, if you will.

Think about this for a moment, for I'll only be
writing until you catch me and blow a fuse, then I'll
turn it back over to you. And you'll be mad. But I
hope you don't throw me out of Alumni Hall, Room 34,
where the walls will never talk and I'll be the first
to tell you I'm grateful.

And you, my friend, will be the second.

This letter is your inspiration, your guideline,
your words of wisdom even though they're coming from
me. I realize you're heading out of town tomorrow to
see the folks and getting away from this place and
that's exactly what you need.

I'm gonna sit here with this pen in my hand until
you get back. And try to get you through this. Hate to
see a senior year (our second one, even!) go down the
tubes because of some girl. Sure, she's probably a
nice girl, but so what?

Okay, time out for an off-the-wall analogy. Are you
ready? Let's say you're on the moon, looking down at
the earth. See how tiny this planet looks? Look at
this college campus from up there. (You can't even see
it, and that's one of my points!) Picture yourself
down there in all that, one tiny little dot, picture

Leigh, another tiny little dot, and realize how crazy
it is to let everything go because of one, micro-
sized, dot on one planet in this huge-ass creation.
    Did you get any of that?
    Probably not, but let's move on anyway, shall we?
I'm full, too, damn it! And my humble apologies for
looking around this room for an extra baseball glove.
Holy shit, I feel like some character from the movie
"E. T." or something. Snooping around, moving sweaters
here and there, lifting up your mattress, opening up
drawers, files, looking under shelves, even peaking
under the lamp shade.
    And in a very large way, I'd love it if I found it.
It'd make me know that there's more to this world than
what we see, feel, hear and whatever those other
senses are. It would be exciting, hopeful, motivating,
a breathe of fresh air and (crazy as hell, but so
what?). And please report me to the nearest rubber
room available. Or I'll place an ad: SWM seeking SWF.
Am a little wacked, but harmless, known to leave
reality from time to time, totally potty trained,
don't smoke, can drink like a fish, recite a complete
sentence while burping and recite baseball trivia till
the cows come home. Not good for much, in a nutshell,
but if you ever have a history question of some kind,
I can just cruise back through time and ask them in
person. Call me at 1-800-BIG-STUD.
    Sorry, let's get back to reality. And school. And
baseball season. And that girl.
    As I said, this letter is your therapy. Another
trip to center field, if you will. A leisurely stroll
through life and time with Fred. And what a scary
thought!
    Another off the wall point: How quick would I get
thrown out of school if I picked up a woman, took her
out to center field and … you know. Hmmmmm. I wouldn't
drive all the way down to Atlanta, though. No way.
She'd change her mind twelve times before we ever hit
I-75. The Jenkins College field would have to do. It'd
have to.
    Sorry, I can't help but laugh. What if I got caught
and kicked out? Wouldn't that be awesome! What an

American way to go! Humping and bumping on the
greenest grass in the world, on a baseball field, with
a babe and please, put your hand over your heart. Even
my dad would've had a happy expression while yelling
at me.

I'd expect a parade when I marched out of the
gates. Standing ovations all around. And yes, you
could set my alarm clock to draw a crowd. And when
security came to arrest me, they'd have to get me in a
rundown of their own! Sixty feet and closing, as you
said, though your only worries were getting a hard tag
on the back, while mine would be getting my naked butt
chased by all six of those security guards. I can see
myself, high tailing it through the dugout (man,
wouldn't those pebbles on the infield hurt your
feet?), jumping the chain link fence (another ouch!)
and sprinting naked through a dark campus with nowhere
to run and even if I did get there, where would my
keys be? Not in my pocket. What pocket?

No, the tag on the back would sound rather
peaceful, especially when compared to a night stick in
my ear, a kick in my bare butt, my balls pushed
against that hard infield and ouch! This hurts just
writing about it; the ache is increasing with every
stroke of my pen.

Don't give up on me, Phil, smile a little. Give it
a try. Come on, that was at least a little bit funny.
This is all for you. Don't let life's events rob you
of your sense of humor, your appreciation for the
abnormal or your ability to convert things, big or
small, into something worth smiling about.

My modus operandi, speaking of, is to feed you some
of this useless drivel about life and baseball, throw
in our past, some humor and then some serious stuff
I've never told anyone before. Some stuff for you to
read and think, "wow, and I'm sitting here depressed
over a girl! Don't I feel like a horse's ass!"

Not saying you're supposed to feel that way, it's
just that your mind is in that rut; that flu-ridden
groove that won't go away with water, orange juice,
plenty of rest and medicine from mom. That groove that
follows you wherever you go, interrupts all normal

everyday thoughts, nudges you in your strongest
moments, just waiting to crack through at the
slightest hint of weakness or the first second of
boredom. And then it takes over.

And over.

And over.

And it won't go away.

And truthfully, it pretty fucking sucks.

Watch my language, you say?

Well, I was. That's exactly why I said it just the
way I said it.

And yes, I can rephrase it, about a million other
ways if asked.

But you get the point.

And I'll move on.

No I won't. I'll get it out of my system, too. What
the hell. You know the stage where you can't turn on
the radio, because the one song that they happen to be
playing was yours and hers? And why in the HELL were
they playing THAT song? Couldn't they have been
playing ANYTHING else? ANYTHING! It's the only song
that group ever released, for God's sakes.

Or you walk to your car in the middle of the night
and she drives by. Why didn't you walk out five
seconds earlier? Or later? Why did it have to be now?
Why?

It's that non-wonderful stage where everything you
do is wrong. Zig when you should've zagged. Say yes
when you should've said no. Turn right. Nope,
should've turned left. Get call waiting, the phone
doesn't ring. Get ready to watch a Braves game. Oops,
rained out. No toilet paper. Cassette tape gets eaten.
It's cold outside. Windy. Don't feel good. Three
tests. No time.

AAAAAAHHHHHHH!

And there's more. You finally do get through it,
you do get over her and literally, the second you do
so, your phone rings. And it's her. Isn't that just
life?

It's the one thing in life you can always bet on,
Phil my friend, is that things like that will ALWAYS
happen. In fact, it is the only sure thing in life.

Count on it.

And you go through your stages: Stage 1: Blaming yourself; what did I do wrong? Should I have? Could I have? Why? Why not? Stage 2: Anger: You're pissed off at her, the world, animals, objects, humans, morning disc jockeys, commercials, you name it. Step 3: Gradual withdrawal/indifference. You're getting there, but prone to repeat steps 1 and 2 if not careful. Drinking is not recommended here. You want to because you're so close, but don't. You're almost there. Stage 4: Indifference. This is your goal, indifference. It's the total opposite of love, you know? Did you? It's not hate, they're too closely related.

But for now, you're stuck in that time where, even if I told you she was outside our window banging a lizard, three goats and a water buffalo, you'd still break traffic laws getting to see her if she asked you over. Wouldn't even say goodbye to your friend, Fred. Wouldn't even laugh at his attempt at poetry.

You wouldn't hear it. Couldn't see it.

It's only Friday night now, and I've got nothing but time. Must be nice, you say? Don't you hate it when people say that? Well, I've got an answer for them. Damn right, it is nice. I planned it that way. And thanks for asking! (Have never had the opportunity to use that line, but when I do, I'll jump with both feet.)

All I'm asking you to do here is read. You don't have to laugh. You can throw this away when you're through, use it for toilet paper, plaster it on the wall at the Pub over all that meaningless graffiti. As Jack Nicholson said in "A Few Good Men," 'either way, I don't give a shit.'

Just hear me.

Listen.

Remember.

Close your eyes.

Take a deep breath for crying out loud! You've looked like you were passing a kidney stone ever since the above "van Slyke; A conversation with" episode.

Let the air come in.

Let it go out.

This breathing is a very underrated thing, probably more so than love, water, laughter and my mother.

Besides, I want you to remember a few things first, and hopefully, this will get you ready for this spring. We need you, you know? Rumor has it, Benjy's arm is shot, Rod's having a little trouble with his grades and that leaves a friend of mine who's initials are - Phil.

Okay. Enough already. Enough introduction. I have stories to tell. I, too, am full.

Center field. My first position in baseball. Ever. Tee League in Michigan. Ages 8-10. Dad signed me up. I was so happy. So excited. Peed in my pants twice the night before our first game. Twice! And I was eight years old already. (And I swear to God, if you ever tell anyone that, I'll beat you so hard, you won't get to read the writing on your Jenkins College diploma and your relationship with that thing will be your last worry).

After the first game, I cried. You know why? Because we didn't get to play the next night; had to wait a whole week. A whole week! Do you know how long a week is in kid's terms? Do you?

I don't think you do. A week in adult time is, "a wink of an eye," to put it in Jackson Browne's words. Or - several appointments, fax machines, calls over the intercoms, traffic, the news, reading the paper and where's the sports section?, going to bed, going to work, going to bed and what's for dinner? Or in our present case, classes, dining hall, intramurals, baseball, dining hall again, pretending to study, drinking, sleeping and wow, it's Friday already! And yes, what did happen to the days when it actually took a year for a year to go by?

Not the case when you're an 8-year-old. Not the case at all. At that age, a week was:

Gilligan's Island episodes, getting pounded by brothers, pulling your sister's hair, Scooby Doo cartoons, Mork & Mindy, The Flintstones, spelling homework on that tablet with those huge lines and science class complete with animals in cages at the

front of the room and oh no, do we have to dissect a
frog? Math teachers with a pointing stick to show you
the way. Short math vs. long math. Geography class, a
globe in front of the room, on it's axis, and would
someone please tell me how the hell you can have a
north, south, east and west when the world is round?
Physical education classes and pulling people's shorts
down when the coach wasn't looking. Tying classmates
shoes together until one of them got hurt and you got
in trouble, laughing at William while in the gang
shower in the locker room, because his anatomy was
smaller and it hooked to the left.

Girls with cooties. Dirt clod battles. People that
picked their nose in class. Baseball cards in the
spokes of your bicycle. Trading baseball cards or the
anticipation of opening a fresh pack and my God, why
don't they put a piece of bubble gum in there anymore?
Putting suds in the bathtub since you've outgrown the
rubber duck. Toys that were loud. Milk shakes from mom
if you were good. Having to stick your nose on the
chalk board for being bad. The teacher asking the
class if anyone wanted to join you. John Thomas
raising his hand and saying he did. The teacher
looking confused, regrouping, drawing John a circle
next to yours; seeing the look on his face when he
volunteered for the wrong job! But my God, what a
friend! What a great guy, John Thomas. Same guy who
swore up and down he wasn't eating in class, swore up
and down, crossed his heart and hoped to die. Had
banana strings hanging off his braces the whole time.
Class tried to keep a straight face. I laughed my ASS
off! Got thrown out of the room again, no circle on
the blackboard this time. No way. I'd graduated. On to
bigger and better things. Like, the principal's
office. Big office. Big man behind big desk,
definition of fear of God when he peered over with
those dark eyes. Sitting in his chair, a big chair,
high back, with wheels, pictures in frames behind him,
lots of words and letters in there and why would you
want to frame those? What's wrong with baseball
posters, pretty girls, monster pictures, or something
like "Party Naked!" I don't know, but it didn't

matter. You just swiveled and felt your palms break
into a sweat while he delivered his sentence. No
entertaining pictures to daydream about while he put
you on detention detail: no recess, pick up all the
rocks on the football field, or sweep up in the
bathroom, and oh my God, you should've have seen and
smelled the condition of our bathrooms! Scientists
could've discovered stuff in there and not even
bothered to brag about it.

And report cards. "Good student, but talks to
much." "Needs to use his time better." "Gets along
with others, but pulls Audrey Harper's hair." "Good
student, better spit ball thrower."

Didn't you hate comments like that? Those ladies
probably laughed their ass off during Wednesday night
bridge parties over that one. Didn't help you one bit.
In fact, speaking of bridge club parties, did you ever
used to put your ear up to the wall and wonder - after
listening to them while they sat down and talked. Did
you ever wonder who was actually listening? How many
people could possibly be talking at one time? Who were
they all talking to? Was there the same amount of
people on the other side listening?

Don't think so.

They were random mouths ready to unload. Full, if
you will.

An illegal walk through the living room where
they'd convened could get you plastered against the
wallpaper. You don't believe me? There was a lot of
horsepower in that room, stronger than a mere breeze.
And you were writing about Higgins and his words per
minute? Higgins was total minor league material. 250
words with gusts up to 400, was that what you said?

Not even close in this case.

But, I'm not faulting these women.

Not in the least.

They all had 8-year-old juniors who just wanted to
run and jump and play, and how well they succeeded
depended totally and completely on how dirty they
could get and how many holes they could wear in their
blue jeans. And the look in your mother's eye when she
tossed them in the hamper, that glance in your

direction while you giggled and hid behind your
Jughead Comic books, that flash of anger, though that
same episode could oh so quickly bring a tear to her
eye at Christmas or birthdays. You? You didn't have
the slightest clue as to what the problem was and how
they could laugh one second, scold in another and cry
later. Didn't make sense.

They'd rolled their eyes and say, "kids," while you
sat there and wondered.

Or you'd crawl under the couch and find your yo-yo
you'd been missing or maybe you'd run off and play
with John and Hunter until they quit being weird.

Sorry, but I'm only on Tuesday, now, just getting
going good. How about opening the washer when it was
going full blast, water flying everywhere? Or opening
the top off the milk shake blender when going full
speed, vanilla ice cream as high as the ceiling? Man,
that would've been great to have backed away from the
whole scene and been able to laugh. Wouldn't it?
Actually, it was, until dad took off his belt and
nailed me a good one.

And did you ever throw butter on the ceiling to see
if it would stick? We did and it would, if you threw
it right. Had races to see who could do it first. It
wasn't fair, though. Sister always won, but she was
taller. Didn't matter, didn't stop her from jumping up
and down in excitement, though mom and dad saw things
a little differently. Did we both know how much it
would cost to clean that ceiling? Or how much time it
would take?

Hell no.

Didn't have a clue.

But that was a kid's job, wasn't it? To take two
objects that haven't been put together before and see
what would happen? Sometimes the results were
interesting. Sometimes they weren't. Costs had nothing
to do with anything.

Did you ever play football on the bed? Did you ever
answer the phone when mom called and told her that
everything was fine except you think John just broke
the bed with an off-tackle run that started at the
pillow, went through your sister at the quilt (40-yard

line) and ended with a dive over little Fred that left
the imaginary crowd on their feet, John's knees in
great shape despite the rough and tough 73-yard run,
but the bed in shambles on the floor; pieces of wood
you never knew existed now warped, bent and totally
unfit for sleeping?

What did we do about it?

What do you think we did?

We started blaming each other, that's exactly what
we did. "It was your idea."

"So, you're the oldest, you should know better."

"Dad's gonna wack you one."

"Me, you're playing, too."

"Was not!"

"Well, what about that touchdown you scored a while
ago that you're still bragging about?"

"Did not."

"Did too."

"Did not."

Did you ever trade your stamp collection for the
single room, then wonder, years later, how your sister
walked away with the stamps, the room and most of the
closet space? Did you ever discover this about eight
years too late but decided that a statute of
limitations didn't exist in your world, so you started
raising hell about it anyway? (Okay, maybe I was just
a total pain in the ass when I was a kid. Maybe you
obeyed mom and dad, brothers and sisters, studied,
made "A's, then went off to college and met some bad
influence named Fred.)

No, I don't think so.

Let's move on. Life is in progress.

Did you ever write notes in class to pretty girls?
Tell them you liked them, did they like you? Put a
little box besides "yes", a little box besides "no,"
and another besides "not sure who you are, please call
again?" Did you ever wonder why the guys, when angry
at you, would always call you by your mother's first
name? Did you ever hide from the school bully? Do you
remember the beautiful feeling of getting the hell
beat out of you in front of God, everybody and the
girl you just sent the note to? That wonderful feeling

of his knees on both your shoulders, pinning you
totally to the ground, rocks grinding into the back of
your head, his body grinding into the front? Do you
know that fighting is a hormone problem, not a sport?
  Did you ever crawl into your locker and get stuck
there? Start screaming and yelling and no one knew
where the hell you were and who the hell was yelling
and what was that noise and man, the second bell has
already rung so we've got to go? Remember how red your
face was when the principal opened the locker and
there you were? Remember what your heart went through
when seeing the look on his face? And losing 25 pounds
because he laughed so hard? He had to. What else could
he do? Ever fall through the roof of your school while
trying to spy on naked girls in gym class? Ever try
explaining that one to mom?
  Did you get thrown out of Six Flags Over Georgia
during a field trip for punching H.F. Puffnstuff and
Fred Flintstone? Big sister ripped me for that one. "I
can understand the H.R. Puffnstuff thing, but Fred
Flintstone? That's totally un-American and I hope dad
pounds you!"
  He did.
  With a passion and with his belt.
  And whatever happened to your first girlfriend, the
first one crazy enough to put a check mark by that
"yes?" Did it scare you? Did your friends make fun of
you? Did they giggle at you when you ate lunch
together, you with your Mickey Mouse lunch box, her
with Goldilocks and the Three Bears, her trading you
her ham sandwich for your Reese's cup. Remember the
first time you got jealous?
  Remember trying to shoot a layup for the first time
and falling flat on your ass? And crying because all
the neighbors were laughing? And pointing? And
doubling over with their hands on their guts? And
knowing you would hear about it all the next day or
any day where any form of conversation had anything to
do with basketball, whatsoever?
  Remember Pee-Wee football and trying to put on your
shoulder pads? Taking the ball down the middle and
getting knocked on your butt by the big boy from

Crawford Street? Now Crawford Street was probably
pretty cool, in itself and from an older perspective,
but since we lived on Park Lane, well, that meant war.
Plain and simple. Battle lines already drawn. The
teams were automatically chosen during Monopoly games,
street hockey or "Smear the Queer" football games.

Are you getting this? Am I wasting my time?

Who cares? It's only Thursday and life goes on,
babe. It's the way the game is played.

Did you put a flashlight under the covers where you
could read? Or a radio under there to listen to the
Braves? Or a Penthouse magazine? Or just some dumb toy
that you just didn't feel like putting down?

Ever crawl down deep inside the covers and hide
when your mom and dad came to wake you up for school?
As if they wouldn't know where you were? As if they'd
say, "wow, Fred must have gotten up early and driven
the car to school today. What a mature kid! Don't
think I knew how to drive at the age of 8, but, you
never know these days. You never know."

Do you remember when part of your manhood was
determined by who would camp out and stay outside all
night? Without coming in? And the ratio that was going
through your head at around 1 a.m., after you'd
already swapped all the lies, school stories and
things you'd never do; the ratio regarding the worth
of staying out. Flies on your face. Mosquitoes locked
on that arm and leg. That rock that always followed
wherever your sleeping bag went. That fire that kept
going out and was it my turn again to keep it going?
And knowing, the whole time, that your bedroom,
complete with teddy bears, baseball cards, familiar
posters, a bathroom and a mattress with the softest
pillow in the land just taunting you from a mere 25
yards away. A stones throw, if you would, or perhaps a
nine-iron shot at that age.

Was it worth getting ridiculed the next day?

Was it?

Sometimes yes.

Sometimes no.

How about camps? And speaking of long weeks, do you
remember laying in bed on a Tuesday night, not knowing

if you could make it through the camp or not, but
knowing completely that the week's end would never,
ever get there. Never. Ever.

Throwing paper wads at your bus driver. Getting
into a fight over a seat. Jumping up and down when the
driver would hit the big bump, throwing you high into
the air (about three inches in reality.) Hearing an
older person say a cuss word and thinking that he was
the meanest, cruelest person in the world and that
hell was coming soon to a theater near him. Getting
laughed at for not smoking a cigarette. Climbing a
tree. Getting pine sap all over those jeans. Those new
jeans! And did you know how hard it was to get stains
out of jeans?

No way!

Not a chance.

But what was for supper?

And can we stay up 30 extra minutes and watch
"Cheers?"

Lunch lines at school. The agonizing pains to
endure until first recess. And second. Classrooms with
a clock in the front, making the hour last for
approximately three days and fourteen hours in adult
time. And that was just one class.

Being afraid to jump off the ledge into water. And
it was only 15 feet high, but do you remember how high
that was in a kid's mind? Hearing the older boys taunt
you, poke at you, call you a chicken and a yellow and
those words you weren't supposed to say yet. And those
thoughts that were flashing through your head; the
pros and cons of life that later some teacher would
explain to you in terms of a balance sheet. And just
exactly how did you practice to become a cliff diver
anyway? Or a stunt man?

Wasn't life supposed to be a trial and error thing?

Ever walk in front of a swing set and get your face
caved in by an enthusiastic swinger who wanted to see
if he or she could go all the way around? Remember
that sound, that pain? That intense effort of not
wanting to cry - because that was another symbol of
manhood, besides getting dirty, camping out and doing
brave things like jumping off cliffs - was not to cry

during painful conditions.

After all, wasn't that always the second question?
What happened? He got hit by a swing. Did he cry?

And realizing all this for a moment, and almost
sucking it up and pulling it off, before feeling that
extra-large head, a little blood and then start
screaming your little ass off. A glass-shattering
scream even, or was it Memorex, that started way down
at your toes, went straight through your balls, picked
up steam around your chest, and came out your throat
at 120, maybe 150 miles per hour. Not to be muffled by
anything, anyone, anytime, anywhere. If you listen
closely, it's still out there. People can blame it on
ghosts or animals all they want to. I know better.

Didn't matter, though, you could always lie
tomorrow and swear you never felt a thing. Could even
get some sympathy for that new crater next to your
eye. Girls would laugh, but you didn't care yet. You
looked tough! Would probably get picked second instead
of fifth when picking up teams for school yard
football. Even though you couldn't punt, pass or kick
and had no trophies to prove it.

Sorry, but I'm getting close. It's Friday now and
do you realize what all I've been through? It's not
even allowance time yet. I've been through all this
crap and haven't watched a single cartoon since last
week.

And what about Game Day?

Quiet!

Moment of Silence.

Tell me this one, Phil, did you ever throw up right
in the middle of class? I don't mean in the hall, the
bathroom, the woods or outside in general, I mean
right slap in the dead center of class? Left-over
pickles, hamburgers, fries, fruit loops, and all kinds
of yellowish-brown funk flying all over the place. In
chunks, liquids and pieces. All over Frank Buyert's
leg? Remember how funny it would've been to see all
your little classmates flying around the room like
bats out of hell? Nothing but arms, legs, hair,
screams, shouts and a teacher who didn't begin to try
and control it all. At first.

Screw politics, the news and the world. Their world was temporarily harmed by all I'd eaten the last week and man, to tell you the truth, I'm kinda chuckling right now as I write about it. While I'm getting up and changing pens.

Speaking of, what did you do with my other pen? Where is it? But don't worry, I ain't opening your closet door again to find one, because it smells very similar to this scene I'm writing about. I'll switch to a pencil, thanks.

Stubbing your toe; did you ever stub your toe? Didn't that just hurt like shit? Wasn't that one of the most underrated pains in the history of the world? Did you ever play nerf hoop at home with your friends and have some smart aleck open the door right as your were driving for the picture perfect layup as time was running down? Remember how it felt when you missed the laundry sacks on the other side and landed face first on the chair?
Now do you understand why I'm so ugly?
Do you?
Getting close now, Phil. Bear with me.
How about arguments with friends over sports? Georgia vs. Georgia Tech? The 49ers or the Cowboys? The argument over when to change sports with the season? And could you believe they were still playing football when it was basketball season? Remember your mother raising hell at you, trying to get you to come inside and do your history homework? Had I done my history homework? Did I know the future consequences of my life if I failed history?
Hell no!
I only knew that we were up 12-8 and Billy wouldn't pass me the ball so I wouldn't throw it to him and I wanted to guard Robert because he was slower than Gene.
Remember the excitement of a Saturday morning? And how other kids would complain because they woke up automatically, already on auto-pilot, thinking they had school? But you loved it. That wonderful feeling

of waking up at 6:30, realizing you didn't have to get up, then permabonding your face right back inside and through the pillow and your mattress and drifting away again? Remember how bad you felt on Monday morning when you thought you could do the same thing?

OOPS, back to Saturday. Did you watch cartoons? Did you fight with your sister over what to watch? Did you ever wonder how you could be at total war with your fellow man as an 8-year-old, then seconds later, be their best friend? Ever wonder why we can't do that now?

Did you used to sneak across the ball and listen in on the other team's plays when playing football in your front yard? Remember how HUGE that field looked, that minimal 30 yard by 10 yard strip of land that dad could cut with a push mower in about 10 or 15 minutes? Remember seeing the quarterback drawing the plays with a stick, using rocks as players, moving the grass with his hand, telling Todd to go down the middle, then cut towards the pine tree, Hunter to fake right, then cut towards the carport and John, well, he had to go long?

Getting caught listening in. Fighting for a few seconds. Either winning the fight or getting the worst of it, then crying like hell just for some sympathy and getting him to stop. Then playing on, becoming best buddies, and who the hell needed adults to screw things up?

Ever wonder why people want to grow up?

Why they're in such a hurry?

Ever have people tell you that you need to?

Ever wonder how to answer?

Well, it's simple - Tell them, no thanks, you've seen grown ups lately. You're not that impressed.

Almost home now, 12 noon and counting: Game Time: 2 p.m.

Wasn't your mom's ice tea the best in the world? Don't you realize now that no matter what recipe you use, you can't top it? Even if you steal hers? Remember how old you were before you realized that mom's way was the only way and everything else was in a different class? Apples and oranges, if you will.

Did you get spanked for sneaking Oreo cookies before and after meals? About 100 times? Ever wonder why you never could get some of those simplest rules through your head? Isn't is funny now?

Skimming rocks, building dams after a good rain, Star Trek episodes, the "Wonder Years", (Columbo even, have it your way!), late night wrestling, both watching and performing it on your neighbors, building forts, spying on people in the woods, your first pet and holy shit, wasn't it the saddest thing ever when your dog got lost or run over by a car?

Feeling that horrible pain and realization - while you stay on your porch, crying your eyes out, snot running out of your nose - that things die.

Let's not beat around the bush here, Phil. Didn't that just suck?

Didn't it?

It did.

Know it.

Remember it.

And I'm almost finished with a week. Almost.

Time to suit up.

Time to walk into my bedroom after lunch, close the door, and see that uniform all laid out on the bed. In order, of course, hat on top, shirt in the middle, pants on the bottom, socks and shoes on the floor.

Now that I think about it, I think mom probably did it that way to keep me from getting confused, not to be neat.

Remember driving over with the folks? He behind the wheel, adjusting the mirror, putting on the seat belts, mom still messing with her lipstick, fumbling through her purse, both deciding between radio and conversation, then flipping off the old FM since junior's in the back, hanging on to the back of the front seat, ready to dive out the window once the ball park was in sight? Was his seat belt on? Were the windows up?

Do you remember that feeling?

Don't you want to feel some of that now?

Remember when the greatest things in life were the simplest?

When you could feel total joy with a candy bar, a glass of coke with or without ice, a box of popcorn, a 30-minute television show or a bicycle with ten gears? Or approval from the folks, tossing the baseball with the family, walking on the beach during vacation? Or the beauty of living in the moment, since that was all we had and all that was needed? And when you get right down to it, it's still all there is.

Are you listening to me?

Do you realize it can still be that way?

Even though "normal" people may think you're out of your mind about three-quarters of the time?

Are you strong enough not to care?

Sorry, let me get on with my game. This is big stuff. Besides, Spence told Todd who told Bobby who told Hunter who told John that somebody heard something about some photographer who might actually take our picture and put it in the paper. THE town paper.

Holy shit! Only eight years old and a superstar already.

Our picture in the paper!

Never mind, it won't come out until next week.

A whole friggin' week.

Jesus wept.

But can I tell you about the game?

Okay, hang on for a second, I'm almost there. So close. But we have to start with the field.

The diamond.

The sphere of influence, if you will.

If I ever went crazy, and many will say that I'm damned close, I'd never go lay on the proverbial sofa in the shrink's office, with my head propped up on a pillow. Wouldn't stare at the strange man or the strange woman and tell them the first thing. No way.

I'd walk out there, on the field. And use nothing more than the senses God gave me.

To smell the grass and even the dirt on the infield, the leather from the gloves, the hot crap pitchers put on their arms and shoulders. I'd hear the spikes being sharpened, bat meeting ball, ball popping into glove, umpires yelling, players spitting,

managers walking, packing and where the hell was the
lineup card?

Yes, that's what I'd do, Phil my man, I'd go to my
own special place to meditate and if everyone else
doesn't have their own, then there's a problem. I'd go
straight out there.

Sure would.

Would walk out to home plate first. Kick some dirt
around the batter's box. Fix it just right. Smooth it
over with both feet. Both sides of the box, mind you,
both sides. Brush the dirt off the plate. A sacred
ritual. If it's clean, brush it again. No brush
required. Use your hand. Get it dirty. So what? Smell
the dirt. It's harmless. Hell, it even comes out with
some soap and water, no lectures required.

Walk out to the mound. Get the dirt straight, even
though I never was a pitcher and have no clues as to
what "straight" is. Toe the rubber, walk around, talk
to myself, scratch my nuts, toe the rubber again.
Check the runner, or runners in some cases. Wind, kick
and fire. Hear the ball hit the mitt, the ump's call,
the batters look on his face as he spits, kicks dirt,
hits bat to cleats, bat to cleats, and steps back in
as I'm messing with the ball and getting ready to
repeat the process.

Walk the bases. Hear the sound of your cleats
moving through the dirt when you're trying to steal
second. Seeing second base, so far away, wondering why
those legs can't pump just a little bit faster, a
little harder. Seeing the second baseman already
there, glove outstretched, eyes locked on the incoming
ball. Remembering your thoughts at this point, "oh
shit, I'll never make it." But you keep picking them
up and putting them down anyway, breathing quicker,
heavier and how far is that base? Arms pumping,
furious, harder, faster.

Feel the pain in your butt or your stomach as you
hit the dirt. Hard. Trying to beat the throw. Feeling
the tag and hoping like hell it's too high up or too
far down, depending on which way you slid. Looking up
helplessly at the ump. Hoping to see those fat arms
fly outwards. Instead of that one hand flying down.

Then cruise out to the outfield. You know, like you did, Phil, just like you did. Hear the grass rustle under your feet. Watch it right itself after your passing, ready for more. Chew on some of it for a while. Have a seat.

Which makes me laugh every time.

Every time.

Because this is what happened.

Second Tee League game. Above week finally at a close and what a week I might add! Crammed a lot in there, did we not? Got $5 allowance and it'll take me a month to spend it. Or a day.

Who cared?

Either way, I'm exhausted.

Actually, no I'm not. Not at this age. Up and at 'em, ready for more.

It was the third inning, the last inning actually, since that's all we played, and we were getting the crap kicked out of us. 10-2 or something like that. I was one-for-two personally; had damned near broken the tee in my excitement the first time, hit what would've been a double the second, but stood there yelling for my mom to look where I'd hit the ball and almost forgot to run the bases. Barely got to first. Some even thought I didn't. Sister laughed at me when I glanced over. Stuck her tongue out at me.

I rolled my eyes back at her.

Whew. I made it, though. Got to stand on first base until Gene damned near broke the tee and left me stranded. Great guy, that Gene. Too bad he couldn't hit for shit with runners in scoring position.

Pissed me off.

But anyway, in the top of the third, Billy Baxter poked one right between shortstop and third base. Right to Spence, who was playing left.

One minor problem, though.

It seemed that ole Spence had gotten a little bored with the game. Decided he was going to sit down with a stick, make a few mud cakes, and build a castle or two. Or yeah, I know! I'll put the stick in the castle, find a few rocks, surround the castle and have my own fort. Great idea!

Spence was somewhat confused when he looked up, seeing people of both sexes and all shapes and sizes jumping up and down, up and down, screaming their faces off. Parents were turning red and yelling themselves hoarse; the coach was standing at the dugout, pointing to the ball, trying to act mad but actually trying to keep from laughing himself to death.

Spence looks around at this point, confused, probably saying something like, "what in the hell is it with these people? What did I do wrong?" Looking around, he spots the ball, now resting at the fence, some fifty feet away. Angry teammates are still throwing gloves, hats, even rocks at little Spence, while others have turned away in frustration.

Inconvenienced, Spence gets up, puts the stick in his castle to mark his spot, makes his dash to the fence and proudly picks up the ball and holds it for all to see.

Meanwhile, slugger has already crossed the bases, high-fived his teammates, the bat boy, his coach and his parents.

Hearing his teammates angry shouts, seeing gloves thrown in his direction, feeling the true wrath that only kids can give, Spence drops the ball, pokes his lip out and starts to cry.

So funny.

So sad.

Such is life.

What was my part in that? I'm sad to say that I was one of those kids throwing gloves and caps at Spence, yelling, shouting, turning red, orange, purple and other assorted colors. I feel bad about it now that I think about it. Will apologize to him if I ever see him.

Probably never will, though.

Do I still have your attention? Are you listening to me? Actually, you probably are and maybe, just maybe, you're starting to realize that, even though you're still depressed, you're starting to see and remember that there's so MUCH more to this world. You're probably even smiling or at least know you should be.

Go ahead, it's okay. You don't have to feel guilty.

Did you start out so young and fresh and alive just to hit a snag like that and let yourself go? Did you? Over a girl?

May I answer that question? The answers are; a) no; b) hell no; and c) all of the above.

You with me?

Good, because I'm not finished.

There's more.

You, you maybe depressed over some damned woman, but I'm just now getting to Little League.

And I ain't taking any shit from anybody.

Little League Baseball Sign-ups Tomorrow!

That's what the sign said. It brought me excitement, as much as the first time but minus the peeing in pants episode that you'll never tell anyone about.

If mother and daddy hadn't driven me to the local cafeteria to sign up, I'd have driven the car myself or at least thrown their butts in the car and pushed. Or maybe gathered mom up on the right arm, dad on the left, and kicked sand in people's faces and hauled us all in there.

They drove. They had to. I would've raised cane, screamed, yelled and generally started throwing shit. Everywhere. It would've come out of my next 727 allowances.

Would've been worth it.

That's the beauty of being a kid. It would've been worth it. Simple pleasures were all there was. Nothing else mattered.

And what if it did?

Some large man asked me when I was born. Didn't have a clue. I knew specifically that my birthday was in May, but how the hell was I supposed to know when I was born? I was too young. Oh, you mean that was the same thing?

They got a big laugh out of that one. Should've seen Tommy Bosworth laughing. Hell with him. He can't hit and he throws like a girl.

He took all the information with lots of help from
mom and dad, then we were excused. Had to go back
home. I remembered seeing another sign on the
cafeteria door as we headed out:

**PRACTICES BEGIN IN TWO WEEKS: MAY 28 AT 4:00 AT
THE FIELD!   SEE YOU THERE AND GOOD LUCK!!!**

May 28! That was two weeks away! Two weeks.
Fourteen days!
And as a 10-year-old kid, you complained about
that, but only for a moment. Because you were tough.
You were 10, in double figures now, growing zits,
muscles, hearing lies about girls, beating up and
getting beat up by other boys, looking at "girlie"
magazines, spending the night at friend's houses,
getting to go to high school games.
You actually knew a couple of the players! You
spend the night with Timmy, who's older brother played
on the varsity football team. A varsity player!
And better yet, you actually got to play some
yourself. Biddy Football Leagues. Soccer. Tennis and
swimming at the "Y". Picking sides, shirts and skins,
getting to play full court on occasion, and man, that
court sure was huge!
But you moved up and down it with ease. Because you
were a kid. But when mom reminded you of that, you got
mad. You defended yourself.
"No I'm not. I'm in Middle School now!"
And you were.
You're past the stage of writing girls love notes
and putting it on their desk. No, you're mature now.
In fact, you laugh remembering stuff like that at
lunch, while trading your chips for a ham sandwich and
asking around if anyone has any M & M's.
Isn't it great to be older?
And now that you are, you ask John to go ask the
girl if she likes you, instead of sending those
stupid, immature notes. You get a little nervous as
John goes hauling ass across the gym during PE class,
you hide behind the bleachers as you see his bow-
legged self pulling Patty out of the line, whispering

in her ear, watching her laugh, feeling shitty because
you'll take that as a 'no', avoiding John cause you
don't need to hear the answer, and forgetting the
whole thing because John, you, Spence, and Cookie are
playing against Ken, Gene, Bob and Timmy in four-on-
four and the hell with everything else.

Did we realize we were supposed to go change and
shower before going to the next class? Didn't we know
we were going to smell bad and affect other people.

Hell no!

Enough already. We've made that point. After all,
it's Little League time. It's opening day. American
Legion vs. VFW There was a 50% chance of rain and if
it did so, we were gonna shoot somebody. Anybody. Or
we'd hide under the bed and never come out. Ever. Or
when they woke me for church on Sunday, I'd hide in my
bed again. Yeah, that would fool 'em. "Wow, that Fred,
he's a mature one, hon. Isn't he great to just hope
right out of bed and take the car into church? Isn't
he great?"

It sprinkled at 4:30, thundered by 5, rained like a
mother by 5:30, but only for five minutes. A few
puddles were still there by 7:30, but we damned sure
didn't care. We held our breath, sucked it in and
almost died while the adults checked out the field.
They walked around, shuffled dirt back and forth,
looked at each other, at the sky, at the infield,
outfield, base paths, home plate, pitcher's mound.

More walking, gesturing, talking, looking back at
our dugout, where 16 sets of eyes told them they'd
have a war on their hands if they canceled.

Sure, they were older. But we were kids. And we
could make their lives miserable.

Seeing the coach walk over to us, probably at a
normal pace, but slow to us.

"Take the field, guys!"

Yes Phil, there was a God.

Don't forget that.

Ever.

We took the infield with a passion. With chants,
noise, chattering, hollering, whooping and whatever

those other words are with similar meaning.

Me, I was so damned excited that when Abe Wyler hit a soft grounder to me at second, I fielded it cleanly and damned near threw it over the first baseman, the fence and the bleachers. In fact, at last sighting, the ball was cruising down Jefferson Street, took a right on Pine, went past the Fuller's house, then cruised over to Poplar Street. It's still going.

I can even see the umpire as I write this, running back to the fence as if I'd kicked a field goal, lifting both hands in the air to signal "good," while everybody laughed and the runner took second on the throw.

But my good buddy John told me to shake it off and it was okay; my coach slapped his hands together and told me to hang in there. The world was good and there was and still is a special place in heaven for people that volunteer their time to help kids in things like Little League baseball. The man with a family and a job and oh no, he had a business trip on Wednesday. The man who stood at the chain-linked fence and encouraged your snotty self even though you had just turned the easiest play in baseball history into a two-base error.

Little League coaches should never have to get sick or die, or be poor or unhappy.

Or friends either, for that matter. Ones who clap you on the back and tell you "better luck next time" and mean it.

I realized something that night, right then and right there, and if I'm starting to sound like a "Wonder Year's episode, then so be it. If I could feel the way I felt on that night and could go there in my mind at will, I'd travel the world giving seminars, having people pay to hear me and not a one would complain or want their money back. Not one.

Do you know what a pure moment is, Phil? Do you?

Either way, I'll tell you.

A pure moment is when you don't want to be anywhere else in the world except where you are, right then, right there. It could be something big like Little League Baseball, it could be a simple high-five from a shy person, or it could be just sitting in a room with a friend.

Regardless, I remember standing there, ready for the next batter, hands on my knees, glove on the left one, dirty hand on the right, a hole already in my uniform though it was only opening night and hell no I didn't know how it got there and couldn't have cared less.

I only knew that this was the place to be. Nowhere else. This place right here, and this time, for no other time mattered. Not then.

I smiled then as a waited for the next ball. (He grounded to short instead of to me, but that's beside the point.) The world was not only good, it was pretty damned perfect.

And why? Because there was no future, maybe that was it. There was no need to get older and be a day late, a dollar short, and oh shit, I forgot a deadline.

Never.

The world was a small field that seemed to go forever, a pitcher's mound that wasn't very high but who cared, a dirt infield with pebbles far worse than Jenkins College's, a couple of umpires, a dirty equipment bag, lights that got the job done, parents sitting on the sidelines in their lawn chairs and a bunch of chattering kids, wanting to run and jump and play.

It was days and nights of slumber parties, getting to stay up until 10 on weekends, ice cream if you were good, free cokes for the winners and the losers of your Little League game (and God help anyone in the path of the concession stand and those boys!), a round of golf, building forts, covering them with dirt, wood, bricks, finding leaves for camouflage and from what I don't remember. Flying kites, bicycle rides, camp trips, swimming …

And more school days. Remember those, from our newly mature perspective?

Remember lingering outside your locker, just beating the second bell and getting to home room on time. Or not and getting sent for detention. Playing thump football during study hall, throwing spit balls, laughing at the guy or girl who fell asleep during class and starting drooling, watching the drool slowly emerge from the corner of the mouth, form a coalition, then slowly seep past the lip and downward, downward, until it found it's home on the notebook or text. Getting called down for laughing, getting sent out of the room, standing in the hall and praying the headmaster didn't walk by. Praying. Praying.

Do you remember the butterflies at this point? Mixed with fear? Dreading the belt that would come off your father' waist, feeling the pain, wishing you'd have put on four pairs of underwear today to ease the pain. And by the way, if it's only one, why do they call underwear a pair?

I'm counting down the last three weeks of school, Phil. I'm getting a good seat next to my buddy John. We're trading stories, passing notes, trying to flirt with girls but not knowing how, then settling for gazing out the window. And wishing we were old enough to play pick up games with the older boys and have girlfriends that were older. Or wondering what we could do to gain their approval and be accepted.

Me, I'd gaze and go inward, hearing the ball crack the bat and reaching first base safely; glancing over at my dad and mom, almost getting picked off for not paying attention. Realizing even then, that the world is full of goods and bads, and you had to stay sharp and pay attention or a positive could quickly turn into a negative.

Are you getting tired of reading this, Phil? Are you?

Do you have better things to be thinking about? Like, that girl? Do you wish I'd leave you alone?

Good, because I'm not.

There's more.

Listen to me, damn it. Listen to me.

It gets better.

And it gets worse.

A brief time out is in order. It's 1:30 a.m. Jenkins College time. The drunks are out drinking,

wondering when they're going to study. The nerds are
studying, wondering when they'll find time for
relaxation. The hall is quiet. Alumni's just sitting
here, uncaring, indifferent, just like that Pub place
I didn't go to tonight.
    It can all wait.

    Because you're in high school now. Adolescence and
hormones at their finest. Zits in full bloom, a couple
of hairs growing around different parts of the body
and now you're really tough shit.
    Some of your friends are shaving. You're afraid to
wash your chest because there's a hair there. Where
did it come from? Where was it yesterday? Will it soon
be joined by others?
    You'll be driving next year, a learner's permit
awaits you, barring disaster. Girls don't have the
cooties anymore, or if they did, you're wishing you
could get closer to find out for yourself. You're
playing junior varsity basketball, kicking footballs
to ease the boredom between seasons and still shagging
grounders around the house.
    Your sister's a babe.
    Friends comment often.
    Behind your back.
    You get very angry.
    You get sent to detention for punching Billy
Herndon in the face. Someone said he pinched her on
the butt during PE class. You saw her crying in the
hall.
    Life is funny sometimes. You used to spend all
waking hours trying to get her to cry. The first time
someone else makes it happen, you get mad. It makes
you sad and makes you laugh at the same time.
    It reminds you of what happened to John, when
someone tried to beat him up in the hall two weeks
ago. His older brother came along, grabbed the guy by
the collar, jerked him up against the locker and said,
"nobody beats my brother's ass except for me. Do you
understand that?"
    He was serious.
    We all laughed, except for the boy against the

locker.

He was scared.

But I want to talk about my sister.

Do you remember your sister? That girl you used to tickle so hard, she laughed until she cried? The girl you fought with over what television program to watch? The girl who told you that Bruce Springsteen couldn't sing for shit, but he had a cute butt; the one who couldn't have cared less what Greg Maddux's ERA was as long as he was cute; the one who took two hours in the bathroom before her first date; the one who looked like a million dollars but you'd damned sure never tell her.

The one who was two years older than you. She could drive. On her own. Openly and freely. The one who would always be older than you no matter how many turtles you found, or hits you got, or "A's" you had on your report card, or whatever. The one you used to beg to take you places. Any places.

She rebelled and took you nowhere.

You got so angry.

You pulled her hair once.

She cried and told mom.

You felt so bad later.

Because no matter what happened, she was your sister. Permanently bonded at the hip. A part of you, your mom and your dad.

Anyway, you're sitting at the table one night, your mother, your father and yourself, just one happy family. You're waiting to eat. You're not allowed to until everyone is present and accounted for, however. Dad is reading the paper at his seat, mom is nervously looking at the clock wondering where she is. You, you don't care. You want mom to pass the peas, the chicken and the corn, then you can start on the apple pie, gulp your tea in two seconds flat and still have time to toss the baseball around in the yard.

You are impatient.

And then … the phone rings.

And you know. You knew something was wrong. Just like you knew when your phone rang at 9:15 or 9:30 or whenever it rang the other morning. And those people

in the world that live their life going only by their
five senses are oh so wrong. There's something else
out there.

    Bigger than you.

    Bigger than me.

    Bigger than Leigh.

    Your mother screams. Drops the phone. Your father
rushes over, concerned, paper flying, the baseball
standings forgotten, crossword puzzle landing face up
and you feeling guilty later for noticing something
like that.

    Your dad takes control of the situation. His voice
waivers. Mom is in hysterics. Screaming. Yelling.
Pounding her fists, first into father's chest, next
onto the wall, pictures flying everywhere, chaos
reigning supreme.

    She'd just been driving home, that was all. Just
taking her friend Beth from the mall to her house,
then back for dinner. All was good. All was normal.

    She took a turn going too fast. The car flipped.
Beth was thrown from the car and turned out okay.
Suffered some scratches. Cuts. Contusions and
abrasions I think was the fancy terminology, but what
was the difference.

    Sister was crushed inside, pinned between the seat
and the windshield.

    Multiple head wounds.

    Internal bleeding.

    Broken neck.

    Crushed spine.

    No chance of survival.

    Dead.

    Did you hear that word I just used, Phil?

    Dead.

    Gone.

    My sister.

    My SISTER for crying out loud!

    My beautiful sister. Such a great girl. Such a pain
in the butt. So prissy. So ugly. So beautiful.

    She'd just left for school this morning, wearing
blue jeans, a cut-off halter top that stopped above
the waist, hair sitting on her shoulders, golden,

beautiful hair and DAMN IT, why didn't I tell her?,
tennis shoes, white socks, a bracelet around her left
wrist, a watch and who cared what kind it was, and a
little belt-like thing that she made; white if it
mattered.

She was just here! At school, in her room, watching
TV, fixing her hair, taking too long in the shower,
humoring me by asking me if I had a girlfriend,
tickling my back, but knowing I was getting big enough
to pound her.

I just sat there. To hell with peas, corn, apple
pie and yes, even baseball. My first true perspective,
if you will. Mouth open. Shocked. Scared. Unable to
speak. Unable to calm mom down. A situation totally
not taught in school, not practiced with fire drills,
tornado watches, or those broadcasting tests you hear
on TV or the radio.

What was I to do? Couldn't she come back? Couldn't
she just get here safely, eat her food, chew way too
loudly, and tell us about her day? About her date for
this Friday? About how she wishes guys weren't so
stupid?

I would listen this time. I swear I would. Every
word. I'd help her. Talk to her. Laugh with her. Not
even ask for a ride to the mall, or to John's. I swear
I wouldn't.

Couldn't I see her again? Please? Is somebody
listening to me? Anybody? Where did she go? Where is
she now? Why? Why? WHY?

Doesn't it scare you to death? Doesn't it make you
wonder? Doesn't it make you want to stomp the shit out
of those people that get so uptight over - what? A
memo? Rain on a weekend? A flat tire? A program that's
canceled for a presidential speech?

A girl?

Are you kidding me?

I said, are you kidding me?

Are you listening to me now?

Are you?

The preacher got mad at me at the funeral. People
would later comment on how I lost it; didn't handle it
well.

The preacher, though, let's talk about the preacher, then I'll get back to life. Or maybe, in this case, there's not a whole helluva lot of difference.

I was shocked. It took me a day before I cried. When I did, I raised hell. Threw things. Didn't take phone calls. Didn't read sympathy cards. Didn't watch TV. Didn't catch the box scores in the Atlanta Journal. Isolated myself from the world. Saw the rays of light for the first time two days later, when walking outside for the funeral.

The funeral.

The limo.

The casket.

So unbelievable.

So gut wrenching.

So final.

The preacher was probably in his mid-30's, a man who my sister would've probably said was cute, probably did but I wasn't listening, because I had my own agendas at the time. He spoke of life, death, life after death, the works. He spoke of resting her soul, ashes to ashes, she'd gone to a better place and how the beauty of death was that it brought us all so close together.

And that's where I had a little problem.

And when he pulled me aside afterwards and tried to talk with me, I told him so. Bluntly, without regard or care.

"If the beauty of death is to bring us so close together, then would somebody please tell me the point of life? Why in the hell do you wait for people to die before you come together? Would some smart person please answer me that one? I can't believe you actually said that with a straight face."

I went on. And on. And on.

My parents came in. Dad apologized, mom just cried. The preacher understood. Accepted. All was well.

My father gave me this look. You know the look. The one that silences you so quickly. Makes you feel so bad.

But this was different, Phil. This was different.

This is another one of those unspeakable things you can't prove, a non-five sensory event, a pure moment in itself. And if someone asks me to prove it, I'll probably pound the sonofabitch into submission and when he gets up, I'll pound him again.

The look my father gave me was different. He was telling me that I was right in a large sense, though taking it all out on the preacher wasn't the way to handle it. He was accepting that I had now grown, that things were different and that we were in this together. He was telling me we were one and we would stick together, just mom, dad and myself. And do you know how I knew that.

I just did. And that was that.

And he was proud of me. And even though I was to shut up, I wasn't on the wrong track. Out of place and at the wrong time, maybe, but not wrong. He told me that with a look.

Nothing more.

Nothing less.

What a great guy, my father.

And do you know what else, Phil? Well, I'll tell you.

When he reached out and touched my left shoulder with his right hand to calm me, it was as if he was holding a cattle prod or a laser. Or something. Goose bumps went over my arms, legs, hair or no hair. My whole body froze and respected.

And my father, in that one simple gesture, went from not only being my father, but to being my friend as well; someone I could now talk to instead of hide from. Confide in. Ask for advice. Know that he was young once, too. He'd been there, done that. I didn't have to think I was so much smarter. Or so much different. Or so much, period.

Because circumstances could all change in the wink of that eye we mentioned earlier. Or sooner.

But dad could help me.

He was on my side.

And the proof was in the moment. When his hand touched my shoulder and I froze. And it taught me the difference between thinking something and knowing

something. Right then I knew. Without question. No
proof required. It was perfect.

I'll never forget it.

Ever.

I just looked at the preacher, who didn't return my
gaze. He looked down at the wall, at the floor, at my
dad and mom. We all learn lessons from people. Of all
forms, shapes, and sizes.

He was just being reminded by a 14-year-old kid,
with scraggly looking hair, tears in his eyes and a
big, huge zit on the left side of his chin. Grew it
right in time for picture day.

We put mom in the middle and we walked out in the
rest of our life. I never saw, heard or felt a thing
from the people in attendance.

Perhaps I wanted to, but I didn't need it.

There's a huge difference, you know. A huge
difference.

My mom, she was so … beautiful. Trying to be so
strong, but her world was totally ripped inside and
out. Dad was doing his best, preparing for the rest of
the haul. They were just human beings, Phil. Human
beings. With feelings just like you, and me, and
everyone else who's ever been here. Ever.

And I realized that so clearly on this day.

And why did it take my sweet sister's death for me
to realize this?

When we were arguing over what to watch, "L. A.
Law" or "Quincy?" Why didn't I know it then? When she
argued with me, but seconds later, put her hands
through my hair and fixed it for me. Asked me about
my day. Told me I'd better be ready after school,
'cause she had to leave at 3:00 sharp!' Teased me some
more.

Can I talk to her, just one more time?

Please!

Lessons are learned, and we move on. My difference
was realizing my parents as people, and one day,
they'd die, too. And now, so unlike before, I could
help them a little.

And I would.

And death would not bring me to my parents.

Life still had that honor.
And I'd use it.
Every bit of it.
Do you understand me now, or do you want proof?
Damn it.
All I could do at that time was hold on to my
mother, support my father and play my role. Even in
little ways. You know, clean up after I spill shit all
over the place. Not argue when it was bed time. Wake
up in the morning when they asked and not hide under
the covers. Help them instead of always asking for it.
Help somebody.
Help anybody.

A brief time out --- for no particular reason. I
have to go to the bathroom. It's getting late. I'll be
back.

Sorry. Let me continue.
It's Saturday morning now, somewhere around 9:30 or
10:00. It's kinda nice to wake up on the weekend
without a hangover. We should try it more often.
When's the last time either of us saw 9:30 on a
Saturday or Sunday morning? Besides when you got up
and took the GMAT or GRE or whatever the hell it was
or when we had that baseball road trip?
It's been a while.
Anyway, you'll be glad to know I'm almost through
here; will turn your journal back over to you, for
better or for worse. Besides, this writing thing is a
little too emotional for me. I'd rather express myself
in other ways; baseball, dancing, jogging; anyway
besides turning and reaching for a pen and a piece of
paper.
It reminds me too much of school; of structure,
organization, standing in lines, sitting in
alphabetical order, speaking only when spoken to,
coming and going only when a bell rings, releasing you
from one organization, sending you to another. And
damn it! Straighten your tie!
I don't know. Writing just … reminds me.
But let's get back to school, and only for a

moment. There's still a couple of things I want to share with you; one, my 16th birthday and two, the summer before my freshman year.

Ah. Sweet Sixteen! Taking the driver's test and barely passing. (Didn't I tell you I didn't test well?) Walking in the house on the big day. A 16-year-old 'man'. A changed person, with nine hairs on my chest, girls to chase and sports to play.

Heaven, in my eyes, but let me elaborate.

I received three presents on my 16th birthday. One was usual, another was sacred and the third, another bond between me and my parents.

John dropped me off at home after school, around 3:45 or so, since we had no practice due to the rain, there were no movies worth seeing, and we just didn't feel like driving around listening to the same old music since neither one of us felt like buying a new tape.

He kept asking me what my problem was on this day; I never told him. I just knew it was going to be weird day at the home front, that's all, and I didn't want to talk to anyone about it.

He didn't press, though. He knew how I was when I hit one of those quiet spells.

I walked into the living room and tossed my books on my bed the way I always did, though I immediately felt … funny. My mother turned her back on me and wiped what looked like a tear in her eye as I came into the living room and saw her heading back to her bedroom.

I didn't say anything.

I just went to my room and read, a Stephen King book I think, about a car that turns evil.

Dad came home from work at around 6 as he most always did. We gathered in the living room instead of the supper table.

My mother handed me a box. A white box, blue ribbon, rather large. Being the curious type, I shook it; it made no noise. None at all.

Okay, it wasn't a jigsaw puzzle. It wasn't round, so I couldn't bounce it to see if it was a basketball.

My only choice was to open it.

I did so.

Slowly. Didn't want to appear too eager. Played hard to get, if you would.

There was a bag. Nike. Blue with white stripes. Small, but durable. It could hold clothes, underwear, bathroom supplies, the works.

"Open the bag, son." Dad, motioning with his hand.

I unzipped it. Slowly still. Looked inside.

There it was - a baseball glove. Brown, leather and beautiful. I pulled it out. Popped my hands inside. Opened it. Closed it. Stared at it. Stared at the Ozzie Smith autograph, smelled the leather, held it up to the light.

I saw the look in my father's eyes. The proud look in my mother's.

It was awesome.

But the evening wasn't over.

Nor was my full investigation of the present.

There was a compartment on the back side of the bag. Probably would hold a paperback novel, letters, even a hair brush if I ever bothered with that sort of thing.

"Keep looking." Dad again, with a weird look on his face.

I unzipped again. A little faster this time. (Sorry, the adrenaline got me. I couldn't help it!)

There it was. I heard them before I saw them.

Car keys.

To my mom's car, who would now be driving the new one dad was going to get.

A Honda. Blue. Five speed. Sun roof. Antenna tilting backward. Good gas mileage and dependable, but I didn't know or care about that, yet.

I held the keys up proudly. Until I saw the look on my mother's face. And the somber look on my dad's.

Mother hugged me, then left the room in tears. Father looked into my eyes so deeply, so sharply, drawing me to them and closing out the rest of the world.

He didn't speak.

He didn't have to.

I didn't either.

I couldn't.

In an unusual gesture, my dad and I met in the middle of the living room and hugged each other. Rather tightly, I might add; and for the first time since I'd gotten stitches in my leg when I was a six year old.

He wasn't one of those touchy-feely type of guys, either, you know what I mean?

He was then. And those goose bumps I spoke of earlier, the ones that electrify your system and turn your arm hairs into needles, once again rose in full salute, unable to be knocked down by anything.

He released me, turned and went into the dining room.

Mom returned from the bedroom, said 'happy birthday' in the best voice she could.

And we ate dinner. The three of us.

In silence.

Well, high school, if you or anyone cares, was sports, drinking, spending the night at friend's houses, more sports, driving around going nowhere, chasing more women, and junior-senior proms, which turned out to be the most overrated event besides the Super Bowls.

Of course, there are passing memories - Debbie Satterfield in the pole vault pit, almost getting caught skipping school, my first fender-bender, missing the front end of a one-and-one against Tucker and losing by a point, playing the last seed in a golf match because we didn't have enough, going to track practice during study hall and baseball practice after school, and drilling a big, fat, lazy, fastball on a 3-2 pitch over the left-center field stands, into the pine trees, interrupting a blue jay and a mockingbird and a cardinal while they were playing, and enjoying the thrill or seeing my dad's big smile as I rounded first, floated to second, came down to earth as I touched third and seeing the beauty of my teammates all lined up ready to congratulate me as I crossed home.

And the road to the state finals. Which actually

ended in the semifinals by a swinging bunt that Taylor
fielded barehanded, but threw low to first. Also, a
diving catch by their first baseman, robbing me of a
double and our team of a run, maybe two. A creative
call by the umpire. Tonya Simpkins playing hard to get
after the game and me telling her to go screw herself.

There's more, but I've dealt with it, as have you,
so I'll bring you high school news no more.

Because spring gave way to summer, graduation
presents appeared on my bed out of nowhere and I got
and accepted my diploma without as much emotion as I
thought I'd have. To me, though, it happened
perfectly. I enjoyed high school enough, but now I was
ready to move on.

To college. To bigger, greener baseball fields. To
women with jugs that defied all laws of physics. To
staying out all night. No curfew. All-nighters. Doing
laundry. Butt slides in the hallways. Flag football.
Intramurals. Which teacher to take and why? Freedom.
Self discipline or lack thereof.

All of which brings us to two weeks before my
arrival at the Jenkins College campus; to August 18th.
Thursday. Sunny and clear. Highs around 85. Chance of
late afternoon or evening thundershowers. Lows tonight
in the upper 60's.

John and I were riding around, not really doing
anything and definitely going nowhere. Listening to
Pearl Jam. Talking about nothing. Do we turn right or
left? Tennis courts or McDonald's? We headed toward
Main Street, where his father was standing in the
yard. Motioning for us to pull in, John steered the
Pinto into the driveway and rolled down his window.

"Wonder what he wants," he mumbled, totally bored
and to nobody in particular. Inconvenienced, we waited
while his dad walked over, putting down his hedges and
pushing the lawn mower to the side to make himself a
path.

It was me he looked at. Not John.

"Your mother's been trying to find you. You need to
get home."

No explanation. No more hint of things to follow.
Just get home.

John tried to make some form of a joke, but he..
had a strange feeling as well.

And he dropped me off.

I walked into the kitchen to a note, stuck on the
refrigerator door, held up by a magnet with a moose on
it. I would've laughed at the time, how smart my
mother was to leave notes in a spot where I was sure
to find them.

Fred,
Come to the hospital immediately. There's been an
emergency.
Mom

Now you're probably thinking: enough already, we
just dealt with that. Can't we change the tempo?

Exactly, my sentiments exactly.

I drove to the hospital rather quickly, breaking
four or five traffic laws, passing in the turning
lane, rolling through stop signs, threatening to stick
a Honda up anyone's butt that got in my way. Got to
the hospital before a different song even came on the
radio. "Some Guys Have All the Luck," by Rod Stewart
still wasn't finished by the time I pulled in.

Wonder why I even kept the radio on, but that has
nothing to do with anything.

I parked. Sprinted inside. Found mom in the waiting
room. Being consoled. By nurses, doctors, friends.

I'll never, ever forget the look on those people's
faces when they saw me. Never. Ever. And are there
words to describe it? Helplessness. Hopelessness.
Frustration. Pain. Anger. Depression. Fear.

They looked at me, then at each other. Mother still
hadn't looked up. Her head was buried between her
legs. Crying was not the term that fits here, either.
Wailing, high-pitched, mixed with screams, mixed with
throat sounds I can't describe would perhaps touch on
it. Her guts, Phil my man, had gathered at her toes,
lifted up from her body and were basically lying on
the floor.

Dr. L. K. Lewis grabbed me by my left arm. Firmly.
He'd grabbed me before; when I'd spent the night with

his son and threw biscuits at his daughter.
    This was different.
    Nice understatement.
    My father had taken his lunch break at 2:00, had a
hamburger and some fries at Baldwin's Drugs at 2:15,
returned to the store at 2:45, shuffled through some
mail and turned on the TV above the counter between
2:45 and 3:00 … and collapsed dead by 3:10 p.m.
    Heart attack.
    A damned heart attack.
    Forty-six years old.
    In decent shape, vibrant, active and very alive. A
busy man, sometimes cold, but always fair. Scolding
but always with a purpose.
    Husband.
    Home owner.
    Proprietor.
    Father.
    Friend.
    Dead.
    Now you do remember your father, don't you Phil?
The man who put you on his shoulders as a child,
throws his dirty socks at you when you fall asleep on
the couch to wake you up, takes time from his busy
schedule to throw the baseball with you in the yard?
The man you busted your butt for, the man you wanted
to impress, to make the best catches and make the most
accurate of throws, not because of any promises or any
bullshit contracts or endorsements, but because he was
your dad and you wanted to make him proud. Remember
the man you looked at after you rounded first after
hitting a clean single in Little League? The man who
would smile ever so slightly and make your whole day?
The man that could make or ruin your day with a look
on his face, the wink of an eye or a gesture with his
hands; the man who raced you in the parking lot from
church to car, who did funny tricks with cards, made
comments while watching the news, enjoyed reading the
paper in silence.
    Are you listening to me?
    Are you?
    Remember the man who took you golfing on Sundays?

Even though Sunday was a day of rest and there were
sports on television and good movies to boot? Even
though he had a world of other stuff to do? And there
was a world going on out there, and maybe he could've
been dealing with it? But he didn't. He drug his tired
butt up after church and, after reading the paper, he
fished his golf clubs out of the closet, told you to
get ready and he took you to the golf course. And me,
I took time off from my busy schedule, you know,
riding around, talking about girls, drinking beer, and
I went with him. Hell yes I did, and I'll never forget
it if I live to be 1,000. Never.

Well, he teed that mother up on the first hole,
pulled out his one wood, reared back, swung… and he
missed the whole ball. The whole damned ball! And do
you know what he said? Do you? Well, I'll tell you. He
just looked over at me, cocked his hat over his eyes
and said, "damn son, this is a tough course!"

Straight face.

Not a smile in sight.

Me, I doubled over laughing and grabbed my gut; the
ultimate tickle, if you will. I rolled on the tee, off
the tee, got grass stains all over my pants and no, I
didn't care!, people in front of me and behind me
staring and who gave a shit? I couldn't stop laughing.
Well, when the dust cleared, he gave me a little wink,
he did, stood back over the ball, made his back swing
and knocked the piss out of the ball. He hit it 250
with a fade, ball following the fairway as if it had
eyes, laid it right on top of a mound, 100 yards from
the pin. He pulled out his wedge, chipped it up and
one putted for a birdie. As if he was bored with it.
And you know, looking back on it now, I know he did
all that on purpose; the swing and the miss thing,
like it was a lesson of some sort. Like maybe he was
telling me not to judge things too quickly, maybe not
to give up when things are going wrong, maybe not to
laugh at people, maybe … Hell, I don't know. But
nobody, nobody played the first hole at Green Hills
Country Club and birdied it that easily, that
effortlessly. Nobody! That was the hole where good
golf games were quickly hung out to dry; or die. The

could've's and would've's usually ended right then,
right there.

Not for my dad.

And mom, oh my God, my mom. Who every single day
fought with the memory of my sister. Who every single
day probably cried merely at the rattling of car keys,
the sound of a horn or an engine, the opening and
closing of car doors. Or hearing me talk of dates and
road trips and be forced to remember. And the strength
it must've taken her to let me go like that, time and
again, over and over, every single day. Every single
solitary day. Are you imagining this?

Can you?

Well I can't. And that's why moms are moms and
they're the greatest human beings that ever put on a
pair of shoes. Ever. The MVP if you will. The people
who just aren't allowed to die. Ever. Ever. If there
is a God, he'd always leave us with a mom, who cooks
for us and cleans after us and makes the best damned
ice tea in the world and you don't even drink the
stuff and who washes your clothes every day and leaves
you notes and congratulates you when you do well and
corrects you when you do wrong and … who knows? I
could probably go to hell for saying this, but I
think God created the heavens, the earth and my
mother, and quite frankly, I don't know what order he
did it all in. Haven't a clue.

And just how do you think she felt at this point,
Phil? Or Fred for that matter? Or do we have more
important things to worry about? Baseball? Leigh?
Combing our hair? Resumes? Careers? Or how to tape
"Columbo" while watching Monday Night Football?

Are you kidding me?

Do you realize what happens at this point? Do you
realize what we learn? And it's not even a learning,
Phil, it's a knowing. A knowing.

Everything comes full circle. What goes around
comes around. You reap what you sew. Period. So
simple. Only made complicated by people who want to
make themselves sound smart and important.

To translate, my mother needed guidance, care,
love, the works. She did it for me, didn't she? Still

does. The roles changed. The worm turned. Up became
down, left became right, whatever. I was helped, now I
will help.

And that's what happened. And that's how I learned
it. And that's what I brought with me when I arrived
at the Jenkins College campus. That's what I don't
like to talk about. Except to you. Now. And that's why
you didn't understand when I wanted to beat the hell
out of Bruce when he made fun of me for looking in the
bleachers at my mom every time I got a hit. And you
didn't understand, but you did. I saw the look in your
eyes when you stepped between us. You knew not to ask.

It wasn't time.

Not it is.

Can you feel my pain and love when I look over? The
beauty of my mom, mixed with the depression of not
seeing two others sitting next to her? They were all
three there during Tee League and Little League, only
two in high school and now there is one.

One.

P.S.   I'll go now. Enough already. My hand is cramping
like shit. I'm hungry. I need to study. I'm leaving it
with you. I'm putting this journal back in your drawer
and burying it again. You'll find it.

But I don't want you to talk to me about it.

Not now.

Your last final is this Thursday afternoon -
history from 2 to 5 p.m. Take it. Do well on it.
Survive it.

Me, I'm not finished until 8:00 that night.

Perhaps when it's over, we can meet out in center
field and have a little conversation of our own. You
can beat me up if you want, get me in the full nelson
or the step-over-toe-hold, or maybe we'll just talk.

Maybe we'll talk about the upcoming spring
semester. Our last semester. Maybe we'll discuss life.
Maybe we'll talk about how horny we are and about how
many women we want to molest.

Or maybe you'll want to talk about Leigh.

Or heck with it, maybe we'll just sit there and
chew on some grass.

Doesn't matter.
But understand me, before I go.
Next semester is our last.
Do you understand that?
Now, before you graduate and say something ignorant
like, "damn, didn't we have it made while we were in
college?"
Yes, Phil, we do.
And we're going to make the best of it.
I got to go. I won't see you much this week. I'll
be studying at various spots and with different
people, you included when I get to the history part of
things.
Hang in there.
Keep smiling.
Enjoy your life.
Help somebody enjoy theirs.
Laugh whenever possible and drink a lot of water.
Don't take all this for granted.
You, like me, are one lucky sonofabitch, despite
anything and everything we've been through.
I love you as much as I can love a guy without
being queer, you sick, perverted bastard.
Peace, love and I'll see you in center field.

                                                    Fred

P.S.S. That was absolutely the longest letter I've
ever written in my life. Please don't make me do that
again.

A Late Night on a Baseball Field

When Fred drove up, Phil was already there. He could see his silhouette across the way, partially lit up by the moon; a waxing moon if it mattered. It was cool out, around 50 degrees and dropping, as fall was finally beaten up and had started giving way to winter. Days were shorter. Jackets were coming out of the closets. People were getting ready to hole themselves up for the winter. Moods were changing.

Fred unlocked his trunk, rummaged through the uncontrolled clutter; books, car parts, antifreeze, an unattached spare tire, more paper, and finally dug it out.

It was a duffel bag. And old, blue with white trim and ugly duffel bag. With a strap that had been chewed by at least one dog, probably two. Didn't matter though, the bag had sentimental value and it stayed, while dogs and anything else that took its toll on it had passed from Fred's mind. Dead filed, if you would.

Closing his hood, he walked behind the fences and came in through the home dugout. Fishing out a key he wasn't supposed to have, he opened the fuse box, fumbled through the switches with both his hand and his brain and he pulled the appropriate levers.

Slowly.

Each one with a purpose.

He looked back as he did it, at each individual pole, as the lights flickered, on and off, then slowly gained strength and readied themselves to shine. A gradual pace it was, but one you could bet the farm on.

Pulling the last one, he closed the box gently,
turned the key, then stood, almost at attention, while
the lights did their chore. The deepest part of the
outfield was affected first, with the warning track
now evident; still hazy but taking shape.

Fred took in the scene reverently as he walked
around the fences and headed to home plate; a coach
going over pre-game with the umpires and visiting
coaches.

He stopped at home plate. Looked outward again. Saw
the lights work their magic, cutting through the
darkness, now fully illuminating the scoreboard and
even the parking lot beyond. He wiped his hand through
his glasses for a better view. Slowly, he walked from
home plate outward, over the pitcher's mound, over
second base, and towards the shape he knew he'd find
before he'd driven up.

Perhaps it was another of those 'knowings' he
referred to earlier. It didn't occur to him that Phil
would or could be anywhere else at this time.

And he wasn't.

He was sitting in center field, arms draped around
his knees, and he was pulling them towards his chest.
Chewing on a blade of grass, he was gazing off into
space and now at Fred, who was at second base now and
still walking.

It was Phil who laughed at this point, as Fred's
direct walk resembled that of a coach who had walked
out to pull his pitcher, but decided somewhere along
the way to cruise on out and shoot the breeze with his
center fielder.

He even walked like a coach, Phil thought; that
slow amble, that non-fluid motion of pulling the legs
in front, one at a time in more of a sideways motion
instead of straight on, as if a corn cob was painfully
inserted into the backside of his anatomy.

Neither spoke until Fred got five feet in front of
him and stopped. Phil just looked up; Fred down. Fred
unsaddled his bag from his shoulder, tossed it at
Phil's feet. Phil looked at it, seemed confused by the
presentation, then finally spoke.

"Perhaps we could get in a tad of trouble for

turning the lights on this late at night?"

Fred shook his head, looked up at the sky. "Yeah, I suppose. Especially since I'm not supposed to have the key."

A quick look of concern entered Phil's face, then quickly disappeared, perhaps overtaken by priorities or no more time to care. Fred plopped himself at Phil's left, grabbed the bag, unzipped it slowly; not for effect, but because the zipper was worn and his mother had had to sew the thing together about ten times already.

"Do you think it's time for a new bag, honey?" she'd always asked. "No, not yet," he always answered and he wondered why she kept asking.

Fishing inside and tossing aside a thing or two, Fred pulled out a baseball. Then a glove. Then another.

He tossed one of the gloves onto Phil's lap.

Looking down at it, Phil picked it up and tossed it aside; an 'are you kidding?' look on his face.

Fred pointed to the glove, then at Phil. "That was my father's glove."

Phil's mouth popped open, then closed, while his hand quickly retrieved the glove in awe and respect. He put it on, rubbed the leather, opened it and eyed the insides; looked over at Fred to apologize.

Fred cut him short by merely the lifting of his finger, while putting on a glove of his own.

They both sat at this point, saying nothing; two college seniors who just happened to be sitting in the middle of center field in the middle of the night with gloves on their hands. The casual observer would take a second look at the scene, wondering just where the hell the other team went, what was the score, or what in the world was going on out there?

It was Phil who again broke the silence, but not before minutes had passed and his eyes had taken in the whole scene before him; the beauty of the manicured field, the smell of the grass, the gnats flying and competing for space in front of the lights, the bases, the mound, the dugout, the fences, the dirt, the backstop, the foul poles, bleachers,

refreshment stand, woods behind home plate, the grass.
The whole picture.
 "Just what kind of person gets thrown out of Six
Flags for beating up H.R. Puffnstuff anyways?" he
said. He didn't even look at Fred when asking it, but
Fred's silence drew a look, front and center.
 Fred chuckled, then laughed, remembering the
moment, but a moment he'd never brought up to anyone
outside his high school circle.
 "He deserved it. He was giving candy to all the
little girls and he didn't give me or any of my
friends jack shit!" He laughed some more.
 Phil gave in and joined him. Tried to picture the
scene in his mind. Failed at first, then succeeded.
Laughed pretty hard; then very hard. He rolled over on
his side and kept going, creating another funny scene;
two college men or boys or who knew, flat on their
backs in the outfield, gloves on, no home or visiting
team, no coaches, managers, umpires or fans, just on
their backs and laughing. In the middle of the night.
No reason known without further investigation.
 They righted themselves after a few minutes, while
the laughter died down and another silence overtook
them; an almost uncomfortable silence. It was Fred who
ended it, by brushing the grass off his butt and
standing, motioning to Phil with his hand, pointing at
the glove.
 "Let's go."
 Phil looked at his friend, grabbed the glove and
the ball, walked twenty or so yards away and faced his
friend. Grabbing the ball from within, he twirled it
around in his hand, found the seam and arched it into
the Georgia sky. A split-finger slow ball it was, if
there was any such thing, and the muscles in his
shoulder rebelled by the sudden order to perform.
 The ball still made a popping sound into Fred's
mitt. Fred smiled, reached in his glove, found the
ball and threw it back; his shoulders making some
small noises of their own.
 The arc of the ball flattened as the muscles got
loose, each ball delivered with more velocity, gloves
popping louder, the follow throughs more complete,

wrists getting further into the act with each toss.

Backing up, the two added to the simple game, not by plan but out of instinct; throwing grounders instead of fast balls, knuckles instead of curves, fly balls instead of grounders.

Now thirty yards apart, warmed up and loving life, Fred got into a full crouch, a center fielder looking in to the plate. Phil wound up and fired, made the crack of the bat noise with his mouth as he threw it high and far over his friend' head.

Racing backwards, cap flying off, tennis shoes knifing through the green grass, Fred outran the gnats, the wind and the would-be-double, making a basket catch over his shoulder with the glove at his gut and a smile on his face.

Willie Mays had made a similar catch in a World Series game back in the '50's, long before either of the two had been conceived. Phil had heard of Willie Mays and had read some about him; Fred had listened to his dad speak of him and had seen a highlight reel or two of what was then known as "the catch."

He smiled broadly when he caught it; turned and looked at Phil, who was now sporting a big smile of his own.

Phil's smile quickly faded. Popping his glove, he crouched down, waiting for the crack of another bat. Fred let it fly. A looping liner, an announcer would say, to Phil's left and in some, dropping quickly, not enough gravity to keep it.

Getting a good jump, Phil moved forward and to his right, backhanded his glove and dove forward, trying to intercept the ball before landing on the green palace.

It bounced off the back of his glove and bounced behind him; a good play turned into a boot. A play that would've been a good one if he'd made, but one where a coach would chastise him if he missed.

But not now.

Not tonight.

Laughing at his friend, Phil dusted himself off, retrieved the ball just short of the warning track, and threw the ball as high and as far as he could.

"A long drive, way back, Fred's going back, back,
back, deep … he MAKES THE CATCH! He made the catch!
Holy Cow! Fred just came of nowhere, his back to the
wall, and speared it just shy of the warning track.
What a play! Saved one, maybe two runs. That Fred, he
sure can make some extra base hits die out there."

Fred laughed again, threw a hot grounder at Phil's
feet. Phil got in front, fundamentally sound as he
was, took a bad hop off his chest, but kept the ball
in front of him. Yes, that's the way to do it if
you're watching at home, folks, keep the ball in front
of you. Block it with your body, keep it from going
through your legs. Use your chest as a backstop.

The two advanced naturally in their passion. More
drives, liners, grounders. A good speed workout, even,
if you looked at it from a runner's perspective.
Eventually, it emerged into a drill.

Fred faced Phil. Ten yards apart. Fred fired the
ball directly over Phil's head. Phil tore back, made
the catch over his shoulder, then fired back over
Fred's head, who was still standing in his original
position. Fred made the catch, fired over Phil's head.
Ditto.

When the two got far enough apart, Fred threw
short, bringing Phil in. Phil did the same. Back.
Forward. Back. Forward. When and if monotony thought
about drifting in, they continued the game, but making
the other move left, then right as well as forward and
backward; a figure eight, almost, in an interesting
drunk sort of way.

Very few words were spoken. Fred respected Phil's
single- mindedness, his desire to do things right and
his ability to shut out everything else in the world
other than what was in front of him or what his mind
was on. A strong point or a weak point, depending on
the situation. The dualism was and would always be
there.

Phil admired Fred's passion for life, his refusal
to obey any rules he didn't think made any sense, his
fly-by-the-seat-of-his-pants, what the hell, let's do
it, philosophy.

Eventually the ball rolled to the pitcher's mound.

Phil retrieved it. Fred held up a finger, a wait-a-
minute gesture, then trotted behind home plate.
Flipping his cap backwards, he got in his crouch and
flashed a sign.
    One finger down.
    Phil shook him off.
    Two fingers down.
    Another head shake.
    Middle finger down, flanked by two bent fingers,
commonly known as "the bird."
    Phil nodded 'yes.' Went into the stretch, checked
the runners, kicked and fired.
    "Way high, ball one!"
    But who cared?
    Thirty minutes passed, then forty five. Eventually,
Fred eyed a security truck driving in their direction
and the two had to cut short their game; had to sneak
behind the visitor's dugout, sneak into the woods and
sit on the hill overlooking the complex. The two
situated themselves behind thick foliage, allowing
themselves full view of the three security people as
they shined their lights around, talked, wandered back
and forth, looked towards the dorms, the woods, even
the sky.
    Eventually, the security people decided not to
pursue the matter with passion. "Probably just a bunch
of drunks playing another prank," the skinniest of the
three said. The fattest of them all reached into his
pocket, pulled out his official key, opened the box
and turned the lights out.
    Phil and Fred both looked up, reverently once more,
as each individual light pole became muted, flickered,
faded then died. Leaving the gnats in confusion.
Leaving the field once again dark.
    The two waiting until the crack-pot security staff
drove off, then emerged from the woods, headed down
the hill and walked the full length of the field.
    Still, neither spoke. Phil almost did. He was
thinking how he wished life could be like this
forever; so care free, so simple, so free of stress
and worry. Just one big opportunity to run and jump
and play.

Fred was on a similar track, but deeper. He'd brushed a tear from his eye when retrieving the glove from Phil, had placed it gingerly back inside the bag. He'd spent the walk just wishing. Period.

For the people he'd lost.

For another opportunity to make them proud.

To glance over at them after he'd singled to left.

To see the expression on his face.

To see his sister give him the 'thumb's up' sign.

To hear her bitch when he didn't let her watch "Doogie Howser."

To see him show him how to make the play, executing it right in the middle of the living room floor in front of the TV he'd been trying to watch; to hear him tell him why he needed to be home earlier and not to pull his sister's hair and how the hell could you make a "B" in history when it was nothing more than reading and memory work, and why did she have to take so long in the bathroom and why was it always his fault?

He just wanted to see and hear.

Period.

He'd learned, though. He really had.

They both had.

Forever was now and it always would be.

They drove off. Entered Alumni Hall, Room 34. Retired to their respective stations. Slept.

Tomorrow was definitely another day.

BOOK THREE:

A Prelude to a Spring; Another Late Night Conversation; A Practice, an Encounter and a Hangover; Lessons; Baseball, Call Her, Don't Call Her; A Late Night With a Picture; More Baseball; An Early Morning With Leigh; A Late Night Conversation With Fred and Leigh; Staying Focused, Friendly Conversations; A Dream; A Day at the Ball Yard; Graduation; Closing Thoughts Because I'm Almost Finished

"I won't hold back anything - and I'll walk away a fool or a king."
  Billy Joel
  "It's a Matter of Trust"

I: A Prelude to a Spring

The world may have been aware of Fred and Phil's past problems, might have even lifted an ear to listen more closely; but it didn't care, or it didn't appear to. In fact, it kept right on going. Santa Claus and his reindeer lifted off, landed, delivered presents and returned home safely. The NFL wound down to only two teams and geared for another Super Bowl. New Year's Eve parties happened, drunks lived and died on the roads, fires burned to keep people warm, people married and divorced, some gave birth; others watched loved ones die.

Even the sun didn't get preoccupied over the residents of Alumni Hall, or their anticipation or anxiety regarding their final semester. It merely rose and fell as if guided, never thinking once about calling role. Jenkins College didn't seem to change it's itinerary, either; it was to begin its spring semester on January 18th.

Not before.

Not after.

Security Chief Bill Kitchens lifted the gates himself at six on that morning, though students wouldn't be driving in until probably 10:00 and at random hours throughout the day. They'd drive in all fired up, horns honking, clothes stacked so high in the front and back seat you wondered how the hell they fit themselves in there, not to mention being able to look out their back window to see anything.

Kids. They'd live forever, or they thought they would. And man, would things ever get noisy this

evening; the first night back after a month apart.
There would be minor damage reports to fill out come
Monday morning. A window would break somewhere.
Fireworks would be shot, though they were strictly
forbidden in the Jenkins College Handbook. Beer cans
would be thrown everywhere. Guys and girls would pair
off and molest each other, and in the strangest parts
of campus. He'd found a couple making it on top of a
grave once; several times on trunks of cars and once
right out on the baseball field, right out there in
front of God and everybody. And that wasn't to mention
the grad assistant who got fired for making it at half
court.

Man, people could be crazy sometimes. And as for
him, he'd have to come along and make sense out of the
whole mess; file it down on reports and memos,
carefully letting the Dean of Students and Mr.
President himself know that he had it all under
control. He knew about it all and had it all typed up
to prove it.

Wouldn't matter that much today, though. He'd be
here until 4:00 p.m., punch the clock, then drive it
on home.

He'd been here for ten years; was known and feared
by the student body, though most of them didn't know
him very well. He had a permanent scowl on his face,
dark eyes, and a scar that ran from his eye, down his
cheek and ended at his mouth. A war scar, the student
body said.

If they wanted to think that way, then so be it.
Actually, it was from running through a glass door
while drunk at a party two years after his own college
graduation.

Regardless, he kept his distance from most of the
students, and if they wanted to treat him with fear
and reverence, he had no problem with that at all. He
took no crap off the drunks, offered no favors for the
needy and generally got involved as little as possible
in student's affairs.

And, truth be known, he loved it when the students
were around. It was so quiet and boring while they
were away. There was nobody to chase down after they

tried to steal the gate off the guardhouse. Nobody to
try to haul in for streaking through the campus.
Nobody to catch for speeding, or rolling yards, or
tossing beer cans, or tossing crabapples at his truck.
Nobody to stop at the guardhouse and question. Nobody.
Just nobody.

They were coming in today, though, slowly but
surely. He pushed the button that lifted up the gate,
put his feet up on his desk, opened his copy of
"Georgia Sportsman" magazine and smiled.

He was ready not to be lonely anymore.

With mom asleep in the next room and with eight
hours to spare to make only an hour-and-a-half drive,
Fred dug out the video tape from the bottom shelf of
their entertainment center. Wiping the dust from the
cartridge, carefully placing the jacket in its place
and ejecting "Die Hard" from the video recorder, he
popped it in.

Already rewound (Be Kind, Rewind!), the picture
began with nine tiny kids taking a small ball diamond
in Ann Arbor, Michigan. Starting at a chain link fence
they called a dugout, the little midgets whooped and
hollered as they ran to their designated spots, pulled
their caps over their eyes, and started chanting as a
batter stepped nervously up to the plate.

Taking a practice swing or two, the hitter bounced
a pretty solid shot to second, and Fred had to gag
himself as the second baseman moved to the side,
allowing the ball to roll right past him. As it did,
the little infielder immediately turned and started
hauling ass after the ball, while most of the other
eight players did the same; some of them even tossing
their gloves away as they gave chase.

The base runner, reaching first, nervously stopped
and looked around. Seeing three quarters of the team
all chasing the ball down and no one anywhere near
second base, he proceeded to second, stopped, looked
around, then cruised to third.

He crossed home just as the second baseman won the
battle with the left and center fielders and the third
baseman for the ball. The second baseman, proudly

displaying his prize by holding it up into the air,
ran off the field in his excitement, showing the ball
to his mother, father, sister and then over to his
coach, who was doubled over pretending to be spitting,
but actually laughing so hard his gut was rocking up
and down.

The coach turned his back for a second, composing
himself the final time, then crouched down to talk to
his little infielder. Holding him by his cap, the
coach pointed at the field, showed him his territory,
guided him with a suggestion or two.

Fred watched as the kid's head dropped for a
moment, probably wondering where he went wrong and how
could things change so fast just when he had emerged a
hero out in right field? But, as the coach kept
talking, junior's head raised a little, a smile
quickly returned to his face as the coach finished his
speech with encouragement and a gentle slap on the
butt.

The kid clapped his hand in his glove, straightened
his cap and, absorbing his new material, sprinted back
out to his position at second base.

Somebody, quick, clone that coach. And don't ever
take the spirit out of that child.

Fred, totally absorbed, watched more, laughed
quietly, almost cried a time or two, but never took
his eyes off that screen. The kid's switched sides,
argued among themselves, high-fived, got dirty,
misjudged fly balls, made mud pits in the outfield,
but always remained focused in their efforts.

Fred feared waking his mother when the left
fielder, name and address long forgotten, stood
straight and still as a statue as a fly ball came his
way. Glove in the air, other hand guiding and a
picture of fundamental perfection, the little kid
stood with his eyes on the ball the entire time. Fred
had to stick a quilt in his mouth as he watched the
ball land twenty or so feet over the kid's head. The
kid, totally confused, chased the ball and explained
to his angry teammates that he'd done everything the
coach told him to do. He swore; crossed his heart and
hoped to die.

The game ended. Both teams were called over to their respective dugouts, given encouragement, patted on the backs and were released into a bee-line to the refreshment stand dead ahead.

Everyone, clear the way. Quickly.

The scene flickered, went off, came back on, and Fred sat in full attention as a man, daughter a little second baseman walked from the field and stood at the intersection. Father, keeping his hands on both his kid's heads, held them there while cars passed; held them while sister took off junior's hat. Held them while junior cried, retrieved hat, smiled again, and father guided them with a gentle push at the back of their noggins when the coast was clear.

The camera shook somewhat as mom had the task of filming, walking, looking both ways and admiring her family, but it always remained on the subjects. Father, son and daughter opened doors to the van, argued over who got what seat, quickly solved the problem with no meeting or memos required, and closed the doors behind them.

The final scene: Father looking over at the camera in the passenger's seat, pointing playfully at the camera with his index finger, cranking the car and winking before the screen went dark. The movie ended and Fred could only sit and watch with tears in his eyes.

It was time to go.

He hugged his mom before she ever got out of bed, told her not to cry and not to worry. He'd be a good boy. He'd write. He'd study hard. He'd try to do all the right things. He'd even try to hit a homer for her, but he wasn't much of a power hitter.

She wiped a tear from her eye, then wondered why as it was only joined by more. He hugged her again and told her he had to go. He would write. And he would call.

And he would make her proud. Somehow, some way, he'd make her proud.

Phil, too, was ready. Christmas vacation had been great; relaxation, getting spoiled, remote controls, couches that you sank yourself into, family outings, the works.

He hadn't realized going home could be so refreshing. How did that saying go? The one about spending half your life trying to leave home and the other half trying to get back?

He wasn't at that point, but he'd re-learned and re-enjoyed the simple pleasures. Playing "Taboo" with sister, trying to beat mom at "Jeopardy," arguing with dad about politics.

His sister about killed over one afternoon, as she was finding her keys and heading to the mall. Out of habit, she asked halfheartedly if he wanted to go with her.

"Yeah, wait up."

Though she covered herself quickly, Phil noticed the widening of the eyebrows and the quick glance between mom and sis. "He does," the eyes said. "Is he sick?"

Nope. Not now, thank you very much. Feeling okay and just wanting to go to the mall.

As far as school, he hadn't spoken to Fred since the above game of catch on the Jenkins College field. Then again, there was no need to. Some friends had to stay in touch; had to do all the basics to constantly remind each other that they were friends. Fred and he had passed that stage. Long ago. They would always be in touch, without having to call or write. When they saw each other, they'd pick up where they left off.

No room or need for small talk. No idle chatter about vacations or Christmas or jobs. Just straight into the insults and back to work. Back to life.

As for Leigh, she had written him a card; and he her. His stomach still did the little dance when he found it in the mail box, he couldn't deny that. The red envelope with Santa Claus in the corner, the smell, the handwriting of hers, the familiar thoughts that would be there for a while all raced through for a while.

Not now, he thought. Just open it and read it.

So he did.

"Hi Phil. Hope you and your family are having a great Christmas. See you at school!"

Leigh

"Who is Leigh, your girlfriend?" sister had said. "Mom, Phil's got a girlfriend, Phil's got a girlfriend!" She had mussed his hair, ripped the card from him and ran in to display the evidence to mom.

Mom just rolled her eyes and told sister to leave big brother alone. Brother got sister in the half nelson and rolled her over for a pin. Sister screamed, but, like always, fought back.

Phil noticed mom walk over and watch out of the corner of her eye.

Pure moment?

Sure it was.

He hugged his mom tight as they walked out the door on that final day. His dad reached across, shook his hand and put another on his shoulder. Phil caught a flash of his own when his dad's hand touched there and he laughed to himself.

Simple gestures that mean so much. He laughed, because he wasn't much into explaining these things. Maybe he'd tell Fred in center field one night. Maybe not.

Anyway, he hugged mom, shook dad's hand, kissed sister on the cheek. Got in his car, buckled his seat belt, smiled, waved.

And drove away.

To college, to Fred, to baseball and to that pursuit of the sheepskin. To late night conversations, pizza runs, spontaneous beer parties, and more baseball. To school. For the last time.

It would all be there when he arrived.

Not before, not after.

He wasn't going to screw it up this time. If not for himself, for Fred and for all he'd shared with him. No, it'd still be tough at times, but what was it Andy van Slyke said? If it was easy, there'd be about six million other jerkoffs playing in every World Series and it would lose its meaning. Something like that.

Thanks Andy. Thanks Fred. And what the hell, thanks Leigh. See you in a couple hours.

And speaking of, Leigh was about nine hours south, packing her bags in West Palm, saying goodbye to mom, kissing dad on the cheek, stuffing bags into her Saturn, careful not to affect the CD player, careful to leave space for two.

But how?

How would she and Dennis fit all this crap into one car? A small, compact car, even. Four doors, her favorite car ever, but a college senior could acquire a lot of crap over a four year period. And damn it! Where was Dennis? It was time to go.

She stood beside her car, waiting on his brother to drop him off, just hanging out with the parents. They wanted to talk, they did, wanted to get in their last few words of advice before she went off, but sometimes the mind just drifted. Away.

Like, to the final semester ahead, if you would. Would it all work out with her and Dennis? Would they get along? Would he leave school again? Could they work it all out? And Phil? Why did that name keep hanging around her brain?

Wasn't he just a transition guy to get her through the whole thing?

But Dennis was back, she wasn't through the whole thing and now this other guy kept finding a way to top in at interesting times.

Phil.

Dennis.

That's what you get, she told herself, as she threw the final bag in while explaining her class schedule to her mom. It was funny, she thought, the way life was sometimes. You never really got away with anything. Not really, not if you sat right down and analyzed the big picture. You always got exactly what you deserved, and you never knew what form it would take or how it would get you.

But it would.

And how could she get mad at anyone but herself?

She played with one guy's emotions to get over another.

Now she had to deal with both.

There was one thing she decided though, before she ever cranked her car and headed north. She would deal with it somehow. Not by blaming the world and lashing out at everyone else, either. And not by being a burden to anyone else. She'd dug the hole, she'd fill it back up. She'd open the worms, she'd stomp the bastards. Or lead them to safe places. Or whatever. She'd take responsibility for her actions. Blame was for losers.

She wouldn't go there. Couldn't. Because what mattered was doing the right thing at the right time. Period. She always heard the voice of her girl's high school basketball coach during times like these.

Leigh had been a point guard. Unfortunately, she thought at the time, so had her coach. Every analogy she had been taught was a reference to her position on the court. When she'd delayed in applying for a college, guess what her coach said?

"My God, Leigh! You're dribbling out the clock at half court, stalling, while the defense is sitting back in a tight zone laughing at you because YOU'RE the one that's losing."

"But what am I supposed to do?" She'd thrown up her hands and said in frustration.

"What does a good point guard have to do? One word. One word only." Coach Ferguson had stared at her after asking this, and Leigh knew damned well she'd better get it right.

"Create?"

"Exactly! You'd better know that after four years, dear." And with that, she'd patted Leigh on the shoulder and she'd walked off.

And Leigh, she had created. Jenkins was a good school, she had good friends, she had fun, and though her athletic career had ended with her high school team's sub-region loss in the semifinals her senior season, the lessons were long remembered.

So remembered in fact, that during Leigh's sophomore year at Jenkins, she'd written a letter back

to Coach Ferguson during the spring semester. Life was
strange, she knew, for all the classes she'd gone in
and out of, all the people she'd been in contact with,
she'd rarely had the desire to pick up a pen and write
anybody, about much of anything.

But this time was different.

She'd worked hard the summer after her freshman
year to set up her roommate with one of her friends.
Worked hard, almost too hard. They were perfect
together. Perfect. But they never knew it. It seemed
it would never happen. They were always dating someone
else. Or wanting to be. Or out of town. Or not
interested. Or whatever.

But in the spring, it happened. The world's perfect
couple, just as she knew, had gotten together. And
Leigh, well she took a lot of the credit. And when she
wrote to Coach Ferguson, she told her so. And Leigh
had even made a copy of her own letter before mailing
it if she ever started to forget the lessons.

Coach Ferguson:

I'm sitting in the dressing room of a church, where
Sylvia Baxter just married Paul Sanders. You don't
know either of them, but that's not the point.

The point is, I used to get frustrated all the
time. I knew this would work between them long before
they ever saw it. Why wouldn't they listen? Did they
not believe me? Couldn't they see something that was
right in front of their very eyes?

But do you know what I learned? If things are
forced, they don't work. You have to understand the
flow of the game and get into it, and you have to
allow other people the freedom to do the same. Things
work that way. Besides, they'll both make up for the
lost time I was always trying to force upon them.

But this is why I'm writing you this letter, Coach
Ferguson, not to bore you with a story of two people
that got married. Happens all the time.

My reason is this: I myself changed from a point
guard who was trying to force the action that wasn't
there, to being a point guard who just dribbled and

looked.. waiting for the right people to make the
right cuts at the right time. When they did,
BAAAAAMMMM, I delivered the ball, right on the money,
right then, right there. And when I stood at the altar
at their wedding and both of them looked at me and
winked, I cried.
    In high school, I'd made some assists that were
scribbled in some score book, filed away and
forgotten. Right here, I'd made one (hopefully!) that
will last a lifetime.
    Now I've cried before, Coach Ferguson. You've seen
me. But it had never been quite like this. It was a
combination of lessons learned and put into action and
seeing the results, all in a split second. Does that
make sense? Probably not. But, it just hit me. Your
lessons, your yelling, instructing, confronting,
teaching. It drilled me right square in the face as I
stood there, all dressed up and crying my eyes out.
    Thank you for teaching me about timing.. And about
creating. And about delivery. I thought and still
think that image is a bunch of overrated crap that's
only good for show and good commercials, but flow,
timing, delivery - that's a different story, now isn't
it?
    Thanks for listening. Better yet, thanks for
teaching.

Leigh Basil (Magic Johnson)
    P.S. I'm still making some bad decisions and
throwing some bad passes, but I'm learning.

    The letter was still in her drawer at school,
underneath her notebooks, photo albums, letters from
friends, ticket stubs to movies, pictures of friends
at parties and the like. It would all make a great
collection one day.
    But the letter had to be a part of it. It had to.
    It just had a way of reminding her that we're all
here for something, we don't do it all for nothing,
and people come into our lives with lessons, for
better or for worse.
    Her thoughts were broken by the honking of a horn,

Dennis getting out of his brother's car, tossing his
bags into her trunk, hugging her parents, and getting
in on the passenger side.

Ready or not, here we come.

II: Another Late-Night Conversation

"If a girl says you're `goofy-cute', is that a compliment, an insult, or both?" It was Phil, somewhere between two and three in the morning, after opening night at the Pub.

Fred rolled over and sat up, getting a feeling this one was going to take a while. He propped his pillows up, threw down the covers, and faced his roommate. "Definitely a compliment," he answered. "In fact, it's the latest up-and-coming category."

"Really?"

"Yeah, and ain't it great? It means there's hope for us." He paused, propped his hands together and placed them behind his head. "Who said you were goofy-cute?"

"Actually, Deah Thompson said it about you. You remember, the girl wearing the beige sweater you spilled a drink on at the bar? The one you gave a "BB" rating to? You should probably call her and ask her out."

"Can't call her just yet."

"Why not?"

"I just met her."

"So?"

"So, you never call a girl you just met and ask her out for a date the next day. It shows you're too eager."

"So you play games and wait a while instead?"

"Right."

"What about all that stuff you wrote in your

letter? About living life and doing good things and
the time was now and pure moments and throwing butter
on the ceilings and all that shit?"

"Shit?"

"Sorry, just kidding, but you're really not going
to wait, are you?"

"Of course I'm going to wait."

"And disregard everything you've said?"

"Phil, you have to understand something," he began,
leaning over to an elbow, facing his partner in crime.
"Just because I know this stuff and you know this
stuff, doesn't mean everyone else does. You know what
I'm saying?"

"No."

"Well, maybe Deah Thompson hasn't gone through what
I have. Maybe she lives with Mr. God, Mrs. God and has
little sisters and brothers all named God, Juniors.
Maybe she never had the privilege of getting caught by
a headmaster for hiding in her locker, or getting her
face pounded in at first recess, or getting caught for
spying on naked people in locker rooms. Maybe she's
different."

"Or maybe, she's had it a lot worse. What's your
point?"

"My point is, the law of averages says that she
probably thinks me calling her tomorrow would be too
eager and would constitute a total breach in the
Handbook of College Studs you so often refer to. It
would tell her I like her and she would automatically
be cautious around me and then the whole thing would
be fu…, I mean screwed. No pun intended.

"So you call her Monday instead?"

"Never Monday. Too early. Never Wednesday or
Thursday, either. Too late. Always call a girl on
Tuesday to ask them for a date."

"I'll write that on my calendar tomorrow," Phil
obliged. "Tuesday is the BEST day…"

"No, no," Fred interrupted, "Tuesday is actually
the WORST day, but it's the best day to ask a woman
out."

"Why is Tuesday the worst day? I thought Monday
was."

"Nope, the Monday thing is a myth."

"A myth?"

"Absolutely."

"Why?"

"Because," Fred began, and Phil had to laugh seeing his friend's silhouette across the room. He resembled a coach or a professor when he got worked up, the only thing missing was chalk, a chalkboard and a diagram to help illustrate his point. He was getting to the arm moving stage, not now, but close. "Because when you get to school or work on Monday, you're not even thinking about the upcoming weekend because it's too far away. Plus, you can still tell all the funny stories about the weekend before while they're fresh on your mind. So, you sit around swapping stories and actually laughing a little about the whole thing and it's really not half as bad as everyone says it is."

"And Tuesday?" Phil himself propped up to await more.

"Well, on Tuesday, you can't tell anymore 'last weekend' stories, because they're stale. So, you sit around and think about the upcoming weekend, but it's too far away. Basically, there's nothing better to do than get into your work."

"Bummer."

"Exactly."

A moment of silence prevailed. Fred sat wondering if Phil understood any of this and actually laughed, picturing the wheels spinning in Phil's head as the information was devoured, filtered, run through the assembly line and reshuffled. Phil, on the other side, after the above filtering, sat wondering where Fred came up with all this stuff. Did he read it? See it on TV? Make it up? What class did he miss when they were giving all this info out? Would they be tested on it someday? Would …

"So answer me a question, Phil my man," Fred interrupted his thoughts, "what did you think of Dennis?" Fred felt a little guilty for asking, knowing there was already too much crammed into that blond head on the other side of the room.

"He seems like a nice guy."

"Huh?"

"Seriously, he does. I mean, I didn't walk over and shake his hand or anything, but from what I saw, he seems like a likable fellow."

"Nice of you to say that."

"You think so?"

"Sure. I mean, I don't know if it'll help you or your relationship, but I hear you get style points for shit like that. Even Leigh herself would probably recommend you to other women. "Wow, that Phil, he's a helluva guy."

Phil wasn't even going to ask about style points, not now. "It always works that way, you know? It's.. frustrating."

"I know what you mean. And I actually agree with you. The boyfriend is always actually a nice guy. I mean, it only happens the other way in movies. In movies, the boyfriend is good looking, but he's always conceited and he's always a jerk. It's so easy to hate him and roll his yard and urinate on his porch and punch him in the head. The crowd even cheers while you're doing it. Real life? Different story. If you had walked over tonight and punched Dennis in the head, people would have stood around and gone, "what the hell did he do that for?" Then, they'd investigate and, who knows, you could wind up being the bad guy and they could end up pissing on our window. Ain't that some shit?"

It was, though Phil hadn't quite taken it to that extreme. He was kinda glad of that, to tell you the truth.

"You handled it well, I thought," Fred added, glancing over.

"I didn't do anything."

"That's my point," Fred interrupted. "You were strong. Didn't ask her how was Christmas or what'd she do over the holidays or wow, nice sweater, or what's that after shave you're wearing or nothing. Nothing. Good for you. If you flirted with Tricia a little more, who knows, she might have actually gotten a little jealous."

"I couldn't. I just can't do that while I'm…"

"It's okay, don't worry about it. I'm just saying if you would have, she would've been jealous or something and put a note in your mail box or called you or burped in your ear or wrestled with you or something romantic like that."

"But she didn't."

"And she won't. Unless you get over her."

"If I'm over her, I won't give a shit."

Exactly, and that's why she'll do it."

"That sucks."

"Search me, I swear I never made up these rules. No one at all consulted me at anytime whatsoever. But, when I become tsar..."

"Okay, okay, enough already. Forget it. Move on. It's going to be a great semester. The best year of our lives. This is..."

"Nope, this won't be the best year of our lives."

"Huh?"

"It can't be. Last year was."

"What?"

"Think about it," Fred began again. "The junior year is great because; first of all, you're settled in at school, people know you and you've found your rhythm. Plus, there's no pressure on you to start looking for a job and no pressure to have the best year of your life since you're only a junior."

"But we were seniors last year, too, remember?"

"Yeah, but we knew we weren't about to graduate. Anyway, in your senior year, besides the fact that you SIMPLY must do it right, you've also got to get your resume ready, even knowing how to fill out the OBJECTIVE part and start to carry it out. You know what I mean - dress sharp, go for interviews, have a great social life, have fun at every single party, get a hit at every single at bat. You have to. It's your senior year."

"Why didn't you tell me this last year?"

"Because then you'd have put too much pressure on it and you'd have screwed that one up, too. It's always a pressure thing."

Frustrated, Phil let out a deep breath and didn't speak for a while. This education process was a little

tough sometimes. Why didn't he know this stuff?
"Forget it, I don't want to talk about it anymore. All
I know is, I had fun on this Thursday night and we've
got a great weekend staring us right in the eye," Phil
added.

"Okay, I'll quit bothering you, but there's one
other thing I'll leave you with," Fred said as he lay
back down.

Phil hesitated. Should he or shouldn't he? Okay.
"What?"

"It's a good thing you had fun tonight, this being
Thursday and all, because Thursday is the best day of
the week." Fred waited for a response but none came.
"Okay, I'll tell you why. Do you realize that if you
went out on Thursday and Friday nights and did the
exact same thing, you would ALWAYS have more fun on a
Thursday. Always."

"Why?"

"Simple," he said and damned glad he asked.
"Because if you go out to some dive or party on a
weekend night, you're thinking, 'we're here? On a
weekend?' There's too much pressure on the weekend. It
always comes back to that. But tonight, we were out at
a perfectly non-decent hell-hole, were we not? But, we
had a few beers, had some laughs, no expectations,
laughed a lot, flirted a little and had a perfectly
great time. And why not? Weekend, as you say, is
looking us right square in the eye!"

"So with your logic, Thursday and being a junior in
college is…"

"The exact same thing."

"Exactly."

"So I guess I made a huge mistake last semester
when I went to ask Higgins to change my history grade
on a Friday?"

"No, you did the right thing."

"What? I thought you said…"

"I know what I said. But you see, not many people
know about this formula of mine. Basically, the
professors, like everyone else, are sitting in their
offices on Fridays thinking, 'hey, this is the best
day of the week. I'm happy!' See? They don't know.

Always ask for raises, grade changes or whatever on
Fridays and just keep the Thursday thing between us.
It's another sacred bond, if you will."
    Silence.
    "Fred?"
    "What?"
    "I think I'm glad we had this conversation."
    "But you're not sure?"
    "Exactly."
    "Good night."
    "Good night."

III: **A Practice, an Encounter and a Hangover**

"Phil! Wake up!" It was Fred, it was early in the morning and it was great to be back in school again. Actually, it took a while before all those thoughts popped in, as the mattress was spinning its web over my body and the thoughts of giving in was a helluva lot better than leaning up and answering Fred.

I did, though, and... wow, he'd changed his sheets. Water buffaloes. Yep, I think it was going to be water buffaloes this semester. And me without animals of my own.

"Get up, it's time for class!"

"Class?" I couldn't help inquiring. After all, since when did class have a thing to do with anything. Especially with us.

"Yes, class. Every semester we've been here we've always said we were going to do good in school this time. EVERY SINGLE ONE."

I put my head back down. According to my most recent grades, I'd made my 2.6, thank you very much, and though there were no dean's list mail outs with my name on it, there weren't any invitations or suggestions that I continue my education elsewhere. Not yet, anyway.

WHAAM!

Sorry, it's hard to describe these sounds in writing terms, but that's the best I can do in telling you what a pillow and two Michael Crichton novels feel when flung across the room by a lunatic college "student."

I popped my head up just in time, as he delivered

another blow; a mythology book I think, but who's book
was that? Not mine.

It struck the window with a whack or a wham or
whatever and I got up, using my pillow for a shield
against further objects.

"This morning we go to class. This afternoon we
have baseball practice. Tomorrow we begin our serious
training."

He was standing, white socks half-on, half-off from
his sleep, polka-dotted boxer shorts barely covering
what they were supposed to, glasses not yet found,
eyes not yet focused.

Not that he was blind, mind you, but his glasses
were so damned thick he could probably see the big
dipper through the roof on a cloudy day. But that's
beside the point.

His hands were on his hips, a great coaching stance
if anyone cares, and he was waiting, waiting for a
response. Any response.

Coach Fred, reporting for duty. Sir.

"Hold on, Fred, wait a minute. Let me wake up for
crying out loud."

These things take a while. Some people can get up
and be fully coherent. Me, not the case. Especially
after being spoiled back home over the break.

I always felt kinda like Columbo; without the ugly
dog and the raincoat, of course. "Let's see now, where
was I?"

Oh yeah, we had rented a movie last night, that's
what we'd done. The "Shawshank Redemption," I think.
Actually, I'm sure it was good, but I was out before
Andy DuFresne ever got to jail. Surely he was
innocent. Wasn't he?

Maybe, maybe not. Regardless, I was out cold,
dreaming something good, though rubbing my head with
my hands didn't help me recall what it was. Anyway, it
was damned sure better than some militant, warped,
Fred throwing books, covers and artillery at me. At
7:15 in the morning no less.

7:15! Do you hear what I'm saying?

"Fred?" I sat back down, shield still in hand,
preparing for battle. "My first class is not until

8:00. Do you actually expect me to like … shower
before class? I mean, I can get up at 7:50 and still
make it."

De-arming himself, Fred retreated to his respective
station, plopped himself right down on the water
buffalo's face, and felt around for his eyes.

"No messing around this time, Phil," he said.
"We're gonna work hard this semester."

"Why?"

I ducked after asking, as he wasn't one for being
contradicted when he was on a roll.

"Just enjoy your day, that's all," he said, rising
and looking for a clean towel in his laundry basket.
"We're starting our training tomorrow."

With that, he got up, slipped into his shower shoes
and headed down the hall.

Okay, training. Tomorrow.

Class at 8:00.

Baseball practice at 4:00.

It's great to be back.

We'll talk again after my nap.

Always remember - if books and flying pillows don't
wake you up in the morning, then hitting a fastball
off the hands in 40 degree weather damned sure will.

Coach Bell was throwing BP (batting practice) and
he can wing it in there pretty good for a 40-year-old
man, mind you. Anyway, he gave me a fastball, down and
in, and me, trying to impress the coaches with my
newly found hand speed (whatever), stepped back,
whipped my wrists around and caught it right up near
the handle of the bat.

And me without my batting gloves.

I won't go into details about how loud I yelled. Or
maybe Fred covered it in his letter when he referred
to the 'getting hit by a swing' episode or maybe it
was the 'stubbing your toe' part. Well, I screamed,
hollered, yelled in a couple of languages and
everything seemed to be clearing up and that heart
beat was moving back out of my hands and back into the
normal place, when I made the mistake of saying
'shit'.

And just a little too loud.

Well, Coach Huff heard me, and he's not the kind of guy to put up with shit - I mean - stuff like that. We run a lap for every letter in the cuss word. Immediately and without question.

And it's a good thing I didn't yell 'motherfucker.'

Coach Huff has been here forever. Head baseball coach. Family man. Quiet. Tall, around 6-5, doesn't say much, but when he does … I guess it reminds me of that old story about Vince Lombardi, the ex-great football coach for the Green Bay Packers. They say that when Lombardi told you to sit down, you didn't bother looking for a chair.

Well, when Coach Huff tells you to sit down, you do look for one … and then you hide under it. I knew I'd screwed up when he stopped from where he was, left his perch on the first base line, excused himself from the first baseman who he was putting through stretching exercises, took off his cap, and walked over in my direction. He cleared his throat first, the way he always did when he was about to cut you down a notch or two.

Normally, I'd stayed clear of the tongue-lashings, generally did my job, worked hard, then went home. This, my second year out for baseball, was my first look, first hand even, at the coach, his molars, dental work and the like.

"What did you say, son?" I think was his first comment, but I was too busy making sure my knees were firm, not shaking, and my eyes were contacting with his. So hard to do at times like these.

"I'm sorry, sir," I managed.

That didn't pacify him. Somehow, I knew it wouldn't. He kept walking, stopped right in front of me. "Let me tell you something, son. We don't talk that way out here. We're a baseball team, not a bunch of trash-talking punks. When you show up out here on my field, you'll conduct yourself professionally or you'll conduct yourself somewhere else. We've got just over a week before we open up, and I'm not going to have to stop practice just to get onto you again. Do I make myself clear?"

*Hell yes. Loud and clear. Roger. Over and out.
Bingo. You're the boss. Where's my hole and can I
crawl in now?*

"Yes sir, it won't happen again."

With that, he put his cap back on, cleared his
throat again, and headed back to the first base side.
*And not a moment too soon, I think I was about to have
to change my underwear!* Me and my red face began
running laps, in silence I might add. Coach Huff was a
great guy, well respected, but don't mess with him.

And there it was, the beginning of baseball season.
Off and running, if you will. Lots of stretches, wind
sprints, distance running, situps and all those other
things you wish you could keep up on your own but
sometimes it's rather tough. Coach's philosophy,
besides laps for cuss words, was that we'd lose some
games, but we would not lose them for being
fundamentally unstable and we *darn* sure (see, I'm
learning!) wouldn't lose them for not being in shape.

And to get to the non-romantic part of my life
(though I promise, I won't take up the whole thing
with it, Fred, I promise!), I had my first meeting
with sir Dennis himself tonight. Actually, I'd seen
him at the Pub two nights ago, but you know, I wasn't
exactly the type to go running over, shake his hand,
and tell him who I was. Sorry, I try to be nice, but
there's a limit.

I had gathered information on him since his
arrival, though. Something about sizing up the
competition, though I doubted I was considered such.
He was tall, thin, good looking *(Damn it! I mean, darn
it!)*, he plays racquetball, tennis, drinks beer, loves
rock and roll AND country music, and strums on a
guitar during his free time.

Hell, he might even like John Denver, but I'll be
damned if I'm ever gonna ask him.

And Jenkins, if you don't know by now, is a small
college. I will probably see them often - walking
from classes, in line at the dining hall, checking
their mail at the post office, lingering between
classes and they just started today, or whatever.
Wherever.

That rule Fred mentioned was definitely right;
things like that will ALWAYS happen. And I've got to
deal with it. And I will. *But they don't seem happy.*
She doesn't seem so carefree when she's around him.
He's smothering her. QUIETTTT!
Fred. He's right. And I love him and hate him for
it. That night after the Pub, I guess it was a couple
days ago now, after I refrained from speaking to her
and just went about my business and my God, can I tell
you how much I hate playing games? Sorry, I keep
wandering.
There was a note in my campus mailbox. The next
day! Like, when did she write this and why? Is there
any particular reason why my head is being messed
with?
What did I do with the note? Well, I opened it, of
course and in record time, I hate to add.

Roses are red,
Violets are black,
I wish things were the same,
But Dennis did come back,

I hope you understand,
I hope you're not blue,
I don't know what's gonna happen,
But I'm still thinking of you!
Talk to you soon!
Leigh

Holy shit, thanks a lot Queen Shakespeare. I needed
that like I needed a size 15 boot straight up my
asshole and I'm sorry for the language Coach Huff, but
what in the hell is going on here, I don't need this,
I can't take this, screw this, screw that, up hers, up
mine, to hell with life, baseball, hot showers with or
without soap, cable TV, room inspections, classes,
being sober, being drunk, ENOUGH!
Sorry, but you know, I feel a little better now.
Even if she does write me these notes while she goes
home with her boyfriend and I go home with Fred and a

hangover. *Should I write her back?*
   Hell no!
   Hell yes!
   You're not serious?
   Of course I'm serious!
   Do it now while it's fresh on your mind.
   Don't even think about it. Don't even pick up a pencil you micro-brained wimp.
   What's wrong with being nice?
   Nice? Nice! What do you want to do? Get dumped again and go back to center field and even have Andy van Slyke tell you that you're a fucking idiot? Or maybe this time we can go back even further. Yeah, that's it! Maybe meet Hitler or Napoleon or somebody. Maybe they can just stick a spear up your ass and put you out of your misery. Or maybe… Yeah, I know, maybe we can… Never mind!
   Decisions. Decisions. To write or not to write. That is the question.
   Okay, I've got it, let's make a hypothetical situation here. If I were to write her back, what would I say?
   Got it! How's this:

   Zippity doo dah,
   Zippity A,
   My ole my I should kick his ass today,
   Break both of his hands, may he never play,
   Zippity doo dah, I think I just may.

   Okay, it's not that good, but holy shit! Roses are red, violets are blue? Come on! I like Fred's version better, the 'hickory dickory dock' thing he tried to get me to laugh at during Higgins' class. As if I was going to laugh again and get called down. Wow, I'm getting called down a lot lately.
   Sorry, I'm back. Fred woke me from my mental anguish. Wanted me to walk with him down to the book store where he could pretend to be looking for a philosophy book because he knew the babe behind the

counter was a philosophy major and maybe that would
impress her. Or maybe it was psychology? Who knew?
Anyway, I'm supposed to be telling you about
running into Dennis the first time. And Leigh. Yeah,
that's her name. Leigh. Leigh Basil. West Palm. Babe.
Okay, okay, this is the story, but it ain't much.
After baseball practice, (or Friday night for those of
you scoring at home), we had one of those golf parties
in our dorms. Do you remember those? If not, you're
sane and may I be the first to congratulate you.
Regardless, I'll fill you in.
    Nine people volunteer their room for a golf hole.
The 'hole' consisted of your choice between a beer, a
liquor drink or a shot. You got one stroke for a shot,
two for a liquor drink, three for a beer. Teams were
drawn for. There were other rules, too, like throwing
up equals two-stroke penalty, partner passing out
equals two additional strokes per hole and there was
some way to take strokes off your score, but I can't
really remember it. Something like taking a shot of
tequila and chasing it with a can of gasoline, hell I
don't know.
    Something college-like.
    A typical game created out of boredom at a college
in the middle of nowhere.
    And was this legal on the Jenkins College campus?
    Hell no! But what else were we going to do? Study?
Classes are only one day in. Even the nerds don't have
an excuse to not go out now. Well, maybe they do. Some
want to get ahead. Me, I've made my vow to keep up
with classes and I almost went to my 8:00 this
morning, but perhaps I should get on with the story
and cut out this useless drivel.
    I'd drawn Benjy, Tommy, Johnny (from the fall
party, the date with … Never mind.) and myself. We
were doing fine, Benjy was drinking pretty hard
because, as you may or may not remember, his arm is
shot and he's not sure if he'll be able to pitch.
Tommy was consistently putting them away, Johnny is a
hard-core pro and don't try drinking with him at home,
ladies and gentleman and me, I was the wimp of the
bunch, mixing beer with liquor with shots and oh my

God, isn't it sad that I did all that and that makes
me a wimp!

Well, I don't really enjoy telling this story, but;
I puked at the turn between holes 7 and 8. *You
bastard! Cost us two strokes! You idiot!* Well, you're
right, I have no excuse, but I'm a little tightly
wound myself if you didn't know by now and … Leigh
wasn't even playing in this, so what in the hell was
she doing there? Caddying? Do you need a caddy for
this game? A scorekeeper, maybe?

Between holes 5 and 6, I found out my answer.
Dennis was playing, hell yes he was. Doing rather
well, now that I recall and for what little that's
worth. But to get through the hazy details, word got
around about ole Phil not making the call for Round 8,
got word that he was in his room, on his couch, being
nursed by Fred, his good buddy Fred and he was okay,
no cause for alarm. He was just lying on his couch
with these little puke chunks caked on his jeans, you
know, that brownish-yellow liquid, nasty stuff and my
God, isn't that sick?

But he'll be okay. Just needed to drink about seven
gallons of water, take 43 aspirin and set his alarm
for next Thursday, but he'll be okay.

And I would've been.

I promise.

But Leigh and Dennis knocked on my door. Can you
believe that shit? They knocked on my door. *Like, hey,
I was expecting you! Good to see you! Perhaps you
should come over when I could at last put two
consecutive syllables together without showing you the
remains of everything I've eaten in the last week.
Perhaps we could talk when I can walk upright without
assistance and actually offer a word or two. Is that
asking too much?*

I guess it was.

I didn't think Fred was going to let them in. He
shouldn't have, but he was a little toasted himself,
and I can't expect him to look after me 24 hours a
day. Could I?

"Sorry Phil, we didn't want to bother you. Just

wanted to come by to see if you were okay?" It was
Leigh, followed by Dennis, *and holy shit, he's
supposed to be on No.9, his team is winning by two
strokes, that bastard!* "We'll only be a second, I
just heard you got sick and wanted to see if you
needed anything."

That was the first time I'd ever seen her unsure of
herself. *And I enjoyed the SHIT out of it.* My
victories are small, but I will revel, roll and glue
myself in them if that's what it takes.

I tried to talk, but give me a break? Let's see
now, where do I begin? *If you look at my shirt, it's
got some nice flavor to it, you know, a combination of
Wendy's, a shake, a Frosty even and then a few
thousands ounces of alcohol, mixed with alcohol, mixed
with shots of … alcohol. I'm feeling good, though,
seriously.*

My mind started cruising through all of this, but,
as usual, nothing actually came out on paper, you know
what I mean. Like if Leigh had to write it down or her
friends asked her, she'd have to just throw up her
hands and say, "he didn't say anything. I swear."

She's right. I didn't. I couldn't.

And wait. There's more. HEEEEEEEERE'S DEEEEENNNNIS!

"Hey man, sorry to meet you like this. But, let us
know if you need anything. I know how you feel."

*Let's see now. Do I need anything? Two bullets,
maybe. And wait a minute! Let US know if you need
anything? Us? Are we attached at the hip now? Well,
now that you mention it, Dennis, I do need a couple of
things. Do you mind? Do you mind running down to the
hardware store and picking me up a gallon of gas. No,
make that kerosene. I'm really gonna torch this place.
And while you're there, you think you could pick up
some rope. You know, to make a noose with? And I'm not
sure who I'm gonna put in it. Maybe me, I don't know.
And do they have machine guns down at the 7-11? Do
they? I'll take a six-pack of those, if you don't mind
and … wait a minute … I've got it!*

No I didn't. I passed out.

Strike one.

Strike two.

Strike three.

And it's probably a good thing. I would've been forced to talk.

And where was Fred during all of this? You might not have wondered. Me, I did. Where did he go? Not sure. I think he was teeing off on No. 7, two strokes down, but it was a dogleg right and if he played his slice just right ...

Fred. Would somebody please clone Fred. Now. Immediately.

He was at my side when I awoke the next morning. Canceled our "training" until tomorrow. Had two non-aspirins waiting for me. (Excuse me a second ... if aspirins cure your headache, what do non-aspirins do?) Made me drink coffee even, though I hated it. Water. Warm rag to put over the head. Bucket next to the couch if I had any urge to pour some more of myself out without warning. Couldn't have been safer at Athens General or Northside Hospital or all those other hospitals I'd visited for better or for worse during my earlier years.

He sat on my bed, while me and my ten-gallon head remained on the couch. And he, as only he could do, told me how things were going to be.

"You're mine," he began, "and I know you don't feel like listening to this right now." I tried to interrupt. Couldn't. He wouldn't have let me, anyway. "I am now not only your friend, but your father, mother, coach, guru, counselor, teammate, classmate and every other thing you can imagine. You will pull all-nighters with me, you'll practice with me, I'll teach you how to smoke a pipe, climb a tree, shoot basketball, steal a base, chase women, both pretty and ugly, work out, sweat, you name it. I'll even teach you how to referee basketball games where you can help me with intramurals. There's some babes out there, you know. As for you, you will remain focused on these things at hand, these little lessons. You won't go near Leigh. You won't go near Dennis. You aren't allowed to speak her name, though on occasion, you will be allowed to speak bad about both of them and

their immediate family - once you've earned it. You
will enjoy this at times and you will hate it at
times. But … are you listening?"
   Nothing.
   "Please nod once for yes, twice for no."
   I gave him the nod, then blacked out again.
   And that, as they say, was that. It's pretty much
up to date, though yes, I did write her back. It was a
cute card, with an elephant balancing an ant on his
trunk. "Always Different, but Always Friends" I think
it said.
   Don't tell Fred. I don't want to start off my
crash course by flunking a test he hasn't even given
yet. Know what I mean?

IV: **Lessons**

Fred's alarm sounded at 6:00 a.m., and could
somebody in God's name please tell me why? Classes
started at 8, 9 for me and I was just getting
plastered a little heavier into those sheets, those
dirty, nasty sheets but guys don't care. My head had
actually melted inside my pillow case, a passing
observer wouldn't have even seen me I was so into what
I was doing. My God man, 6:00 in the morning!

Regardless, my whole body shook and rose off the
bed at the sound of that explosion, kinda like those
cartoons, when somebody gets scared and they fly
straight up. Well, that was me, five feet and lifting,
no fuel required.

And Fred, that BASTARD, just kept right on snoring,
no problem, a peaceful little smile on his face, and
he'd mumble every now and again, sometimes in English,
sometimes in God knows what else and sometimes he'd
even sit up and raise hell at you, all the while
totally asleep. Funny thing is, he'd call you a liar
if you told him what he did.

Me, I wasn't going to let him get away with this
one. Peeling the sheets from my skin, I walked across,
screaming at him, cussing, (Whoops, more laps), and I
took those brown, buffaloed sheets and I hurled them
straight behind me. They landed in his closet, the top
shelf catching them and suspending them there, like a
shower curtain.

Fred, he just reached down for his sheets. Finding
none, he began his non-English assault on me,
jabbering away, sounding nothing even similar to any

language that existed on any planet at any time at any place. Ever.

Turning the alarm clock off, I had to laugh. I had to. Sure, it's early. But my God, can you believe this man? His sheets are hanging from the closet, his alarm just woke up an entire city, possibly a country, and he's just sitting on the end of his bed, raising total and complete hell, mattress marks stuck all over him.

Doesn't have a clue.

And could someone please loan me their video camera? I'll split the $10,000 with you once we win, I promise I will.

Finally, he finished his sentence, or whatever it was, scratched and clawed at his face a few seconds, then opened his eyes. Blinked them, looked around, blinked again.

"What are my sheets doing in the closet?"

I laughed, which made him madder.

"Fred, your alarm. We've got to do something about that alarm. Who made that thing and why?"

"My alarm went off?"

"Yes, and like usual, it woke everyone but you."

"Wow," he managed, then walked up to retrieve his sheets. "Is there any particular reason why you threw my sheets in the closet?"

I didn't even answer. Just walked back to my bed, pulled the covers up over my head, and tried to continue my dream, something about me and three women in Jamaica.

"What are you doing?" Fred again, but why?

"It's 6:00 in the morning, what do you mean 'what am I doing?"

"Get up, we're going running. Now."

Laughing, I rolled over and faced the opposite wall, viewing my 1995 World Championship Atlanta Braves poster instead of micro-brain.

"Phil, I'm serious. We're going running. I'm your coach, remember?"

I waited for the punch line. None given. Rolling back over, I watched in awe as he got up, put on running shorts, a T-shirt and his running shoes. Reaching into my closet, *that brave bastard*, he threw a pair of shorts, a shirt and my shoes at me.

"Don't you think we do enough running at baseball practice? Wasn't the two-mile for time enough for you?" I leaned up at this point, still shocked, still tired.

"We're not going for time, we're going for therapy. You need it."

"I need sleep."

"Up!"

And with that, he walked over, yanked my sheets, and threw them into my closet. They hung there. Like a shower curtain.

"Is there any particular reason why you just threw my sheets in the closet?"

He laughed.

But we ran.

Three miles.

And I'm still not sure if I'm a better man for it.

-Some Random Notes That I'm Not Going to Let Fred Read-

I was sitting there, all dressed and non-fresh from my run, feeling sore and I think you can imagine. Sitting in English class, waiting for the teacher. Students were milling in, some already there when I arrived, others choosing their seats next to their friends, others looking like it was too early for any form of socialization.

This, of course, was my favorite day of class. The first day. It means, if nothing more, I'm not behind. I'm just as good as the next guy. My syllabus will be the same as his. Or hers. Sorry.

Guess who walked in? Are you guessing? How long did it take you? Can I borrow your ax? Did Dennis ever get back with those machine guns? No?

Guess not. What the hell, I'll just sit here and take it.

"Hi Phil," she said with a big smile. *Nice teeth. Probably has one helluva good dentist down there in West Palm.*

"Hi Leigh, how are you?" I said, but not too eagerly, thank you very much. She plopped those books

right beside me, to my left. Had established her plane
of space. Right by me. All semester long. My last
semester even. But we've already covered that.
"You look nice," I said, but why did I say it?
She looked genuinely flattered. "Thanks, I
appreciate it."
I started laughing at this point. Sorry. But I had
to. It was funny. Usually, you expect or you at least
hope that the person would say something like, "you
look nice, yourself." But, she looked me over and
didn't say a word. Just started arranging her books,
stuffing them in her book bag. Plus, it reminded me of
the time that Fred all but offered his liver, kidney
and spleen over the table to this girl at the Pub. She
just gathered her keys and walked off. Just like that.
I laughed harder.
She cut her eyes over at me. There was a trace of
that curiosity there, that roundness of her mouth,
that inquisitive squint in her eyes. I just waved her
off. Didn't want to explain. Didn't have to.
*Good job, jerkoff, now she's really glad she dumped
your goofy ass. Maybe you could bust out laughing
while the class is in progress. That ought to turn her
on.*
Anyway, I stared straight ahead the entire class,
looked Dr. Taylor right square in the eye. Didn't even
notice Leigh - *blue jeans, flannel shirt, little bitty
earrings, no lipstick, Florida State hat, Nike tennis
shoes - what a babe - didn't* give her the time of day.
Just stared dead away, zoning in on the teacher.
Didn't hear a thing.
It's the first day of class.
And I'm behind already.

"And tonight we're going to study." Fred, standing
in the middle of the room, boxer shorts with lizards
on them, pecker hanging out, books in his hand, waking
me from my nap.
"Fred, I've been up since..."
"Since six this morning, just like me. And we're
not going to get behind this semester in the books.
Rumor has it, we're actually on the list to graduate."

I rolled away from him. He walked over and rolled
me back.

"Okay, fine, just lay there. Daydream a while.
Think about that girl. Great idea. Come on. GET YOUR
ASS UP!"

I did. Our own study hall, if you would. He on his
side and thank God he finally put on some shorts, me
on mine. Communications, English, another History
course, Marketing.

Game. Set. Match.

Two miles, then three, by Friday it'll be five.
Three mornings a week, plus baseball practice, plus
study hall, plus … *Could somebody please bring me a
beer? Miller or Miller Lite? I don't give a shit, just
bring me a beer. Deliver it to my room. Don't they
have people that deliver. Dial-a-Drunk? Something like
that.*

Oh yeah, and while we're in this "lessons" chapter,
I'd like to make a comment here. (And yes I hope Fred
does read this.) He taught me the ugliest jump shot in
the history of the game today. THE. UGLIEST.

Didn't want to hurt his feelings, though. He's
doing his job well. Keeping me busy. Keeping us in
training. Keeping us sober. *That bastard!*

Let me go now.

We open tomorrow.

Put your hand over your heart.

Fred has.

A non-capacity crowd of about 64 showed up today
for our opener. Baseball was big here in the 80's,
but Jenkins has hit a string of bad luck since.

Regardless, Eastern University, conference
champions last year and the year before if my memory
served me correctly, and I do believe it did, was our
opponents. We'd lost to them, for five straight years,
at least twice per season, but today we were hoping to
turn over a new brick. Or leaf.

The field was in good shape and we were all
excited as our bunch took the field to start off our
year.

Dave started on the mound, Johnny at first, Bruce
at second, Fred at short, Terry at third and Tommy,
Jake and Willie started in the outfield and Ward is
our catcher. You got all that?

Me, I sat more to the right third of the bench,
didn't want to sit all the way on the end. Something
about being the last one down there. I don't know.
It's kinda depressing. Didn't matter anyway, though.
Once the game started, we'd all be up and chattering,
offering encouragement and making damned sure we
stayed out of Coach Huff's way.

Simple rules. I would follow them.

Well, big Dave did a helluva job. Mowed the big
Eastern hitters down through the first four innings,
allowed only one hit. Problem was, we had only one hit
ourselves. Fred got it, a soft liner that dropped in
front of the center fielder. I watched him as he
rounded first, followed his eyes as he looked into the
stands.

She was there. Bundled up in a blanket. Sun glasses
on so I couldn't see her face. Clapping loudly for her
son. I've never met that woman but I love her. May he
bat .850, make a trillion bucks and send you traveling
around the world to enjoy your last years.

Anyway, trouble began in the top of the fifth. Not
to bore you with more names, but a very large man from
Eastern swatted a 2-1 curve ball somewhere up between
Lupton and Hearst. Fans (all 64 of them) are probably
still looking for it.

Then, with two out, Bruce made a throwing error,
the runner stole second and scored on a single to
right. We were down by two, but we were still in it.

In the bottom of the seventh, we fought back. Bruce
doubled, took third on an infield grounder, scored on
Willie's sacrifice fly. Johnny came up next and belted
one of his own, not Hearst-Lupton depth mind you, but
enough to clear the 315 fence in left and tie the
game.

Dave got through the eighth, but his arm was
wearing out. He had run the count full on three of the
four hitters and looked weary as he stepped into the
dugout. Coach Huff walked down towards my end of the

bench, checked his scorecard, looking for available
pitchers.

My stomach started raising total and complete hell.
*Surely he doesn't need me? Does he? Or maybe he does.
We've got a doubleheader tomorrow on the road. He's
got to save some pitchers, you know. But, you never
know.*

"Phil, get warm," he said, eyeing me for a second,
then heading out to his perch on the third base line.

Remember that chair I told you about earlier? When
I was telling you how fast you act when he tells you
to do something? Well, I tripped over it. Damned near
sprained my ankle and busted my ass, all in one swoop.
My teammates started laughing. Coach, he just turned
around for a second, gave me that look. You know that
look?

I knew it, anyway.

Will and I made a little walk out to the bullpen
to play a little game of catch. This time for real.

Fred got robbed of a double, center fielder made a
diving catch *and man, maybe that's why these guys are
conference champions,* our next two batters went down
swinging and I made that long, slow walk out to the
mound to take my warm-up tosses.

So, after seeing limited action last year, there I
was. All dressed up in my pretty uniform; and feeling
oh so lonely. *Call 911! Quick!*

My stomach was acting up a lot worse now, kinda
like that time I started to kiss Leigh the first time.
*NOOOO, keep your head in the game, but speaking of,
there she is, sitting right there with Dennis, both of
them laughing and joking with each other, not even
watching the fucking game and … perhaps they'd like to
put me on a leash where I could see them all the time.
NOOOOOO.*

I finished my warm-up tosses. Fred walked over as
the catcher threw the ball down to second and had a
little word.

"How you feeling, hoss?" he asked, a slight smile
on his face.

"I'm scared shitless."

"Quiet, you don't want to start running laps now,
do you? 'Shitless', that's eight laps. My God, you'll
miss the ninth inning."
     Leave it to Fred to make fun out of this. Seeing
the concern in my eyes, he changed the tempo. "Don't
worry, man, you can do it. Keep the ball down and away
on this first guy. He likes the high heat."
     "Batter Up!" the ump yelled.
     And with that, I silenced my voice the best I
could, spun the ball around in my glove, spit a little
bit for effect, and slowly walked up to the rubber.
Getting the sign from Ward, I wound, kicked and fired.
"Strrriiikkkeee One!" the ump yelled, and thank God I
might add.
     The arm felt good. It really did. *That was
probably a 90-mile-an-hour fastball. Actually about
75, but who's counting. Nobody has a gun in the
stands, do they?*
     The next two were wide of the target, but on the 2-
1 pitch, the hitter belted a shot to Fred's left.
Taking two quick steps to his right, Fred fielded, got
the ball out of his glove at an incredibly fast pace,
and fired to first. Got him by a step.
     My eyes went up to mom in the stands. She stood and
applauded. Beautiful. God, I hope I don't let you
down, honey. Please, God. Not now.
     The next hitter was one of those tall, gangly
Darryl Strawberry looking kind of guys. Not an ounce
of fat on him. *Christ, what do they do to these guys?
What do they put in their food? No, not now.
Concentrate.*
     Anyway, I missed down-and-in with a curve that
never curved, then Darryl or whatever his name was,
dug in, swung hard at a fastball, but got under it too
much. Willie cradled it in center and there were two
away.
     *Come on, one more out. Get this fucker and go sit
down. Bear down. You can do it. Concentrate, damn it,
concentrate!*
     Sorry, but my innards were raising total hell at
this point. Feeling good, I gazed into the box at the

next hitter - who was perhaps the largest, meanest, green-teethed young man I've perhaps seen in my 22 years.

He was 6-4, well over 200, and the look he gave me when he spit that nasty shit that was in his mouth, I'll never forget. Just begging me to bring it on. Give him my best shot.

Sensing my fear, Ward called time and jogged out for a chat.

"You've got to keep the ball in on this guy, otherwise he'll tattoo the damn thing," he began. *Nothing like a little encouragement*. "Start him off with the breaking ball."

The breaking ball missed, as did my next one. At 2-0, I gave in to him, obeyed Ward's sign to throw the heat and I wound, kicked and fired.

CRAAAAAAACCCCCKKKK!

I think that's the way it sounded, but can I try again? Or maybe he hit it so hard, there's no spelling available, in this language, or any other.

I didn't even look. Couldn't, though rumor has it, the ball is still going, past the dorms, student center, outdoor volleyball courts, gym, out the front gates, past the Pub, past …

I heard the cheers from the opponent's dugout, heard the guys spikes as he kicked up dirt running from first to second to third to home. Heard the high-fives as he crossed.

3-2.

So close.

Just one damned pitch.

Anyway, the next guy lined to Bruce, who made a good play and speared it.

We take our turn in the bottom of the ninth.

But we went down in order.

And we lose.

I sat at the end of the bench. Watched Fred take off his spikes, saw Leigh and Dennis laughing about something and wrestling with each other and leaving the park, saw Coach Huff kicking at the dirt. I apologized to Dave, he pitched such a good game.

"Hey man, don't worry about it. We got a whole
season to play," he told me. Class guy. But I think
he's pissed.
Slowly, I got up and walked off the field. Head
down. Hoping a train would perhaps jump the track and
squash me, right as I walked, right here between home
and the pitchers mound. Or maybe Charles Manson broke
out of jail somewhere and wanted to transfer my body
to the non-living.

"Hey Phil, get over here." It was Fred, releasing
me from my misery.
He was standing on the third base side, by the
visitor's dugout. Talking to that beautiful woman
you've heard so much about.
And if she can be strong after all of this, I think
I should be able to handle a baseball game.
"This is my mom," Fred said, a huge smile on his
face. Mom, glasses off, gave me a big grin, ear to
ear, walked over and gave me a hug. She was small,
around 5-3, thin, but had a rather powerful look about
her. Her eyes were narrow, slanting, but when she
looked at you, they had that way of cutting right
through you, know what I mean?
"Tough luck, son. We'll get 'em next time." And
with that, she gave me a big hug. A powerful hug. I
almost lost it, right there.
"Ma'am, I hated to ruin that game Fred played, he
really did good." She just smiled again, an honest,
genuine smile.
"Don't worry about that, young man, you two have a
lot of games yet to play."
"Yes ma'am, we do." Fred slapped his arm over my
back on that one, patted it a couple of times,
released me from the conversation. "I'll see you back
at the room."
"Ma'am," I began before I walked off. *Careful now,
I'm not real good at this.* "It's really a pleasure to
meet you. I mean it."
I wish you could have seen the smile on her face.
It was worth it all.
"Thank you, son. It was nice to meet you, too." She

smiled.
    Fred smiled.
    I smiled.
    A pure moment and I'm glad I was there.
    Anyway, we're 0-1 damn it, but don't give up on us
yet.

        We worked harder. Fred made me. And I made him.
    He taught me how to smoke a pipe and may I tell
you, that's probably the nastiest shit I've ever put
in my mouth in my life. Didn't even look fun when he
did it. We kept running. And shooting ball. And
studying. He saw me walk over to talk to Leigh in the
library one night. He hid behind a cubicle, watched,
then followed me when I left; kicked me right square
in the ass. He never let me just sit.
    Lift.
    Run.
    Read.
    Shoot.
    *Where does the pipe fit in? Who knew, I guess we're
allowed some small vices.*
    Boredom was something he would not allow. Boredom
was shit, I think was the way he put it. Do something.
Anything.
    Except talk to that girl.
    Have three 'B's' and an 'A' so far.
    My stomach's getting hard. *Beer, does anyone have a
beer?*
    The soreness is gone from my legs.
    I even know something about World History and the
World Wars.

    But you can't stop. Got to keep pushing. No time
for ordering that extra pizza, calling that girl,
watching that movie on cable (Well, maybe just one and
my God, how do they get in positions like that? Are
those humans? Could someone untangle all that? Should
I be taking notes?)
    Well, look at it this way. I can watch the movie
and I don't even need volume.
    Anyway, my curve ball needs work, my fastball is

rather slow, my stomach still does funny things when I
see that girl - but wasn't it great to see Fred's mom
the other day? Wasn't it?
I told him that during yesterday's run.
He thanked me. Told me he appreciated it. No
problem.

V: Baseball, Call Her/Don't Call Her

I was in the back of the dining hall, eating my mystery meat, sitting alone, just thinking. Fred and I had jogged, he had us a double date set up for the evening, two tests were coming up early next week and our baseball team was on a roll. Too early to think about playoffs, but …

But over she came.

"Hi Phil," she said with a smile. "What's up?" She looked withdrawn, haggard, tired, not her old self. She had already eaten, had collected her books and walked over. A passing chat, I guess you could say.

"Oh, hi Leigh, how are you?"

"I don't know, hanging in there I guess. You doing okay?"

"Yeah, just getting through school. How are your classes?

I hate small talk. I hate small talk. I hate small talk. I hate small talk.

"Okay I guess, except for that English class we're in. I'm kinda behind."

"Yeah, me too." *Perhaps we should start a talk show. Excuse me a second.* "How's Dennis?"

OOPS. Caught her off guard. Perhaps we should've stuck to the…

"He's fine. He's got three tests this week so he's pretty busy." She started twirling her hair around with her hand here, started looking around. Feeling uncomfortable. "Maybe we can get together and study sometime?" she asked, looking at me with - not sure what that expression was; a studying expression for lack of a better word or words.

"Phil! What are you doing?" It was Fred, hauling ass into the dining hall, short pants, running shoes, sweat all over his face, angry scowl on it and what had he been doing?

Leigh and I both looked around, questioning.

"Excuse me?"

"We've got an annual staff meeting right now! McKenzie's been waiting on us in his office for 15 minutes. Let's go."

I had absolutely no idea who McKenzie was, had no clue I was on the annual staff, didn't have the slightest idea where this mystery person's office was.

"Now, let's go!"

I went - and we argued. He raised hell at me as we walked up the steps, I raised hell at him as we crossed the student center, we raised hell at each other walking to the parking lot and by the time we got to our car, we were friends again.

No foot up my butt this time.

The baseball team kept rolling, reeling off four out of five, three of them conference games. We were actually thinking about the playoffs, though Coach Huff warned us to just stay focused, one game at a time.

Guess that's why those adages stayed with us in sports; most of them made sense.

Anyway, our school paper did a feature on us, put our picture in there. Even the town paper took notice, though the article was well hidden in the back of the sports section.

Fred, well he was playing like Fred, hitting .435, stealing bases, committing virtually no errors and leading the squad in about everything. Me, well I sat a lot after serving up the longest homer in man kind, but rumor has it they actually found the ball, (our school paper even mentioned that, too), and things moved on.

I've pitched twice since serving up "the shot that's still going." One a mediocre outing, another a three up-three down kind of thing. I'll never forget that one, even though it wasn't a big deal. After getting the last batter to fly to center, Fred was the first one over. Usually, you know, it's the catcher you greet first, then you form that little line and everybody high-fives everybody and you go change clothes. Who knows when all that started? In most other sports, the two teams shake hands.

Anyway, Fred got there before Willie gloved the ball. Gave me a bear hug. Looked in the stands at Dennis and Leigh and shrugged them off with a gesture that he probably shouldn't have made. Huge smile on his face.

My teammates joined him in their enthusiasm. Positive things can take hold just like negative ones can, you know? All I remember was that I felt like a million bucks in that locker room that day. Got more knee pats and high-fives and congratulations from my teammates than I ever have. Or probably ever will.

When I walked out of the dressing room, I, out of habit, looked into the stands. Didn't see... those two people, but I saw Fred's mother and she gave me the biggest smile I've ever seen and a 'thumbs up' sign.

I almost lost it. I really did.

Don't look now, but things are starting to improve.

And English class: There are always those tests that life offers, aren't they? Well, I went to that damned class; sat there every time it met. No more withdrawing from things, thank you very much. Actually have notes that I can read. Teacher about fainted when she asked me a question and I knew the answer.

Actually knew it.

Leigh, I guess, was in that hard-to-get mode at first, but then … she started disappearing. Not showing up. Missing a class here and there. Not like her. And deep down, I wondered.

Oh shit, not again.

I just want to know where she is, that's all.

Why do you care?

I'm just wondering, is that so bad?

It can be if you let it.

So, am I supposed to be a jerk about the whole thing?

No, just indifferent. Would you wonder if the girl six rows down started missing class?

No. But, I mean, I don't know.

Thinking, like boredom, can be a very dangerous thing.

So I didn't do it.

Run. Sweat. Read. Lift. Jog. Study.

I ain't smoking that damned pipe anymore though, damn it. I'll take my 'F' in Pipe-Smoking 101.

Sitting in the library, reading about Napoleon. Rattling dates and places and figures through my head. Needing glasses. *Need to make good on this test, babe, if you screw the pooch on this one, you'll be right back in your old ways. You can do it. You can do it. There she is.*

Big fucking deal. Study!

I'm studying for God's sakes, I just said 'there she is', I didn't say we had to walk over there.

I ain't even thinking about walking over there.

She walked over here. To me. To my cubicle. Out of habit, I looked around for Fred.

Didn't see him.

Anyway, there she was. Jeans, a brown sweater, no hat, hair a little messed up, books in her hand. "Have you seen my roommate?" Terse. Bad tone. Unfriendly almost.

"No I haven't."

"Shit!" Pretty loudly. People looked over.

Silence.

"Where've you been? We've missed you in English class." I marked my place in my book with my hand, looked up at her.

"I don't want to talk about it right now," she said, looking away.

"I'm sorry, I wasn't prying. Just asking."

"I got to go," she said. And she did. Quickly. Head down. Pissed off about something.

WHAT A BITCH! Was it something I said? Was it? Read, Jog, Lift, Sweat, Study, Remember seeing Fred's mom at the baseball game. That smile. That hug. Those eyes.

I actually smiled to myself. Two weeks ago I couldn't have done this. I'd have followed her. Asked. Pried. Two months ago, I'd have been sitting on a baseball field in Atlanta or God knows where. *What if I popped in in the middle of the game? That'd be some shit, wouldn't it?*

Nope. Not now.

Not this time.

I stayed on course.

But I have to admit, I did wonder.

What the hell happened?

Was it something I said?

I like you, do you like me? Yes or no. Please check one.

You better read faster if you're thinking shit like that.

Don't worry, don't go there.

Deep breaths.

Concentrate.

Breathe in, breathe out. Wow, sounds like a great long term goal!

Went back to Johnny's room to study with Fred and Johnny. Fred informed me I was growing a mammoth sized zit and Johnny teased me about my curve ball, or lack thereof.

Whew! I feel better already.

I excused myself after an hour or so, left them to their hard core calculus (was there any other kind?) and headed back to the room to study some Communications. After all, my resume wasn't finished yet.

Resume?

Oh shit.

Yeah, just a friendly reminder.

So there I was, sitting alone, shuffling papers on the couch, English papers here, history dates there, a McDonalds wrapper, a newspaper, some dirty running shorts, you name it.

Let's see now, where were we? Oh yeah, resume. The part that says 'Objective.'

How in the world did all those people in the class

know that one except for me? And so easily and
effortlessly? They did, though, I watched them; saw
their little hands just writing away when it got to
that part. Cruising at warp speed, no time for talk,
no one looking around the room except me.
Impressive, I thought.
Or depressing.
One of the two.
Professor Tompkins called on me today, too, and I
got kinda pissed. I mean, it's not really anybody's
damned business what my objective is, is it? "Go ahead
Phil, we're waiting," he said. "Read us your
objective."
Twenty-five eyes just stared over. At me. What did
I do? I turned red again and it seems we've done this
before. We have and I have.
"I haven't finished that part, yet," I eventually
told him. And leave me alone, damn it.
After a few more seconds of embarrassing silence,
he did so. Thank God.
Anyway, Fred was still gone, would be for a while,
I had the room to myself and I wasn't going anywhere
until I came up with one. Any one.
It was so quiet.
No stereo.
No television.
Not much noise.
Check your messages.
What? Where did that come from?
Who cares? Just check your messages.
So I did. Getting up, I turned the machine on and
it rewound while I got back on the couch.
The first one, they hung up. *Don't you just hate
THAT SHIT!*
The second - from Billy to Fred, they need to
study, or eat or something.
The third - "Phil, this is Leigh ... Please call me
when you get a chance. I really need to talk to you."
*Heeeellllllll no. Don't you call her ass back.
Don't even think about it.*
*Why not? She probably just wants to apologize.
What's the problem?*

Don't do it! Don't! Do! It!

No one will ever know. No one. And besides, it'll be the last time. I promise. Fred's not here. You're all alone. Just call her.

Call her what, a …

No, just call her.

Why in the hell would I want to do that?

She was upset tonight, don't you want to know why?

Maybe, but I also wonder who shot JFK and what happens to all those ships on the Bermuda Triangle. So what?

Okay, tough guy. Don't then. Let her sit up there all alone.

Alone my ass, what about Dennis?

What about him? Call her.

Shaking my head, I picked up my pencil and filled in my objective: To not call Leigh for the rest of the semester, to mind my own business, to study, work out, play baseball and graduate. Getting laid not a priority, but it wouldn't hurt. A job wouldn't be too bad, either. 20K through 90K a good starting point.

So call her. She needs to hear from you.

I put my pencil down, got up and walked to my bed. Sitting on it, I reached over and picked the phone up. Then I started laughing.

I pictured this Point-Counterpoint show in my head. You know, all the girls on one side, all the guys on the other, and two experts arguing. Right when I picked up the phone, all the guys yelled, "wimp, pussy," you know, stuff like that, while the girls looked appalled.

"What's wrong with calling her? He's a nice guy. Is there anything wrong with being a nice guy? one of the experts said.

"Noooooooooo," all the females yelled in unison.

"Oh, come on Sylvia, he needs to call her like he needs a hole in the head. She's already told him to get lost. What more do you want?"

"Yeah, right on brother, you got it. Be strong, babe, don't let us down." Guys in audience. With

passion.
    "I think you're being a typical male." Cheers from
the girl's side.
    "Yeah, right, it's always the guys fault." Cheers.
Guy's side.
    *"It has nothing to do with that. Can't you just put
aside your chauvinism for a second and realize that
the girl NEEDS SOME HELP?"* Louder ovation, from lots
of girls.
    *"Then let her go get it. How can you expect Phil to
be the one? He was messed up so bad a couple months
ago he went time traveling for God's sake! Time
traveling. I mean, I've been pretty messed up over a
woman before, but I ain't ever gone backwards three
years and had no conversation with a god damned
baseball player. Hell no!"* Ovation. Just as loud.
Guys.
    "Bastards."
    "Bitches."
    "Bastards!"
    "Bitches!"
    "Penisheads!"
    *"Okay, okay, enough, we're going to take a break
for a little commercial, but we'll be right back with
Call her/Don't call her!"*
    Cut to commercial as the guys and the girls meet on
stage and start pounding each other.
    I just stared at the phone.
    And picked it up. *Yeah. Do it!*
    And put it back down. *There you go, big guy. Knew
we could count on you!*
    And picked it back up. *Yeah. Nooo. Yeah.*
    And dialed.
    Wimp! Some guys got up and left. Girls cheered and
shooed them away.
    She answered on the first ring.
    "Leigh?"
    "Yeah?" Not much energy in the voice, but maybe
that was a chauvinistic opinion.
    "This is Phil. Did I call at a bad time?"

"Phil, oh my God, I'm so sorry, I tried to call you earlier and I was just about to call you again."

Bullshit! Bullshit! Bullshit! You're not buying that shit are you? Are you?

"I just wanted to see if you were okay." More guys threw in the towel and walked off. The girls smiled, crossed their legs and leaned forward to listen.

Leigh smiled. "No, not really, but it's really good of you to return my call. I'm so sorry I snapped at you tonight. Man, you're the last person - I mean, it's totally not your fault. There's just been a lot going on, lately."

"Sorry, my ass," one of the remaining guys yelled as he walked out of the room. "I'll show her sorry if she does that shit to me."

A silence.

"Phil?"

"Yeah?"

"Do you forgive me?" *BOOOOO, don't even think about it.*

"Yeah, I forgive you. Don't worry about it. Just hang in there."

"Okay, thanks, and I got to get back to studying. But, it was great of you to call."

"No problem."

Silence.

"Bye."

"Bye."

Cut to commercial. Phil puts phone down, walks to couch, dodges objects thrown at him by men. Accepts pats on the back from women. Tries to fill out objective.

Has trouble.

Puts it down and studies some history.

Didn't see her much for a while after that and when I did, she was usually alone. No Dennis, no friends, no one at all. Just her, walking to class, a far off look on her face. Or in the dining hall, eating and running. Or at her intramural basketball game. Or just around. But I'm not supposed to be noticing anyway.

After all, I've found some therapy of my own.

VI: A Late Night With a Picture

Run. Lift. Read. Study. Sweat. And a picture.

I stole it … from Fred. Took the negative right out of the package, drove down to Moto Foto or whatever the hell it was called and made myself a copy.

What the hell. It couldn't hurt. He had his baseball field. Patients had their couches. Drunks had their drinks. Addicts had their poison.

I hung it up in our room over my study cubicle. Right next to my picture of my own parents and brothers. Even bought some of that stick-stuff crap at the book store, pasted it to the back, and hung it right up there. Made damned sure it would never fall. Ever.

And that was my plan of action. Okay, so it won't make the headline news or make it's way into any action-drama plans in the future. But that was my plan, and I did it.

And I'll tell you the results.

I was laying on the couch that night when he came in and saw it. Purposefully, I didn't face him. Looked straight ahead, while actually looking at him thought the mirror. He had been off in the girl's dorms, lucky guy, and I didn't think he'd spot it at first. But, out of habit, he looked over at my bed. While looking, his peripheral vision took it in and froze him.

Just a mug shot, that was all, from the waist up. A lady standing outside her home, flexing her muscles as a joke, laughing at the camera. Glasses on and a hat. Probably for gardening, but who knew? Sunny day. Good picture.

Great picture.

He stood there, a deer blinded by a car light. Stood for minutes. Totally unusual for Fred. Walked closer. Stood there, at attention. Totally reverent, in awe. Didn't move. Not one muscle. Probably didn't breathe.

I watched him watch.

If the phone would've rang or if someone would've walked in, I'd have pulled the chord or thrown a nearby baseball at the intruder. Eventually, he actually leaned forward, hands on my desk; a closer look. Drawing strength. From her. From me. Or the fact that the picture was there. Or from himself.
Or from wherever it was that people went in their heads to draw strength or however they had to do it.

I shivered, had to close my eyes, didn't want to say anything. I remembered that quote from some coach somewhere that said that, sometimes, knowing when to keep quiet was just as or more important than knowing what to say.

Don't know who said it.

Don't care.

He eventually walked over to his closet, took off his coat, hung it up. Turned off the light. Folded his hands behind his head. Stared at the ceiling. How do I know this when the lights were off, you say?

I felt it.

I knew it.

It's more than a five-sensory world, babe.

Remember that.

And know it.

Remember all those late night conversations? Well, of all the times I've laughed, questioned, wondered and spoke to him in our years at Alumni Hall, Room 34, this one was my favorite.

By far.

And not one word was spoken.

Yes, Jesus did weep.

This time in happiness.

And before I move on, I'll tell you this. We never, ever spoke of that picture. Never. Not as a joke, not

being serious, not in our heartest-to-heartest of all
of our talks. It would never, ever be mentioned.
And it shouldn't be.
Words can cover a lot of ground.
Some things or events don't need to be covered.
Leave them as they are.
Appreciate them.
And keep getting up day after day, putting one foot
in front of the other, and keep moving.
So we did.

VII: **More Baseball**

"I can't believe you put me up to that!" It was
Fred, at baseball practice, the day before a road trip
to take on Georgia Central; a team that, like all
others, seemed to finish ahead of us in the standings
year after year.

We were tossing the ball back and forth, talking
quietly, not wanting our coach to think we weren't
concentrating on the task at hand.

A win tomorrow would improve our post-season
chances greatly, though a loss would by no means end
it. Eastern was unbeaten, Central, us and North
Bulloch were all in the race for second. Any team
could come out of it. Or not.

"What are you talking about?"

"Deah, you know, the goofy-cute girl you wanted me
to ask out."

I caught the ball, attempted a curve that actually
did so, a little, and I admired the pop in his glove
as he caught it. "So what's the problem?" I laughed as
I said this. I was actually starting to sound a little
like him.

"She switched teams, that's the problem."

I waited for an explanation. None given. He just
gripped the ball and threw me a knuckler that bounced
off my glove and into the dugout.

"Let's go Phil, wake up down there!" Coach Huff had
apparently sensed our conversation and didn't seem to
like it. *Okay, concentrate. Playoffs. Motivation.
Hard word. Switched teams?*

I had to wait a full twenty minutes before I got my

explanation. Davis was throwing BP again and Fred,
Willie and I were in the outfield, shagging flies.
Fred made an over-the-shoulder catch, hit the cutoff
man and waited for the next ball, while I, chasing
down an earlier hit ball, popped the question.
"What do you mean 'switched teams'?"
He cut his eyes at me, glanced over at right field
where the next ball was hit, then smiled and answered.
"Yeah, you know, switched teams. She's a lesbian."
"Wow. How depressing." I tried to picture this.
Tried to be open minded but couldn't. Different
strokes for different folks, so to speak. A lot of
guys would suffer over that one.
"How do you know this?"
He acted as if he didn't hear me at first; hated
when he did that. Then he glanced over again, shifting
his bubble gum from right to left in his mouth.
"Because I asked her out, that's why."
I started laughing. I had to.
"You called her?"
"No Phil, you never, ever call a girl and ask her
for a date."
"Huh? Why not?"
"Because, you always have to ask them out to their
face, that's why. If you ask them out over the phone,
it's too easy for them to lie to you. You know, can't
go out, have to stay in and study, have to wash the
hair, or, have to watch 'Star Trek', or something.
Anything.
I shagged a fly; kept listening.
"If you ask them to their face, it's a lot tougher
on them. They're on the spot. Can't lie to you. Or
they can, but it's tougher. Understand?"
I did, sort of.
"Why didn't you tell me this when I called you-
know-who earlier this year? Where was this expert
advice then?" I paused. "Besides, she said 'yes'."
"Yes, and look what happened."
He tried to trot away, but I followed. He did have
a point, though.
"You mean you're not going to fill me in on the
details?" He stopped, pulled dirt out of his cleats

and laughed. Didn't say anything for a while.
    "Promise you won't say anything?"
    I just looked at him.
    "Okay, this is what happened: I went to her dorm
the other night. She and Teresa Locklander were
there."
    "Teresa Locklander? She's definitely into her own
sex."
    "I know that and you know that. But how in the hell
was I to know that Deah was? You know? Especially
after she made that comment the other night at the
Pub." He paused to catch a grounder. "Anyway, I called
her outside the room, asked her for a date and she
politely declined. Got this weird look on her face,
but she was cool about it. Anyway, the next day,
Teresa passed me in the hall and bumped right into me,
knocked my books over. Me? I'm figuring it was an
accident, but while I was bending down to pick up all
my crap, I looked back at her and she just kept right
on walking. Gave me the dirtiest look I've seen in a
while. And then, BOOM, it hit me. My God it hit me.
And didn't I feel like a horse's ass."
    "FRED! Take off. That's three laps. NOW!"
    You know, sometimes I get the feeling that Coach
Huff isn't that impressed with our conversations. But
at least three laps is the least you can run as far as
cussing punishment. I think.

    - *Game time - versus Central - on the road and in
front of a hostile, drunk crowd -*
    It was one of those crowds that found some feature
of each and every one of our players and ripped into
them about it. One of those crowds you don't mind
being a part of, but man, when you were on the other
team, it was different.
    Well, Fred, now dubbed as 'The Golden Child with
Glasses' in honor of his short, practically bald, hair
cut, and Dave, 'Pillsbury Dough Boy' in honor of his
gut, put us out in front early with a pair of doubles
that muted the crowd for at least ten to fifteen
seconds.
    But Central fought back, touching Johnny for three

runs in the fourth and two more in the fifth. Down 5-1, I was put in for damage control and pitched two good innings. Giving up only one hit and a walk, I struck out one and avoided any form of disaster - even if those drunk pansies did refer to me as 'nerd' and 'Phyllis.'

We scored one in the seventh, two in the eighth and another in the ninth on a solo homer by Bruce to tie the game. But, the bottom of the ninth proved our undoing, as Benjy, now feeling better after his arm problems, gave up a lead off walk and a homer.

We lost it 7-5.

That was the bad part.

The good part was we're still healthy and we'd see them again at our place. In front of sane fans, even.

And we ripped them up 10-2. Everybody hit, the defense was awesome and the school was taking even more notice.

Things were starting to click.

Fred and I are still focused. Running. Sweating. Reading. Studying. Shooting.

The baseball team's got a chance.

I've gone on two dates and almost had a good time on one of them.

There's no looking back.

It's our last semester.

Keep going, full steam ahead.

And if you need help, read the letter, stare at a picture, open your eyes, live a little.

No problem.

Until, early one morning ...

VIII: **An Early Morning with Leigh**

I found her crying outside the girl's dorms at
about 2:30 in the morning. What was I doing out that
late? Studying. Do you believe me? I don't blame you
if you don't.

But that's what I was doing and that's where she
was. Sitting on a step in the back of the dorms. Head
in hands. Bawling her eyes out. Leigh, this once on
top of the world, crazy, off-the-wall, give-and-I'll-
give-it-back kind of girl. Crying.

Not at her own dorm either, but I wasn't going to
ask.

I had taken the short cut from the library, had cut
down the path that was now well lit (and our school
paper had told us so!), and I was in kind of a hurry
because I was freezing my nuts off on this mid-March
night.

The weather wasn't giving in. March was supposed
to be windy but warming, and sometimes it was. Others
it wasn't. Our weather man, though, had promised
clearing skies and a warming trend. He promised. I
heard him say it.

And it was about time.

And I probably needed to see this girl sitting out
there like I needed to throw another fastball to that
Eastern batter with green teeth. *Things are going
great now. Keep going. Don't even stop. It's not your
problem. She dumped you, remember?*

*But does that mean you don't help people? Just
because of what happened to you. I mean, what is all
this 'me' shit anyway?*

*Okay, so wander on over, fall in love again, get
dumped, hit three batters and lose the game because
you can't concentrate, go sit around and talk to, hell
I don't know, go back in time and talk to Jimmy Hoffa
or Marilyn Monroe or somebody. Always wonder what
really happened to them anyway.*
    She's crying. She's in pain, damn it.
    And you weren't?
    What goes around, comes around.
    *I'm not saying don't be nice. Do. Teach them how to
play a sport. But don't ever let them into your soul.
Isn't that what he said? Something like that?*
    I almost kept walking. I really did. Almost just
tucked those books into my waist, put my head down,
put left in front of right in front of left and moved
on. Forward. Full steam ahead.
    At first, I succeeded. Made the turn towards the
guys dorms, away from her and her tears and her life.
Carried forward, back to her, into my own world. *Get
away fast. Quickly.*
    And then, pictures formed in my head, one after
another . One was of a family, sitting around the
dinner table. Another was a sister and a brother,
pulling each other's hair. Another was of three people
sitting in lounge chairs, watching a baseball game. A
conversation in an outfield. An old lady in the
stands. A smile. A letter. A friend. And then I heard
a voice.
    Oh shit, you're probably thinking, whose voice was
it this time? Is Andy back?
    Well, I'll tell you, I don't have the slightest
idea whose voice it was. But I'll tell you what it
said.
    Help somebody.
    That's what it said and nothing more.
    Nothing less.
    No argument from the male side of the auditorium,
either. I guess that's what I was waiting on. And I
waited. Heard nothing. Waited some more. Still
nothing.
    So I stopped. Turned towards her - a 20-second time

out if you will. I walked over. Stood beside her.
Didn't know what to say. My out-voted rational voice
popped in as I drew closer, asked me if I should leave
since she was crying. After all, some things were
private, you know? But …
Help somebody.
Damn it.
Help somebody!
So I did.
I stood for what seemed like hours, (probably about
10 or so seconds), she looked up. Tears rolling down
that Florida face. Frustration, pain, shame, anger, I
wasn't really sure what that face showed.
Doesn't matter, just help.
It's funny as I think of this. I mean, where did
this come from? Didn't know. Didn't know the ways of
God's workings or if it was a he or a she or a being
or how it worked. But that's what happened. And that's
what called me back to her side as I froze my nuts off
on this not so wonderful March night.
"Leigh?" That was what came out in the real world.
Just that in this pressure filled moment. *Man, you
have a way with words, you should become a … Please,
not now.*
She looked up at me, wiped her tears away on her
sleeve, looked down, then back up. Stared at me some.
For hours. (Five seconds.) "Phil." She answered. And
she laughed. And she wiped her sleeve again.
I sat down. Didn't wait for her to move over. *It
seems we've done this before.*
"I know you hate me." She said after she had
herself together. She was staring off into the night
now, at the Big or Little Dipper or I wasn't sure,
because I never could see patterns in all that
perfection. She said it softly, almost as if to
herself.
I started to speak. She stopped me. "I've got to
get my shit together. God, I'm sorry. Dennis and I
broke up, I've been drunk for two weeks, my grades
have gone to shit, I just got into a fight with my
parents and my fucking tire is
flat." *Fix a flat if it's flat. Holy shit! I think*

*that was the rest of that phrase that Andy was talking
about.* "My roommate's about to disown me, I've got a
paper due tomorrow." She paused, shrugged her head,
looked back up. *Calling role in the sky.*
"I'm just so tired of dealing with all of this
right now. I can't do this. He's trying to mold me
into this … I don't know. I understand that he's so
perfect, but he gets pissed off when I'm not the same
way. I just couldn't take it anymore. And look at you,
you should've kept right on walking. Why should you
sit here and listen to my problems? Me, of all
people."
        I still didn't say anything.
        But this time, it was on purpose.
        "Why am I telling you this? You're probably
laughing inside." Pause. "And I don't blame you." She
looked over at me again. Stared into my eyes. I didn't
look away. Stared right back.
        "I'm really proud of you guys, you and Fred," she
said, her voice changing tones and catching hold. "I
was so happy that day you pitched and got those guys
out, I swear to God I was. Dennis and I fought over
it. When you got that fat fuck to fly out to Willie, I
jumped up and cheered. I swear! It was awesome. You've
come a long way. God, I see you and Fred out there so
determined and, I don't know, it's great to see that.
You guys are intense. I'm proud of you, envious and
jealous all at the same time. You seem so determined,
so focused. I could never in my life do that. Shit, in
high school, I'd be dribbling the ball down the court,
calling a play with one hand and wondering what was on
TV later. I don't know. I can never focus like that. I
can never…"
        I interrupted.
        Do you believe that?
        If not, it's okay.
        "Quiet." Her mouth opened. Rather wide. "You need
to quit putting so much pressure on yourself. Relax.
Take a breath, for Christ sakes, you look like you're
about to pass a kidney stone. Stop getting so caught
up in so little. Get out of yourself!" *Holy shit, who
is this guy?* "I mean, listen to yourself. I mean, I'm

sure that Dennis is a nice guy and all, but think of
all the other stuff that's going on in the world. Man,
look around you, there's a bunch of great people and
things around here." *Sorry, I had to improvise a
little. Can't copy things word for word. That would be
plagiarism. I learned that here. OOPS, hold on a
second.* "Are you listening to me, Leigh? Are you?
Okay, so you're having a little run of bad luck. Big
deal. You can handle it. Shit happens. You can deal
with it. You're a reasonable, sane, intelligent
person. Your tire is flat? I'll help you fix it. You
have a paper due? Do the best you can on it. You're
behind academically? You can make a comeback. Come on,
these are the best years of your life. Don't blow it
by sitting out here feeling sorry for yourself."

Leigh was just staring at me at this point, mouth
open, wide open and for just a brief second, I was
back in a car in fall semester, explaining Bill
Buckner and snack pack puddings to her. Her tears were
dried and I think she was about to start talking, but
...

But I wasn't finished.

"Don't worry about Dennis. If it don't work, it
don't work. Fuck it, move on. If it's meant to be,
it'll happen. Be yourself. Live a little. Go jogging.
Read a book. Lift weights. Go to a movie. Talk to a
friend. Eat some ice cream and I don't give a rat's
ass whether it's Yogurt, Baskin Robbins or whatever
other brands there are out there. Call home. Talk to
mom and dad. Say hi to your brother and sister. If
you don't have one, then say hi to someone else's.
Doesn't matter. Get out of this! What are you doing
out here? It's cold as balls out here and your flat
hasn't jumped up and fixed itself yet. And your paper,
what in the hell is happening to your paper? Is your
computer on auto-pilot? Holy shit, are you listening
to me?"

She was. I could tell. Maybe it was her mouth and
how much bigger it got, how it could not only catch
flies, but a bird or two. Maybe it was the fact that
no noise was coming out, but she really wanted to say
something. Maybe ...

"Phil?"
She said this as if asking, 'are you Phil?' Did
someone else stop by in your body?
"Leigh," I answered.
"I'm so impressed. You've really grown up."
Don't say that. I've been watching grown ups
lately, I'm not that impressed!
She stared at the sidewalk a while, then continued.
"I don't deserve a friend like you. Not after…"
I shrugged her off with my hand.
"I'm so confused, I don't know anything anymore."
"Well," I started again, "this is what you need to
do." And she watched and listened, while I continued.
And wow, perhaps I should tape this conversation
because not even Fred is going to believe me. "Don't
worry about Dennis. Don't worry about me. Don't worry
about relationships for now. Put it on hold. If it's
worth a shit, it ain't going to run off anywhere
anyway. Get your life back in order, a step at a time.
Don't let yourself go. Quit thinking. Period. Quit
feeling sorry for yourself and start living again."
She reached over and grabbed my arm. I started
laughing because, believe it or not, I didn't think,
"holy shit, she just grabbed my arm,", but actually I
did, so I started laughing.
"Will you be my friend? Will you help me through
this?"
"Of course I will," I answered quickly. No thought
at all.
"You don't have to believe me, but you …"
I cut her off. Again.
"Don't even say anything like that.
"No 'buts'."
"But what is Fred going to say? You know, with you
and me being … friends? He'll probably shoot you or
something. I saw his little gesture after the game
that day. Not that I didn't deserve it."
I thought about this for a second. Paused. Looked
at the constellations or whatever they were called.
"I don't know what he'll say. But why don't you
drop by, have a talk with him and ask him?"
She looked at me, questioning at first, a 'you're

crazy' look on her face. Then it calmed, she smiled a
little, looked back at me and agreed. "Maybe that's
not such a bad idea."
      "You remember where I live, don't you?" I asked.
She smiled. "Alumni Hall, Room 34."
      I punched her playfully on the arm, then walked
off. She sat a while longer, smiled, wiped the dust
off her behind and headed back to her room.

IX: A Late Night Conversation With Fred and Leigh

I wasn't invited to this one, so I don't know what
was said. What do you think I am? Nosy?
An added footnote: We never spoke of that
conversation either. Ever.
All that needed to happen was a simple gesture,
when I passed him in the academic quad the next day.
He gave me a big smile, clapped his hand on my
shoulder, and walked on to class. Remember his scene
when his father touched him? Do you?
Well, maybe it wasn't quite the same as that.
Actually, it wasn't. Lacked a whole helluva lot of
that intensity. But it had an effect. It froze me for
a second. Made me feel good.
So I went on to class.
So did he.
And Leigh was there in English.
Drove there in her car.
Still has that key ring with Mickey Mouse on it.
And remember that sun up there? It kept right on
going, still rising, falling, rising, falling.
That bastard doesn't get affected by anything, does
it?

X: Staying Focused; Friendly Conversations

We split with Bulloch, lost again to Eastern and beat the dogshit out of Central. Fans started to come out. This time, we got our picture in the *town* paper. Should be out some time next week.

Next week. A whole seven days. A week consists of … Never mind, we've already done that.

Leigh was back in class, struggling, but hanging in. She was still - *beautiful, pleasant to be around, prone to drifting away at times* - but she was sticking it out. Her grades were returning to normal. She smiled more often, laughed again, slowly but surely recharged. Drew strength. From somewhere.

And when she'd fade away and drift off. I'd never ask.

Or pry.

And I'd never ask the talk show hosts what they thought about it, either.

She even wrote me notes again. In English class.

"There's something hanging out of your nose. Please remove it at once and refrain from grossing me out."
        Love always,
            Leigh Basil

Sorry, but studying or no studying, I wasn't going to take a perfectly humorous letter like that and not respond. I had to. I'd been challenged.

    "I think that it's red,
    "But that's just my hunch,
    "I'll keep it in my nose,
    "And have it for lunch."
        Love always,
            Phil

    That was sick, wasn't it?
    She replied:

    Phil,
    "On the outside, you and Fred are perfectly normal,
sane human beings. Once you get right down to it,
though, you're both perverted, demented, sick and
obnoxious."
        Leigh
    PS "Don't change. That's why I like you guys!"

    There were others, but you get the idea.

    Winter finally caved in and died. Weathermen told
us it was going to stay warm and we believed them.
Sweaters were placed back in the closet with the wool
socks, stocking hats, scarves and the like. The winds
eased up, car windows rolled down, the sun made it's
reappearance, and this time let us know it.
    Volleyball games emerged out of nowhere. Joggers
returned. Recreational tennis players blew the dust
off their racquets and hoped the varsity didn't have a
match where they could play. Soccer balls were kicked
around. Golf balls launched behind the upper quad.
Students walked outside and looked around, finding a
hobby to get into. Anything to keep them outside.
    The girls were all babes.
    Soap operas were taped, to be watched later, when
the sun was at rest.
    People would take rides in their cars. Stereo
volume increased louder with the increase in
temperature. Suntan lotion could be smelled as easily
as the honey suckles. The noise factor rose. Studying

was tougher. Days were longer. Sitting inside wasn't
an option.
      Even the nerds studied outside.
      And complained only a little about the noise.
      Because it wasn't going away.
      Classes were held outside at times. Couples would
pull out a blanket and drop it at a moment's notice.
Throw the books on it, pull out a cooler and start
drinking, or studying, or just gazing off into the
college atmosphere.
      Bicycle riders covered every inch of the campus and
then some. Farmers' tans were everywhere. Windows flew
open. Stayed that way.
      People laughed more. And meant it.
      Winter was fine, if you were into that kind of
thing, but winter was over. Good looking women emerged
everywhere, never before noticed. Guys, in heat,
noticed, made their moves. Couples split. New ones
were formed. One night stands more frequent.
      Hibernation was over.
      For better and for worse.
      Parties happened everywhere and all the time.
      And for no particular reason.
      It was spring - and that was enough.

      "That must suck for you guys. I mean, all this
partying going on and you two have to stay sober all
the time." It was Leigh and it was around 10 and we
were in our room. We were studying for an English test
and Fred was hammering away at some calculus. A lawn
party was going on, just outside our room, and the
noise that filtered in created more than an urge
inside me and I listened.
      Fred didn't respond. Me, I was staring out at the
lawn, wondering just when this couple was going to get
a room. They had their arms around each other, and
their legs, and they were bumping and grinding and …
Oh well, I'd catch something similar later on TV.
      Leigh looked from Fred to me, back to him, mouth
curled up, wanting an answer, a response, something.
      "What would Coach Huff do if he caught you guys out
drunk?"

Fred looked up. Over at me. "I think he would hang us up by our nuts," was his response. She looked at me for backup. I pointed to Fred, a 'yeah, what he said' gesture.

"Really?" A curious girl, she was.

"Well, actually he tells us to use our discretion. I mean, he doesn't go around checking our rooms, but he doesn't exactly endorse it, either," I said.

"He's never had to hang either one of you by your nuts?" She smiled. Looked at us both, again.

"Actually, I've lost both of mine." Fred, laughing.

"And I with only one left," me, flexing my muscle or lack thereof.

"Aren't you guys a little nervous? I mean, about the Eastern game." She put her papers down, folded her arms, put her feet up on our end table, or whatever you called it.

"Shitless," Fred said.

"Yeah, my side of the bench is getting tough to hold up," I added.

"What happens if we win?"

"We go to the playoffs."

"Really? That's awesome."

With that, Fred got up to go to Billy's room. Taking his papers with him, he excused himself and headed out. Leaving us there.

Alone.

I didn't start laughing this time, but almost.

I felt awkward. I studied. I read.

She felt awkward. She studied. She read.

After a while, she spoke, "You know, you have this gaping crater on the left side of your chin. What in the hell happened to you?"

Okay, what did you expect? Something romantic?

"Always been that way. Mother fell down a flight of stairs when she was pregnant with me."

"Really?"

"I swear."

"Are you mad at me for saying anything about it?"

"No."

"Sure?"

"Yeah."

"I hope you guys win." Leigh. And a quick subject change, I might add.

She looked around the room. Saw a picture hanging over my study cubicle. "Is that your mother?"

"No, it's Fred's."

"Seriously?"

"Yeah."

"You have a picture of Fred's mother on your cubicle. Does he have yours on his?"

"Huh?"

"Does he have a picture of your mother on his cubicle?"

"No, he doesn't know my mother?"

"Why do you have one of his?"

"She's been through a lot."

"What's in the green notebook under the picture. That one right there." She pointed with her head. Looked at me. Waited for my answer. Perhaps I should …

"It's my … uh … journal."

"Of what?"

"It's just something I keep for fun."

"Can I read it?"

"No."

She looked at me, waiting for the punch line. Wasn't one.

"Really?"

"Yes."

"Wow, how neat." She paused. Stared at it a while, then back at me. Sensing I didn't want to talk, she looked back at her books, then back up.

"Thank you."

"Huh?"

"I said 'thank you.'"

"For what?"

"For helping me. And for not asking questions that you may or may not want to ask. And for being there when I needed somebody. I appreciate it. I really do." She hugged me. I hugged her back.

"I really hope you guys win this weekend. Wouldn't that be great?"

I just smiled at her.

She just looked at me. And as if sensing

something, she looked back over at my cubicle; at a
picture. Stared at it for a while. I pictured Fred
that night, staring, reflecting, in awe. I didn't
interrupt.
      Eventually, she returned to her book. And I to
mine.
      We studied.
      And that was all.

XI: A Dream

Fred couldn't sleep. Not a chance. He wanted to
call over to Phil, to start a conversation, to get it
out in the open. Phil was awake, he knew he was. After
a couple of years, you could tell by the breathing
whether your roommate was asleep or not.
He was tossing and turning as well.
But, for some reason, Fred refrained from starting
yet another late night conversation. He had to get it
all straight in his head.
Something was bothering him. Eating at him.
Following him to the dining hall, across the campus,
into the bathroom, even in the morning when he tried
to read the Atlanta papers and work the crossword
puzzle. Or the jumble even.
Pressure.
Not much at first, but steadily increasing as the
season unwound.
After all, they'd come so far. They'd worked so
hard. What happens if he let everyone down? What then?
Could he come up with a joke that would make everyone
happy? If so, how would he make himself laugh? Could
he?
His mother would be in town for the game; maybe a
couple of relatives as well. Phil's folks couldn't
make it, but they had been calling after every game.
Who won? How'd you do? How many hits did Fred get?
That was it: how many hits did Fred get? What
happens if he didn't get a one? What happens if his
mother walks away depressed? Again? What happens …
It had been so much fun up till now. Seeing the

look on Phil's face when he woke him up at 6:00 a.m.
The disgusted look in his eyes when laying down under
the bench press bar. Hearing him break out in
Tourette's Syndrome the first couple days of their
three and five mile runs. The sweat. The lifting. The
running. The studying.
    And now this.
    Time to play.
    Time to pick it up yet another notch. Time to make
his mom and Phil proud. Time to lead.
    But …
    He stared more at the ceiling; kicked some covers,
propped up on an elbow, stared out the window, locked
his elbows behind his head, pulled them back down.
Rolled over some more. Made his eyes stay closed.
Opened them again.
    And again.
    Phil had depended on him, needed him. His mom
deserved … everything. Was it too much to ask for one
trip to the playoffs? Couldn't he play well, carry his
weight and keep carrying forward?
    It was getting late. 1:35. How long could this go
on? Could he still see the ball out of the pitcher's
glove as well as he had been? Did they work hard
enough turning the double play? 2:49 . Would Phil get
to pitch? Could he clear his head? 3:14. Would we
graduate? With or without honors or would we care?
What then? 3:40. Was he going to stay up all night.
    No, he didn't. At around 4, he rolled face down,
put his head on his pillow, and…

    And there he was. But where in the hell was he?
    It looked like an airplane terminal, you know, the
runway where you walk down after you finally get to
board, after you've given the robot in uniform your
pass, but before you actually get into the bird
itself. There's probably a name for it, but damned if
Fred knew what it was.
    But he was there. But why?
    It was so loud, so much louder than a regular
airport. What was going on? Why was he here? Where was

he? Holy shit, he had a game to pitch. Where was Phil?
And then he saw them; seven of them, all walking
forward, right towards Fred, dressed in full astronaut
attire. White compressor suits, white shoes, helmets
in hand, an intense yet excited look on everyone of
their faces. They walked straight, faces held high,
similar to a golfer after clubbing the shit out of a
one wood and proudly flipping the club to his caddy.
None of them seemed to notice Fred at all. Which was
strange, Fred thought. Like, hey, isn't it everyday
that some anxious college boy just stands in the ramp
with his T-shirt, docksiders and hat on? He and his
dirty socks and his wrinkled up boxers? Where was
security anyway?
Better yet, where was he?
Fred got nervous as they came closer. Closer.
Twenty yards and closing, if you will. Not a one
looked up. No one, that is, except for one. A woman.
She looked right at Fred and smiled. Genuinely. Oh
shit, Fred thought, what now?
And in an instant, he knew. He just knew.
"There you are," she said as she stopped and
grabbed Fred by the sleeve of his shirt. Looking
ahead, she let her companions walk on as she pulled
him aside. "Sit" she ordered.
"Oh my God," Fred finally spoke. "You're not going
to get on that thing. It's gonna…"
"Fred! Relax!" she ordered. "We're here to talk
about you, not me." She smiled again, so pleasantly,
and it made him … scared, nervous, frightened, upset.
"You're Christa McAuliffe, I know you! You can't
get on that damned ship. Don't you even…"
"FRED!" She grabbed him again, rather forcefully,
possessing far greater strength than he could ever
imagine. "I need for you to listen to me and I need
for you to listen good."
Fred started to counter, then stopped. If she could
smile and talk at a time like this, the least he could
do was listen.
"This isn't about me," she continued, "it's not why

you're here. But hear me out and I'll tell you why you
are." She paused, sat down on the floor beside him,
plopped right down, right out on the ramp of a Space
Shuttle. Fred's thoughts took off. Hmmm. Where's Phil?
He and Andy van Slyke should be
coming along any minute. This happens all the time.
Miss McAuliffe, do you know Andy and Phil? They're
really nice people.
She pointed to her ship with her right hand,
bringing him out of his daze. He looked at her,
reverently, while she spoke. "The final destination
isn't always what matters. You seem to be having a
little trouble understanding that," she said, patting
his leg while putting down her helmet with the other.
True, Fred thought, right now I'm definitely having
some trouble.
    "You see, it's the things you do along the way that
make as much or more of a difference as the outcome.
The people you see, the examples you set, the people
you teach. For me, just the fact that I'm here right
now is my message. It's not what happens here, it's
not whether I make it back and become famous or if I
don't and I won't. People don't understand that. They
get so caught up in all this 'me, me' stuff. You have
to understand, Fred, that maybe we can't always expect
it to be our lives that go to the stars. Maybe our
role sometimes is to help someone else get there. Do
you see? Are you listening? Are you? God, people
don't ever seem to get that!"
    Fred's face registered nothing, just an open mouth
ready to catch more flies or whatever happened to be
flying around in a NASA terminal.
    "If even one of my kids can see my example and
learn from it, even one, then maybe that's my purpose.
Maybe that's why I was put here. Don't you see? What
if this thing makes it back and I'm all over the
papers? I used to see that as a large part of it. Now
I know it isn't and how wrong I was for letting any of
that in. The point is, Fred, is that I am a teacher.
My being here is my teaching, my example. Regardless
of the outcome."
    "About this outcome, Miss McAuliffe ..."

She put her hands on Fred's lips, muting him. Fred
wanted to continue, but the look in her eye told him
to put a lid on it.

"You are a teacher in your own way. You make people
laugh. You put them in a better mood. You don't think
that's big? You don't think people need that? Your
problem is, you're starting to see it in the wrong
light, wondering what good it's going to do you. What
happens if you run out of jokes? What happens if you
strike out four times and lose the big game? What
happens if you don't make the playoffs? What happens
to me… me… me? Get out of that mind set! I'm serious.
Do you think God created all this for me and you? Do
you? Who are me and you to think it's supposed to go
all right all the time? What kind of person are you?
You're not that selfish!" She paused, looked at her
watch; had somewhere to be.

"Use your gift, that's what I'm saying to you now.
Just use your gift. Don't worry about the outcome so
much, just do it."

Fred shrugged, looked at the ground, then spoke.
"I'm sorry, ma'am, I just don't think I could handle
letting my mom down. Or Phil. I try to be happy and
all and to cheer people up, but sometimes…"

"It's hard," she finished. "And who's supposed to
cheer up the court jester? And doesn't he have
feelings, too?" Her eyes peered solidly into Fred's.
Fred looked back, couldn't have looked away for three
state titles and a grand slam.

"Simplify. Do your best. It's not the end of the
world, whether you do or you don't. Get some
perspective on this."

"I don't know if I can."

Smiling, the teacher looked away, then back at
Fred. "Well, do you want to come with me?" The smile
faded; her eyes looked at, inside and through every
inch of Fred.

Fred's mouth opened. No answer. He tried. But
couldn't. And finally, she got up and walked away, she
did, a teacher to her destiny, filling her purpose,
playing her role.

And Fred, just stared, didn't move. He watched as

she walked up the ramp, stood at the door, looked back at him. And smiled.
"This is my message," she said. "Go deliver yours." The door closed and the last thing he saw was a peaceful yet intense look in Miss McAuliffe's eyes.
"Fred! Wake your butt up! Good God man, turn that alarm off!" Fred jumped up, cleared his eyes; looked around. He was back in Alumni Hall, Room 34, clearing cobwebs out of his brain, looking at Phil, who was sitting up in bed, throwing pillows and blankets across the room, trying to wake him up.
"Man, I'm gonna shoot that clock after we graduate," Phil added before falling back down. "Jesus Christ!"
Fred laughed. Turned off the clock and laid his head back down. He had this strange, peaceful feeling, but didn't know why. After all, he'd been up until … how long? Three? Four? But he didn't feel tired. He'd had this dream, apparently, but couldn't quite recall what it was, or what had happened.
He had spoken to someone, somewhere, about what? He closed his eyes trying to recall, but it didn't happen. His mind only caught Phil's snoring and the ticking of his clock.
Still, whatever it was, it had made him feel … focused. Relaxed almost, but how? He'd been so edgy last night. So nervous.
Why ask why? Right now, he felt alert, sharp and ready for a new day. Ready for the world.
"Phil?" he finally said. "Wake up damn it! Are you ready to play some baseball?"

XII: A Day at the Ball Yard

"Get the picture," as Larry Munson would probably
say. "Jenkins College, well, it's a do or die
situation for those fighting Jaguars. If they win
today, they move on to post-season play for the first
time in 17 years. If they lose, they go home. It's
that simple, folks. It's just that simple."

But actually, it wasn't just that simple. For our
opponents on that fine April afternoon was that team
from Eastern, that team consisting of large men that
could launch homers and did, almost on request, that
team that came in with a record of 23-2, 13-0 in
conference play, that team that had already clinched a
post-season berth.

That team was already in. And that team that we
hadn't beaten since 1990. Five years.

Coach Huff reminded us of that as we sat in our
dugout before the game. It was the last home game ever
for us seniors, win or lose, as the conference
tournament would be at Eastern. That was so
depressing, for Fred and I were used to our schedule,
our workouts, our rituals.

It had gone from "are you kidding me?" to "okay,
I'll run," to "get up, you asshole! Five miles today!"
And it had gotten ... fun, believe it or not.

Believe it or not.

Well, baseball fever had finally caught on at
Jenkins. People that followed sports knew what was
going on, but even the ones that didn't started
asking. Or saying things like, "I hear we're pretty
good this year." And even the ones that had given up

on us, figured we'd had a streak of good luck early,
were now back in our corner.

Looking into the stands, it showed. There were
over 1,000 people out there, not bad considering our
student body is only made up of 1,200 or so. The
biggest crowd we'd ever had in my four or five years
here. Signs were hung up everywhere, banners in the
dining hall, interviews with Coach Huff were on our
campus radio station and even in the city paper.

People had begun to stop their Frisbee golf games
or volleyball games or jogs to stop over at the field.
Even if it was just a 'what's the score' type thing.
They knew. Or they asked. The rumors that had started
had now filtered over to fact, turned heads and caused
action. Tape Columbo, damn it, I'm going to the game!
Are we at home or away? How far away is Bulloch?
What's Fred hitting these days? How'd we score? Who's
pitching? When's the next game?

A couple professors even canceled a class or two to
sit out at the field, but to watch the game this time.
In olden times, a prof could sit up there in the quiet
and grade papers, only occasionally getting
interrupted by the cracking of a bat or an umpire
making a call.

Not now.

The campus radio station interviewed players
instead of told corny jokes. The school newspaper
saved us our own page. A couple of town sportswriters
were starting to become familiar.

Fred was a God.

The beauty of it, though, was that he was still
Fred; keeping his distance, remaining easy to know on
the surface, but allowing few to penetrate any
further. He made you earn it. And me, I got goose
bumps every time, watching him single, look into the
stands while brushing off his pants, seeing his mom's
face, hearing the crowd; louder and louder and louder.

Goose bumps for mom, goose bumps for Fred, goose
bumps for run, work, study, sweat. Nothing but juice.

And it had spread, gone ye forth and multiplied.

Pure moments. Everywhere.

And most knew about Johnny, Dave and Willie, too.

And Bruce and Ward.

People like myself, they didn't know the details, but they knew I was a part of them, so that made me okay in their eyes. Sometimes, people I didn't know would call me by name, wish me luck or give me a clap on the back. Made me feel good. Me, the nerd, with the gaping crater on my chin, about to play in the big game. Or sit in the big game. Whatever.

And I was nervous. As was most of the rest of the team. Even Fred looked a little antsy on this day, even showed some signs the last couple days of practice and in our room last night.

"I'm ready to play the DAMN game," he'd said the night before, while staring at the ceiling and tired of not being able to sleep.

That summed it up pretty good. Let's do it. Now. Enough already. This attention is nice, but … let's take it to the field.

The rest of the guys were ready as well. Coach Huff put it all in perspective as we sat out there on that day. "You people have to know, that all of this ends right here, right now if we don't get it done today. All this hoopla is over. Gone. We've got a game to play."

He was a genius that way. Getting to the point. Knowing when to push what buttons. Knowing when to yell, when not, when to stare, when to look away. A lot of coaches would've probably written a speech for an occasion like that.

Not him.

He knew.

He saw.

He was a veteran.

And we knew, too.

It was, after all finally time to play.

Our fans erupted as we took the field. Ninety percent of them were Jenkins people. After all, why should Eastern be here? They were already in, they hadn't lost to us since Bush, or was it Reagan, was president and this was just another game for them.

The field, speaking of, was in the best shape ever.

The field, speaking of, was in the best shape ever.
Outfield grass remarkably green. Immaculate. Infield
dirt smooth. Baselines straight. Pitchers mound arced
over just right. Dugouts freshly painted and shiny.
Foul poles painted bright yellow and who knew why they
called it a foul pole since hitting it made it fair?

The field, like the fans and the teams, was ready.
Dave, our ace, beer belly and all, got the nod on
the mound and the only difference in our lineup now
and at the beginning was that Benjy was now completely
healthy. He was our closer and he'd be used, if
needed.
     The coaches and umps met at home plate. They
talked. Pointed to foul poles and lines and pitchers
mounds and things. Traded score cards. Shook hands.
The ump reached down, pulled a brush out of his
pocket, and dusted off the plate. Made it nice and
white. Coach Huff returned to the dugout, cleared his
throat, straightened his hat. The Jenkins College
defensive unit got into their crouch. Dave kicked at
the dirt on the pitcher's mound, straightened it with
his foot, fixed his hat.
     An Eastern batter took some more practice swings
while Ward fired down to Bruce at second and they all
whipped the ball around the infield.
     The batter stepped into the box.
     Ward put his mask over his eyes and into place.
     The umpire leaned in and did the same.
     "PLAY BALLLLL!" he yelled.
     The crowd stood up. More goose bumps. More energy.
More juice.
     A pure moment in process, for better or for worse.

     Our fans, once strangers, now oh so beautiful, went
delirious when Dave struck out the first two, then got
the third hitter to ground out to Bruce at second.
Quieted a little as the Eastern pitcher, also their
ace, forced two weak pops ups and struck out Fred to
end our half of the inning.
     Nothing major happened until the fourth, and
unfortunately, it wasn't us that made it happen. With

two on and two out, Eastern's lead off man tripled,
bringing home two runs to break the deadlock. The next
batter then singled to right field.
    3-0 and oh shit but we ain't quitting. Not now.
    Dave got through the inning, though; swore he felt
fine when he came into the dugout.
    Fred singled to lead off our half. Glanced over at
Coach Huff at third, who flashed him the 'steal' sign.
Studying the pitcher, Fred took off on the first
pitch, head down, feet churning, arms rotating back
and forth.
    The catcher made a snap throw without ever getting
out of his crouch, a perfect throw, beating Fred by a
step.
    But the shortstop dropped the ball.
    And Fred dusted himself off with a smile as he
stood on second, safely.
    And smiled even bigger when Johnny pasted a 2-1
pitch over the center field wall.
    3-2.
    Hold on to your hats.

    We tied it in the bottom of the fifth on a triple
by Bruce and a wild pitch. The crowd was delirious.
Sober. Drunk. Always loud. Most of the time standing.

    Things started to come apart in the sixth.
    Dave got the first guy to fly out, but then allowed
a walk, a single and a walk. Working from the stretch,
he delivered his first pitch to the next batter and
his arm snapped louder than the catchers glove when
the ball hit there. Rolling down in pain. The umps
called time as Coach Huff and our trainer walked the
big man off the field.
    I looked around the bench as Coach Huff walked
over. Didn't know who would get the nod, but I knew
his mind was already made up. He never looked up, just
walked, all the way to my side of the bench. *Oh shit,
oh shit, oh shit, oh shit* and he grabbed me by the
sleeve.
    "Get warmed up, son. You're in there." His eyes,
those dark, piercing eyes, locked into mine, way in,

and I couldn't look away. Intense, yeah that was a
word, but it didn't quite cover it. Not sure what did.
Energized by the touching of his hand, I got up,
made my warm up tosses. And made that long, slow walk
out to the middle of the baseball field. Stood up on
the mound, saw Fred and Ward, all out there waiting on
me.
And a crowd that was cheering. Actually, they were
probably saying, "who the hell is this guy?" but who
knew.
Didn't matter.
Time to pitch.
Damage control.
The role of the middle reliever.
Keep Eastern at 3.
Don't do anything stupid.
Fred flashed me a smile as I completed my warm-ups.
Stood around the mound, brushing it with his feet,
getting it just so.
"Get the picture. Phil really needs to get out of
this inning. You can't afford to get behind by too
many runs to these guys. But my God, there's not a
weak spot in this lineup. One through nine, this team
is solid! Anyway, Phil has inherited a bases loaded,
one out situation and a 1-0 count on the batter."
But why was I hearing Larry Munson's voice in my
head as I stepped up there?
The crowd was standing. All of them. I looked out
there, while fixing the mound a little myself.
Parents, fans, students, Fred's mom, Leigh. *Wonder
how she did on her test today?*
Stepping off the rubber, Fred looked over. "You
okay man?"
I nodded. Let's play.
That Darryl Strawberry looking guy was up again.
That tall, gangly, man with the non-nonsense diet and
the muscles in his teeth and his armpits. I've seen
this man before.
Our infield was drawn in, hoping for the double
play.
"Let's go, get this guy. You can do it!" Fred,
from short, getting me ready.

I paced the mound, rubbed the ball, looked around, got this mean look on my face, meanest I could muster for the nerd that I am.

Okay, you're not allowed to think out here. See the sign, throw the ball, nothing more. You got that! Wow, why didn't you say so, that should be simple. Enough!

I gave the place one long, last look before I stepped onto the rubber. Checked out my teammates, the crowd, the dugouts, both tense and waiting. *I ain't writing shit in that fucking journal if I don't get out of this one.*

I stepped on the hill, toed the rubber. Ward flashed me the curve sign. I obeyed and let it fly.

CRACK!

A sharp shot to short, to Fred's left. Spearing it, he pivoted and threw home to get the force. Ward, avoiding contact, threw to first to get the double play. SAFE! No runs had yet scored, but Eastern was still alive.

And still had the bases loaded.

And that large man that hit the homer off me earlier in the season was coming to the plate.

Slowly.

Still had that mean look in his eye.

Still spitting that nasty shit all over the place.

Still ugly.

Ward called time.

Fred walked over.

I walked off the mound.

"How are we gonna pitch this guy?" I asked.

"Don't throw him a fastball," Fred offered.

"Are you kidding? Last time I threw this guy a fastball, he hit it to the fucking library," I answered.

"What do you think, Fred?" Ward asked.

Pushing his glasses up on his nose, Fred glanced towards the outfield, left then right. Walking over, he grabbed us both by the collars. "The wind's blowing from right to left field, thank God, so pitch him away. Don't let him pull the ball, we'll never find it. Make him hit to right field. Everything's away and no fastballs. Make him hit the breaking shit."

*Gotcha. No problem. Just fire that fucker from
sixty feet, six inches away and place it on a dime
three straight times without this large man cracking
it to the next area code. Should be easy. Why didn't
you just say so?*
    The fans were up. All but one, and I kinda wondered
why he wasn't standing. *Great, nice concentration! Way
to have that mind on the game! And while it's
wandering, Leigh's over there. You want to walk over
and say 'hi'! Great idea, she'll think that's a nice
gesture. Strike the guy out and pick up some style
points, all in one big swoop.*
    The batter stepped in. Kicked some dirt. Flipped
his bat. *Wow, how does he do that?*
    Ward gave me the sign. *Breathe damn it. If you
don't breathe sometime in the next three or four
minutes, you're probably going to die. Right here.
Right now. In THE big game. With a diploma that you've
almost earned. With ...*
    Canceling the thoughts, I grabbed the ball, rotated
it, checked the runners. The batter gazed out at me,
ready, eager. Toeing the rubber, I wound up and let it
fly.
    Low and away.
    Too far low, too far away.
    "Ball one!" The ump bellowed.
    *That fat bastard! Sure, why don't we blame the
umpire. It's his fault.*
    I looked back to Fred. "You can do it. Come on,
damn it! Throw it in there." The crowd was still
noisy, still standing, *except for that one. QUIETT!*
    I paced off the mound. Picked up some dirt. Popped
the ball in and out of my glove.
    "Come on, you can do it. Get this guy! Come on."
It was Fred. Intense. Fire in his eye.
    Run, sweat, lift, jog. I could feel it, flying off
the man. I gathered strength.
    Looked to an old lady in the bleachers for more.
    Stepped back on the rubber. Rotated the ball.
Another sign from Ward. Same one actually. Kick. Fire.
"STRRRIIIKKKKKEEE ONE!"

"Yeah, my man! That's what I'm talking about."
Fred, excited at shortstop. Major roar from the crowd.
Fred's mom lifted herself on her tiptoes. Leigh
smiled. *Big smile. What a smile. Holy shit.*
        One ball, one strike. Tie score. Big game. *I'm
scared. No. No. Use the adrenaline. Breathe damn it.
Don't aim the ball, throw it. Throw it, damn it. Throw
it!*
        No more thinking.
        Off the mound. Back on. Rub the ball. Feel it. Look
in. No, glare in.
        The sign from Ward.
        Same sign, same place, *and don't they think this
guy's gonna catch on? Don't think, just throw. Maybe,
but for now, how about at least breathing. Good idea?
Living would be a good idea regardless of the game,
don't you think?*
        Adjusted the ball in my hand, rotated it in the
glove, got the grip, kicked my legs. Fired again.
Outside corner, but too low. "BAAALLLL TWOO."
        *Damn I hate those over-enthusiastic umpires. Just
call it, damn it, you don't have to get so excited.
Right, you weren't complaining on that last strike.
Dennis, did you ever bring me that ax. Seriously, I
have a chance of striking this fucker out if we can
just cut off my head.*
        "Keep your head up, Phil. Come on, hum it by him.
YOU CAN DO IT!" Fred, and I love that bastard.
Seriously.
        Crowd still noisy. Still up. Still behind us. Even
the drunks seem to have temporarily sobered up. *Maybe
their next drink depends on my pitch. Hmmm. Never
thought of it that way. Good thought, though.*
        I peered in. Meanest look I could muster. If he's
gonna crack one off of me, at least I'm gonna look
pissed off about it. I spit. Nothing to spit, but what
the hell. Seemed like the thing to do at the time.
Spit again. Wiped my hands on some dirt, any dirt.
Walked off the rubber. Gazed in. Glared, that's the
word. Glared in. With a passion. *Maybe I should've put
on some of that dark shit that players put under*

their eyes. That would do it.
Sorry, I'm back. Gaze. Concentrate. Breathe. *Aim.*
No, don't aim, damn it, just throw!
I did.
"STRRRRIIIIIIKKKKKEEEE TWOOOOOOOOOO!"
Damn it, don't you just love those enthusiastic
umpires? They really put some excitement into the
game. Man, that was awesome.
"Yeah, Yeah, Yeah!" Fred, hopping around now, up
and down, up and down. In shape, too, mind you. We
didn't do all that running for nothing. The crowd, oh
my God, the crowd. They're out there. *Look at Leigh,*
she has her pretty little hands together, never seen
her do that before. That looks … cute. Maybe I could
take a picture and haul ass down to the Moto Foto and
- Dennis, the ax damn it. Bring me the ax.
"Just one more, Phil, just one more." Fred. And
everybody else on the team. Coach Huff was kicking
some dirt. Players in both dugouts were up on the top
step, either on one knee or walking around. Clapping
their hands, shouting, looking nervous. Or excited. Or
both. Tension everywhere.
I rubbed the ball some more. Paced around the
mound. Looked up. Looked down.
Maybe I should throw him a fastball? Man, are you
on drugs? Perhaps I should toss it underhanded and let
him stand closer to the home run fence. Good idea?
Gazed in at Ward. He set up, low and away. Again.
Same sign and same place.
Low and away, baby, low and away. Stepped off the
rubber. Glared. Picked up dirt. Threw it back down.
Breathe. Glare and stare. Gaze. Play with your
shoelaces. *Where'd that come from? Who cares?*
Got on the rubber. Toed it. Looked in at that big,
mean bastard with funk coming out of his mouth.
Gritted my teeth. Fired.
"BAAAAAAALLLLLL THREEEEEE!"
Sorry umpire. Fat bastard.

"Well, I guess all the crap is pretty much out of
the way, ladies and gentlemen." Some announcer that

didn't exist.

3-2 count - bases loaded -tie score - big game -
Need I remind you? Or myself?

A collective murmur went through the crowd at the
'ball three' call. Not sure exactly what a collective
murmur is or was, but we'll settle for that.

And we'll move on.

Walked off the rubber. Fred gave the 'thumbs up'
sign. "Come on, man, you can do it. YOU CAN DO IT.
COME ON." The outfielders and infielders looked at me,
shouting encouragement. Fred's mom, Leigh, Coach Huff,
cheerleaders, *we don't have any cheerleaders you
stupid shit.*

The stomach was cruising. As bad as the attempted
kiss episode of fall semester. Michael Jackson was
doing a serious moonwalk in there. Jumping all around.
Grabbing his crotch. Jumping up, landing, jumping
sideways. Landing. Zigging. Zagging.

I stepped back up. Meaner look this time. Much
meaner. Pissed off. *Everything that happened in my
life to this point is this batter's fault. Everything!
Come on! Strike this guy out. Now. Come on!*

I adjusted the ball behind my back. Twirled it
around. Found the grip. Stepped on the rubber. *Did you
ever throw butter on the ceiling just to see if it'd
stick?* Stepped off the rubber and holy shit, where did
that come from?

Fred called time. Walked over. "Quit thinking, get
this guy. Come on."

He's right. No time for a brain. Get him. Get him
now.

I stepped back up. Ready. Focused. Breathing. No
aiming, just throwing.

And I wound.

And I kicked.

And I fired.

And that big bastard fouled it off.

*Oh my God, he did not do that! Excuse me, are you
allowed a time out to change your underwear? Can you?
Excuse me, coach, I'm having a little problem.*

"Concentrate. Come on!" Fred, reading my mind. Poor

guy. "Get this man. Now!"
    Walked around the rubber. *This is getting old.*
Sorry, I didn't invent the game. If it were up to me …
Grabbed the ball, rotated it, felt it in my hand. It
felt small, aerodynamic, ready to rock. Peered out
into the crowd, up at the sky, down at the dirt.
Rubbed the ball some more.
    The crowd, a sea of blue, all up. All one.
    Ward's mitt, still there, low and away. Ump, ready,
play ball.
    Got the sign. Nodded my head.
    No thinking now babe, just bring it to him.
    CRAAACCKKKKKK! *Oh shit!*
    "There a drive down the right field line … FOULLLLL
balll!"
    "Oh YEAH!" Fred raised his arms up on that one.
The crowd murmured more collectively and more loudly.
Some of them sat down and put their heads in their
hands. Some of them had their eyes closed, me
included, and cheered when they heard the news. That
one guy stood up. *About time, meathead.*
    The umpire threw me a new baseball.
    And they all got ready.
    Again.
    One big Jenkins College student body; friends or
enemies, still yelling. Coach Huff shuffled some more
dirt from the dugout. Even the ones that were on one
knee were now up, standing, pacing, some covering
their eyes. All eager.
    Ward shouted me encouragement. Couldn't make out
the words. Looked at me to ask if I needed a time out.
    No.
    Not now.
    Fred looked over, peered into my eyes. No words
this time. Nothing. Just that look. That look that
can't be explained.
    I looked back.
    Into the crowd. Over at my coach. Over at Leigh.
Over at Fred's mom. Breathed a little slower. Gathered
my wits. Got rid of my thoughts. Focused. Walked
around some more. Paced a little. Took the ball.
Rubbed it down. Rubbed it more. Harder.

Glared a little. Stared. Looked mean. Saw Ward's mitt. Big mitt. Felt so alive. So glad to be a part of this. So lucky to be here. *Enough! Breathe some more. Don't think, just pitch.*

Stepped up to the rubber; Ward gave the sign. Set up outside. Curve ball. No surprise from me, I knew it. I wanted it. So be it.

The batter took the bat off his shoulder. Spit. Might have winked at me, but maybe not.

A silence fell over the crowd. Total, complete silence. Not one blessed word.

From anybody.

Isn't this fun? I mean, if this weren't you out here, wouldn't you just be loving this shit?

Stepped back off the rubber. Picked up some more dirt. Glanced at Fred. Glanced at home. Stepped back up. Felt and even heard the silence. Breathed slowly.

Took one last look at the stands. Fred's mom. Nervous. Standing. Beautiful.

Gazed in at Ward. Saw his mitt. My target. For better or for worse, here it comes, damn it.

Kicking my little Q-tip leg, I wound and fired that bastard as fast as I could throw it.

He swung.

He missed.

The ball popped into Ward's mitt.

"STRRRRRIIIIIIKKKKKKKKKEEEEEE THREEEEEEEEE!"

Fred jumped straight up. His mom cried. Leigh hugged six people, didn't know four of them. Coach Huff smiled. Fans started throwing things at each other.

Me, I turned towards the outfield, cocked my fist and yelled, "Sit down, MOTHERFUCKER, SIT DOWN!" No one heard me, but I'll run those laps, Coach Huff, I'll run every one of them.

I swear.

Benjy came on to replace me for the final three innings. He was ready. I was still shaking anyway, couldn't have pitched to another man. Fred carried me from the mound to the dugout. Coach Huff just patted me on the butt and said, "good job." Coming from him,

that's the equivalent of a normal man picking you up
in his excitement and hurling you across home plate
himself.
The noise level increased, on our side of the
dugout, anyway.
High pitched.
Loud.
Intense.
One.
Neither team scored again until the ninth inning.
The top half, unfortunately, when their lead off
hitter, who only had one homer all year, connected on
one of Benjy's fastballs and took it over the right
field wall.
Home run. 4-3.
The Jenkins fans were now quiet. Sitting again. The
opponent's dugout had emptied, going berserk. Us a
little quieter now. A lot worried.
Settling down, Benjy mowed down the next three in
order and the home team came to bat.
The crowd stood and yelled for us as we came to the
plate.
Coach Huff called us over. "Hey, listen up. This
has been a great season, guys. Do you want to quit
now?"
A rather enthusiastic 'no' came from all 21 of our
mouths as we started our half.
They brought on their closer, one of those left-
handed, junker ball throwers that didn't look that
good, but man, he was hard to hit. Hadn't blown a save
since February. Only one earned run had crossed the
plate with him out there. Regardless of this outcome,
he had plans of continuing his baseball career after
graduation.
For us, though, it was our last shot.

Willie led off and hit a liner that looked like it
was going through the hole between third and short.
The shortstop dived, caught it in the air.
One out.
Our crowd got quiet. Muttered obscenities. Some
sat.

But stood again as Tommy drew a walk. Fouling off
four straight 3-2 pitches, he finally got his free
pass on a pitch in the dirt.
    And he took second on a wild pitch. One out, a
runner on second. All we needed was a hit.
Bruce didn't supply it. He flew to deep right
field, advancing the runner to third on the tag.
Two outs, a man on third, Eastern up by a run.
    I thought they were going to throw babies out of
the stands when Benjy stepped up the plate and
doubled. The first pitch! Holy shit, a double! Scoring
Tommy. Getting the crowd into another frenzy. Objects
hurled. Programs thrown. Voices hoarse but still
croaking. Goose bumps on my arms. All over. Juice.
More juice.
    Two outs, one on, winning run on second.

    "Come on, Fred, you CAN DO IT!" I clapped him on
the back in the on-deck circle. Everybody was on their
feet, both teams, both dugouts, all the fans, all
thousand or however many of them. All nervous.
    Fred, he remaining kneeling in the on-deck circle
while their manager walked out to talk to their
closer. He motioned me over.
    I went.
    He looked so ... calm ... had this peaceful look about
him. I knelt beside him. Pushing his glasses up again,
he looked me in the eye. "Don't you just love this?
Don't you?"
    I looked back. "Huh?"
    "This," he said rather angrily. "This right here.
This day, these fans, these people. Isn't this ..." he
paused to make sure Coach Huff was out of ear shot ...
"isn't this fucking great?"
    Me, I'd be faking an injury to not have to bat-
would've pulled at my own crotch and moonwalked right
out of there.
    "We've come a long way this year, Phil. We really
have. You should be proud of yourself."
    "Well ... thanks, Fred."
    "Leigh about had a stroke when you struck that guy
out, you know." He looked back at me, again. Peering.

Then he smiled. "I about came in my pants, myself."
"He's not used to having to hit anything that
slow," I countered. Fred laughed, stared at his bat.
"You'll never forget this day, man, you'll never
forget it." He looked at me again, got up, threw a bat
down, tossed me his towel - *holy shit, he just tossed
me his towel* - walked up to the plate, winking at me
as he went.

Fred took the first pitch outside, the next one
for a strike. It was silent again at the ole ballyard,
it really was. You could hear the ball strike the mitt
on both the first two pitches, could feel and sense
the tension on both the pitcher and on Fred.
"One ball, one strike, score tied, bottom of the
ninth. Jenkins College trying to save themselves."
Fred stepped out of the box, looked into the
stands, dusted his hands off. Stepped back in. The
pitcher walked around, took the sign, stepped off the
rubber, paced a little more. The ump took off his
mask, wiped his forehead. The catcher fidgeted at the
plate.
The crowd stood.
And watched.
The pitcher checked the runner, got the sign,
nodded his head and fired.

And everything went in slow motion, from that point
forward. I'll never forget it, Fred's right, I never
will. Can see his head oh so perfectly, watching the
ball all the way in, releasing his hands, getting his
wrists around, bat contacting ball, making that sound,
that CRAAACCCCKKKK ... of the bat.
Can see Benjy. Pumping those arms. Touching third
base. Coach Huff winding his arms, windmill style,
frantically gesturing towards home. Our dugout, up,
trotting towards home, waiting to mob Benjy if he ever
made it. And Benjy. Ninety feet and closing. The
center fielder, scooping up the ball perfectly,
kicking his leg, releasing it quickly but with speed
and with accuracy. Benjy, still pumping, Coach Huff,
now walking towards home, the umpire, taking off his

mask to get a better look. The catcher, already with no mask on, crouched in the dirt, waiting ... waiting for that ball. Benjy, running, running, running, 70 feet, 65, 60 ... 55 ... The crowd, standing, screaming, some with their fingers in their mouth, too tense to speak, others running towards the bottom of the bleachers to get a better look. Fred already on first and just standing there, waiting ... waiting.

The ball left the center fielder's hand. It's still going as I write this. Over the second baseman and shortstop's head, over the pitcher's mound, striking the catcher at about waist high. Benjy, head first, hook sliding around from the third base side, trying to sneak in behind the catcher. The catcher catching the ball in the mitt, turning, tagging Benjy on the back ... but too high up.

"SSSSSSSSSSSSAAAAAAAAAAFFFFFFFFFFFFFEEEEEEEEEEE!"

Fans poured onto the field. Players mobbed Benjy. He's still down there. Covered up. Bodies, arms, legs, hair, teeth, all over him. Dirt, too, but who cared? Parents, student body, maintenance people, registrar employees, bookstore workers, people off the street that just wondered what the hell was going on, friends, ex-enemies, staff. All of them.

The other team watched from their dugout. Didn't move. Just watched.

The umpire picked up his mask and started off the field.

The few Eastern fans grabbed their car keys and drove home.

The few sportswriters in attendance quickly typed away, beating their deadline.

The catcher picked up his mask and joined his sullen teammates.

Coach Huff took off his hat and smiled.

I grabbed Leigh and spun her in the air.

Fred knelt down on the first base side and cried.

XIII: Graduation

It was early, 8:30 or so, and I'd set an alarm of my own. Fred popped up before I did. Funny how our alarms would wake up the other one quicker than ourselves. He cleared his eyes, stared at his clock, wondered.

"What are you doing? Graduation's not until 10:00."

"Paying severance." I answered, throwing my sheets off and hitting the floor.

"Paying who?" Fred leaned up, grabbing his glasses.

"Remember? I still owe Coach Huff some laps. You know, from the game."

He smiled, rubbed his mattress marks, understood.

I was going out of here on a clear conscience. Had approached Coach Huff in the hallway at season's end, walked up to him and stood. His eyebrows lifted as he sensed my presence, wondered what I wanted. Still, he had this smile deep down, you could tell after a while.

"Coach Huff, you're going to think this is kinda strange, but I owe you 12 laps for something I said during one of the games. I'm going to run them before I leave here."

He kept tacking something up on the board, some announcement for the faculty, then cut his eyes over. "What game?"

"Eastern. The clincher." He kept tacking, smoothing over with his hands, staring at his work. Then he smiled; looked at me.

"You know, I may owe a few for that game, myself." He laughed louder. Clapped me on the back. Went back

in to his office, a slight wave with his hand before
he closed the door.

Anyway, the baseball season, unfortunately, didn't
end with any more Cinderella endings. We didn't win
the national championship, have parades down Main
Street, get mobbed by millions.
Nope, we lost in the conference tournament, to
Eastern even, in the final game. Still, we had nothing
to hang our heads about. We'd overachieved, I think
was the term, and we'd earned some respect. Made 'em
proud as fathers would sometimes say. Even had our
picture in the city newspaper. In color even.
Fred had a copy enlarged and sent his to his
mother. That along with his certificate for making
All-Conference, and his trophy for earning MVP honors
at our banquet.
I had my picture enlarged, too, but I didn't know
where to send it. You know, you get copies of all this
stuff, but sometimes you just don't know exactly what
to do with it.
For now, I've got it filed away. Still have it.
Saving it for … I don't know; perhaps for the right
time or the right person or the right place. Or maybe
I'll just pull it out some night when I'm bored or
feeling sentimental.
Whatever.

"I'm going with you." Fred, too, got up, put on his
shorts, a T-shirt and some shoes.
"You don't have to," I told him, "I'm the one that…
you know … sounded off."
He paused, unfolded his shirt, then glanced at me.
"Yeah, you did, and I heard you. But I believe I at
least owe a few from the thoughts that were going
through my head. From innings six through nine, now
that I recall."
I stood at the door and waited while he dressed;
never took him long, bedside to ready in 2.3 minutes.
"Let's do it," he said, clapping his hands together as
he walked towards me.
But then he stopped.

"Phil?"
"Huh?"
He had this faraway look in his eyes.
"Get your graduation robe."
"No, we've got plenty of time to ..."
"Don't matter. Get your robe."
We pulled our robes out of the closet and headed
out of Alumni.

Some official people were already out at the
graduation site, straightening chairs, testing
microphones, shuffling papers. The weatherman promised
a beautiful day for Jenkins College's graduation, and
the sun was already up and wasn't going to make him a
liar. The lawn was well-kept, no vandals overturned
the chairs the night before, and everything seemed to
be in working order for the final event.
Jenkins' president looked out over the setup and
smiled to himself. Yes, it looked good. Yes, we were
ready. A couple of potential snags here and there, but
I think we're okay. But he got a little nervous when
he glanced over at two soon-to-be-ex- college men as
they walked past in running gear, carrying their
graduation clothes. Got a little more uneasy as they
began loosening and stretching in center field.
All four of the men on the podium stopped, gazed
across the lawn at the field and wondered. Actually,
no one, students or alumni, were allowed on the field
during the off-season. But, students got antsy from
time to time, pulled pranks, broke some rules. That
was the nature of the college student.
The Prez started to speak up, yell across at the
two, then thought better of it. "Hell, they ain't
hurting nothing," he muttered to nobody in particular.
"They just going for a little run, that's all. What's
the worry?"

"How many are we doing?" Me, while stretching.
"I don't know, how many letters are in
'motherfucker?'"
"Twelve I think, unless you can think of a way to
shorten it."

"Why don't we make it 20?"
"Why 20?"
"Why not?"
So off we went.
We left our graduation gear at the fence and off we went. Slowly at first, then picking up the pace. Feeling the sweat running down our faces. Hearing the muscles pop, then adjust. Hearing our feet knife through the grass. Looking back and watching it right itself after our passing, ready for more. Staring at the field, the bases, the foul poles, the pitchers mound, the total picture.
That was us, just running - and hearing noises and voices and people and ghosts that only existed inside our heads, but would be there for a long, long time.

Leigh came out at around Lap 8, or 9, put her hands through the fence, and peered in. She was already dressed in her graduation togs, had her tassel all straight and everything. Shielding the sun with her eyes, she followed our path as we cruised from right towards center field, then yelled at us as we made our turn towards left.
"Excuse me, but are you two nuts?"
Fred looked at me; me back at Fred.
"Well … yes, now that you mention it."
"Aren't you guys graduating?"
"Yes, we think so."
"Well, I hate to be so blatant, but is there any particular reason why you two are running around the damned baseball field?"
I looked to Fred. Fred back to me.
"Not particularly. Come join us." Fred beckoned her with her arms. Come on. We just have about 10 or 11 more laps. Come on." Laughing, Fred and I continued.
Challenged, she gave Fred a look, thought about it, looked back towards the graduation site, walked to the fence.
Finally, she hiked her gown up, grabbed it with one hand and climbed over at the lower part of the fence in left field. When we came around again, she fell in stride.

"SLOW DOWN FOR GOD'S SAKE. Are we in a hurry?"
We both laughed, until I finally answered. "I don't
know, what time is graduation?"
"We've got an hour or so, I think."
"So, let's run."

So we did. All three of us now. Two of us in
shorts. One in a graduation gown. Even as the cars,
parents, brothers, sisters, friends, alumni and
graduates began to fill the parking lots and fight for
good seats. Even as the president and some of his
peers kept looking over in curiosity. Even as Coach
Huff walked up to the podium himself.
"Coach, do you want me to kick them off," the
president said.
Coach followed the president's eyes, saw the
three running around the field. He smiled. Then he
laughed.
"No sir, they're fine. They'll be finished in a
minute."
Coach Huff walked away. The president shook his
head, but didn't ask.

We finished our run with plenty of time to spare.
Still had a good 35 minutes before the ceremonies
would crank up. Plenty of time to fall into our
alphabetical place once the seniors began their walk.
You know, I knew then that I'd miss those runs. A
good form of therapy, they were. A good head-clearing
jog could probably solve a lot of problems, or keep
them from happening.
Anyway, we all plopped down at the end of ours, a
little post-run stretching in center field, if you
would, though Leigh had a little problem getting down
on the grass with all that graduation crap on.
None of us spoke. No need to.
Fred was in his palace, and I wondered for a second
if I could get him up for graduation. He was gazing
toward home plate and up in the stands. Back to home
plate, back to the stands. His eyes were far away and
gone, not even close to Leigh or myself, but he'd be
back in time.

And if not, so be it.

He saw his mother, his sister, his father. Heard the crack of the bat, saw outfielders making mud pies in center field, saw perhaps an entire Tee-Ball team chasing a ball down in right field, saw a kid grab the ball and show it to his parents, heard the chatter, the noises, felt the grass.

Saw a video, remembered a game of catch on a late night his senior year.

Wondered just how did he get butter to stick on a ceiling, how did he get out of that locker, why did he hit H.R. Puffnstuff and why did the Eastern pitcher throw him a fastball instead of a slider.

He saw. He heard. And he remembered.

Leigh, she had leaned back on both hands, had put her graduation cap back on despite the sweat. She was gazing around, taking it all in. This was new to her, this sitting- on-a-baseball-field thing, but she looked comfortable. She had this, "so this is center field!," look on her face, if that makes any sense, and she leaned back further, propped up on her elbows. Eventually, she lay all the way back, taking her cap off and resting her head on her hands, just gazing up at the Georgia sky.

A serene, far off look about her.

Me, I felt the grass with my hand, even though it was sticking to them and to my shorts and probably making one helluva stain. Even if it did itch a little. Eventually, I turned over on my side and just watched both Fred and Leigh.

That was all. Just watched. I was tired of me for now. Enough of my problems. All I knew was that I'd always want to be around people like this forever, somehow or another.

And I knew the difference between friends and acquaintances.

And how fast this year seemed to go.

And how if time could somehow be made to stop, I'd stop it now.

And about how soon we'd have to all get up, put our gowns on and go grab our diploma.

But for now, we'd sit, thank you very much.

Right out here in the outfield.
And how would you explain this to outsiders?
Or for that matter, how do you explain it to
anyone?
Or to our own classmates and their relatives, who,
as we speak, are probably wondering just what in God's
name are we doing out here?
I don't know.
I can't speak for Fred or for Leigh, either, but
for my part - I don't know - it just feels so ...
peaceful.
Yeah, that's the word.
Peaceful.

XIV: Closing Thoughts, Because I'm Almost Finished

    I hung around a while after the ceremonies; didn't want to drive home just yet. Had to walk around, had to see things again. Had to 'get weird' as Fred sometimes called it.

    I won't forget this year. These people. Yeah, I guess you do learn a lot in college after all, whether you want to or not. It's funny how different colleges offer different prices for their education, and that's kinda strange to me. Who can put a price on it? How much for a good friend, a relationship, for better and for worse, conversations in center field, getting to see a mother smile when her son gets the key hit? Tell me, what price do you pay to see Fred whack that ball straight up the middle, take off his helmet and start bawling right out there in front of God and everybody? How much does Leigh cost? How about bonding, late night pizza with the gang, road trips, rising and falling with the opposite sex, no pun intended?

    Oh, I know, I've got it. Maybe you get three for the price of two, or if you get Fred at the regular club price, you can get Leigh and baseball memories for $14.95 plus 12 dividend dollars.

    Who knows.

    Anyway, I drove past the ball park just a while ago, Fred's sphere of influence, my therapy, Jenkins College's playing field. I got goose bumps as I saw it; rolled down my car window as I approached, and just sat there, pulled over, staring at a baseball field. Like, if somebody had driven by, they would've thought, 'wow, look mom, there's some weirdo just

sitting there staring at a baseball field.'
    Yeah, that's me. Pulled over staring at a baseball
field. And 'getting weird' about it, might I add.
    But give me a call sometime. Come see me in center
field even. I'll be there, with my memories of Fred,
his family, Leigh, and even famous baseball players.
I'll be sitting on a glove, yes I will, propped up on
my butt, knees pulled together, and I'll be chewing on
a blade of grass. Will pick a blade up, toss it back
down, pick up another, and chew on it awhile.
    We'll talk. Or maybe not. Maybe you should bring
your glove. Maybe we'll just stand out there and chunk
the ball around. Or maybe you'd like to get me in a
full nelson or a step-over-toe-hole or whatever Fred
was talking about. Why not?
    There's things I've learned this year, you know.
Like I sat out there and received help a lot this
year. Maybe it's my duty to give some of it back.
Maybe the roles change as we go along. Maybe the worm
really does turn.
    Oh, don't think you're too busy or too important.
You're not. No such thing.
    And don't think you're not good enough either. You
are.
    Isn't life great that way?
    And if you don't think so, it'll remind you.
    It's kinda funny – and yes, it all is if you look
at it in such a way. But anyway, Leigh and I were
having dinner the other night, and we overheard this
couple arguing. Each was trying to convince the other
of their importance, how one was so much busier than
the other, one had such a hectic schedule, life was
tougher on her than him or on him than her or
whatever.
    You know what? I don't think anybody ever has a
right to do that. Ever.
     You're alive, that's what you are. And with that
contract, comes problems and snags and disappointments
and tears. You can try to convince yourself that it's
tougher for you and your luck is bad and things and

*the world are stacked against you and we should all
feel sorry for you.*

Well, quite frankly, you're wrong.

Period.

Flat out wrong.

*We're all busy. We're all hectic. We're all
scatterbrained at times, nice, mean, ugly, beautiful,
naive, tough as nails, weak, hard as a rock, flimsy,
you name it, all rolled into one body.*

So quit griping about it.

Help somebody.

*What did Andy say - help them fix a flat if it's
flat, teach them how to play a sport - I think that's
what he said. And I'll paraphrase: Be patient enough
with people to know and understand whether you should
let them into your soul or not. That's it. Something
like that.*

*And remember, you don't have to convince anyone of
anything. They're them. You're you. We're all
important. And we're all not.*

And that's life.

So deal with it.

*Anyway, I must go. Leigh's waiting on me at the
dorms. I'm full no longer. I feel sorta peaceful now
that I've talked to you, whoever you are, wherever you
are. I've never met you but I know you. And you me.*

*Maybe Fred summed it up best, in a letter he wrote
to me as a junior. I was having a stroke of bad luck
and jokingly, I told him I wanted to jump off a cliff.*

*He got this funny look on his face when he read my
note, a real far off look. With a smile quickly taking
over his face, he jotted his reply and passed it to me
without even trying to be discreet.*

*"Maybe we all jumped years ago … we just haven't
yet landed."*

*I wasn't even sure what it meant at the time, but
now I think I like it. It fits.*

*Well, I hope I didn't bore you. I'll be back soon.
Life has a way of filling us all up. Hopefully, there*

will be more stories to tell, more lessons to learn.
Anyway, thanks for listening. Seriously.

   Leigh helped me throw my stuff in the car, helped
me empty my room. Yeah, it was a task and a rather
depressing one. Fred, he'd gone already. Told me he
didn't like good-byes, didn't make any bones about it
and wasn't going to make an attempt. Besides, we'd be
seeing him again and often. He graduated, grabbed his
stuff, cranked his car and went.
   Leigh and I, we stood outside the door of Alumni
Hall, Room 34 for a second, just stared at a closed
door. Eventually, we too, turned, headed down the
stairs and out into the Georgia afternoon. We were
silent as we headed to the parking lot, both in our
own worlds. We walked through the quad, stared at the
buildings, the field, the lawn. We didn't stop, just
walked, looked and remembered.
   She brushed her shoulder against me as we walked,
hooked her elbow in mine, grabbed my hand.
   I grabbed hers back.

ORDER AN ADDITIONAL COPY OF

ALUMNI HALL, ROOM 34

send check or money order to:

Patek Press, Inc.
2193 Capehart Circle, NE
Atlanta, GA 30345

Number of copies @ 11.95, which includes shipping and handling: _____

Name _____

Address _____ **Apt.** ___

City/State/Zip _____